ALL HER LIFE SHE HAD WANTED
TO BE SCHAHRIAR'S WIFE.

And now she was. Not that it mattered to him. He seemed to have vanished.

Would she not even get a chance to talk with him? Her entire plan revolved around spending the night with him. She needed to see him, to talk with him.

She knew that once he remembered who she was, he would not harm her. He couldn't harm her. He had cared for her too much.

A clicking sound caught her attention. At first she thought it part of the music because it was so soft and faint. Then she realized it was coming from one of the archways.

Schahriar stood there, in the shadows. She had no idea how long he had been standing there.

The flickering light hid his features from her and accented the strength of his magnificent body. He held a beaded necklace. He had been hitting it lightly against one of his palms.

Scheherazade swallowed. She was nervous. She hadn't expected to be. Her father had been right. The boy she remembered was not present in the man. Not even his eyes—the eyes she had watched so closely in the ceremony—held any trace of that gentle child. Instead they were sunken and dark, filled with an intensity that had flared into hatred when he held his brother in his arms.

What had happened to her Schahriar?

ARABIAN NIGHTS

Kathryn Wesley

based on a screenplay by Peter Barnes

HALLMARK ENTERTAINMENT BOOKS

HALLMARK ENTERTAINMENT BOOKS are published by

Kensington Publishing Corp.
850 Third Avenue
New York, NY 10022

First Hallmark Entertainment Books Paperback Printing: April, 2000
10 9 8 7 6 5 4 3 2 1

Printed in the United States of America

For Kate Duffy,
with thanks for bringing us to the party

An Introduction to
Arabian Nights

Dear Reader,

The stories in *Arabian Nights* have entertained people worldwide for at least 13 centuries. The history behind this remarkable piece of literature is just as interesting as the stories themselves.

Scheherazade, that wonderful storyteller whose ability to weave a tale saved herself and ultimately a kingdom, seems to be a fictional character. She and her husband Schahriar appear in an ancient Persian book called *A Thousand and One Nights*. But this book differs from the collections of tales we know today.

In fact, a lot of the books that are called *Arabian Nights* or *A Thousand and One Nights* differ from one another. Scholars have found no original collection of stories that can be called authoritative. For hundreds of years, these stories were kept alive by world of mouth. The only thing these stories have had in common is their narrative frame—and the delightful Scheherazade.

Many of these tales were first introduced to the court of Harun al-Raschild, the Caliph of Baghdad, in the latter part of the 8th century. The Caliph loved stories, and was a scholar and poet himself. The storytellers in his court loved to flatter the Caliph by making him the hero in many of their tales.

You'll find Harun al-Raschild in this book as well, although he isn't a hero. He appears as the Sultan Abraschild, who disguises himself and moves among his subjects in search of jokes. The real Harun al-Raschild used to disguise himself and move among his subjects as well—but not for jokes. He was trying to learn more about his people.

Other stories in the collection came from other countries. Scholars break them down this way: the fairy tales probably came from Persia; the beast tales came from India; the anecdotes and stories with morals are Arabic; and then there are tales that clearly came from China and Japan.

Arabian Nights first made its way to Europe by way of a French scholar named Antoine Galland. His translation was never completed—although he told many of the stories orally. Among the stories he brought to Europe were "Ali Baba and the Forty Thieves" and "Aladdin."

The Egyptians continued to collect *Arabian Nights* tales, and by the time the British discovered them in the 19th century, there were more than 200 in all. An unknown Egyptian editor gathered them into a manuscript, and all subsequent editions of *Arabian Nights* are based on this collection.

Three Englishman translated *Arabian Nights* into English. The most famous version was compiled by Sir Richard Francis Burton in the 1880s. If you'd like to read this version, you'd best go to a library. The Burton translation takes 16 volumes.

However, there have been shorter versions of the work, many of them published as children's editions, some with spectacular art. As movies and television developed, a lot of the individual stories—like Ali Baba's—became films of their own. But to our knowledge, no one has tried to integrate the true spirit of Scheherazade and her desperate storytelling into film before.

This too is a shortened version of *Arabian Nights*. The legend has it that Scheherazade told stories for a thousand and one nights. That's 2.7 years! So instead of trying for the world's longest miniseries, we had to pick and choose a bit.

Favorites, like Ali Baba and Aladdin, are here, along with some of the lesser known tales. And of course, our heroine Scheherazade, who enchants us and ultimately the man who would kill her, with her ability to weave a storyteller's spell.

But we have tried to stay faithful to the international nature of these tales. We've also tried to show how stories influence everyday life.

And if you enjoy this, look up other editions of *Arabian Nights*. You'll find enough great stories to keep you entertained—maybe for an evening or maybe for a thousand and one nights.

Robert Halmi, Sr.
Chairman, Hallmark Entertainment Inc.

Prologue

The boys sat cross-legged on the bed, pillows at their backs. They both had dark curly hair and dark eyes. People usually took them for twins, even though they weren't. They were ten months apart.

They lay near each other on the large, soft bed, looking sadly at the sunlight streaming into the room. They could hear the murmur of voices outside.

It was too early for everyone else to go to bed. Only the boys had to, and only because they were so young. They hated that, and usually fought it. Tonight, though, they had gone to bed easily.

They had a different plan for staying awake.

A woman set down a tray on a small table beside the bed. The tray held their usual bedtime snack, biscuits and some juice.

As she stood, the oldest boy caught her arm. "You promised us a story!"

She smiled at him. It was a teasing smile. "I did?"

"Yes!" he shouted.

His brother joined in. "You did! You did!"

She laughed. Even though she hadn't promised a story this evening, they were being good. Usually it was difficult to get them near the bedroom when the sun was still up.

"May I join you?" she asked, looking at the edge of the bed.

"Please," said the oldest, scooting aside to make room.

"What kind of story are you going to tell us?" the youngest asked.

"A story about stories," she said.

The oldest frowned. "What does that mean?"

"You'll see," she said, settling her robes over her long legs.

"I want wars and battles," the oldest said.

"You'll get that," she said.

"And murder," the youngest said.

"That too," she said. Then she leaned toward them, her eyes bright. "But this is a very unusual story."

"Why is that?" asked the oldest.

"It doesn't start in a real place," she said.

"Where does it start?" asked the youngest.

"In someone's mind," the woman said. "In a dream."

"How can a story start with a dream?" asked the oldest.

The woman's smile was mischievous. "Let me show you." She clasped her hands together. "Are you ready?"

The boys punched their pillows and nestled in. Then they nodded.

"Well," she said. "Once upon a time . . ."

Chapter One

The dream seduced him, the way it always did. Only toward the end did the dream go bad.

Which seemed to be the way of things.

But Schahriar could not escape the dream, no matter how hard he tried.

First, he hears music. Drums and flutes playing a vaguely familiar tune—one he feels he should know, one he once enjoyed. Then he sees colors, faint, blurring—golds mostly—and as he focuses on them, he realizes that some browns are mixed in. Browns with jewels along the middle, jewels that move.

As he stares, he realizes he is watching a woman dance. All he can see is her belly. Her hips are covered with tassels and beads, and a jeweled tassel rises toward her breasts, which he cannot yet see.

She has the most beautiful stomach, flat and brown. He longs to place his hands on it.

Slowly his world widens. It is as if he is looking through a peephole, and then a door, and then from a vast distance. He can see her body now—her entire body except for her face. He stares at her full, round breasts, her legs encased in harem pants, the veil flowing down her back. Her lithe, supple hands move with the music. Her hands are stunning. They remind him of someone's—another woman's perhaps? His mind shies away from that, as if he has touched a barrier, and the barrier is too hot, even for him.

He is drawn to the dance, to her slender form, moving just for him. And then he realizes he is not alone. *She* is not alone. For she is dancing on someone else's hand.

In the logic of dreams, he accepts this as normal. The hand is huge and a strange reddish brown, like clay badly dried. The fingers have lines and wrinkles, and they curve upward, protecting the woman. The nails at the ends of the fingers are long, like talons, but shaped as if they have been manicured.

The giant hand breaks the seduction, for just a moment. Schahriar feels a twinge; then he finds his eyes drawn to the dancer once more.

Now he can see her face. She has brown eyes and a wide smile with more than a touch of whimsy to it. Her hair is long and falls down to the middle of her back. She is so striking, so enticing, and the way she laughs and moves, the way she smiles, is just for him.

His vision widens again, and he suddenly sees the owner of the hand. It is a huge demon with the face of a man. The demon's skin is more red than brown, and he has two horns growing out of his head, curling over the back of his skull like ram's horns. His eyes are white, frightening on a face larger than most buildings, and he has a thin, sloppy mustache that trails over his upper lip. He wears a single earring made of gold, a loop that bobbles as the woman dances.

As Schahriar's vision continues to widen, he realizes that the demon sits in a desert, near an oasis. His legs and feet are hidden in a trench so deep that Schahriar cannot see the bottom of it. At the edge of the trench is a large iron box—a box that disturbs Schahriar, although he cannot say why.

The dream holds him now, tightly. It takes him deeper.

When he realizes he is in the desert, he feels hot. Sweat covers him despite the fact that he is hiding in the oasis itself, in the branches of a palm tree that provide him some shade. The tree's leaves scratch him, and he knows—even though he cannot stop it—that soon the dream will turn bad.

The dancer waves her arms with a flourish, the music cascades, and she folds herself down on one knee, hands outstretched. The music lasts a moment longer, and then it too ends.

The demon grins. Schahriar bites his lower lip, fearing for the dancer's life. But the demon brings his hand closer to his square and oddly pointed ear. The dancer climbs onto the earring's loop, leans toward the demon, and speaks.

Schahriar cannot hear what she says, only the faint, husky rasp of her voice. The demon looks startled. Then he smiles.

"In the twinkling of an eye," the demon says, granting whatever wish she has just made. The demon's voice is low and powerful, shaking the entire oasis so hard that Schahriar thinks he might fall from the palm tree.

Then a hole appears in the sky, and through the hole, Schahriar sees clouds so blue that they hurt his eyes. The demon lifts the dancer so that she can see through the hole. Schahriar, through the power of his dream, sees what she does.

A city, a great city, floats in the sky. He sees the palaces, minarets, and towers, all dazzling white, sparkling in the sun. The roofs are made of gold—white gold that is worth more than all the wealth of Schahriar's kingdom combined.

The dancer claps her hands in delight. "More! More!" she says, like a child who cannot get enough.

The city gates open and a horse whinnies. Schahriar lifts his head so that he can see better.

A horse comes out of the gates, heading toward the dancer. The horse is even whiter than the buildings, looking pure and perfect, too perfect to exist. It stops in front of the dancer, who laughs with delight.

She bounces on the demon's hand and says, "More! More!"

The gold of the minaret's roof peels off into millions of jewels and coins. They float through the air like water, falling on the dancer. She laughs again.

It has been a long time since Schahriar has heard a woman laugh with such pure enjoyment.

She holds up her hands, gathering all the riches that she can to herself. "More," she says. "More!"

"Later," the demon says, his voice rumbling through the entire desert. "Magic is very exhausting and I am 542 years old."

"You don't look a day over 200," the dancer says insincerely. Schahriar feels a pang at her flirtation. He wants her to be better than that, to tell the truth always, no matter what the consequences.

"Yes," the demon says, agreeing with her, obviously delighting in her compliment. "I'm as bad as I ever was."

Then he laughs. The sound rolls over the desert like thunder from a storm. "We'll continue after I've slept."

Schahriar catches his breath and parts the fronds of the palm tree even farther. The demon does look exhausted, as if something essential has drained out of him, something that only time and sleep can replenish.

The demon glides his hand toward the box. The dancer

does not look at the demon's face. Nor does she look down at the box. Instead, she surveys the desert and the oasis as if it is her world. There is a smugness to her features that Schahriar has not seen before.

It is a warning to him, a warning he will not heed—has never heeded, in all the different versions of the dream.

She sees him hiding in the palm tree. He tries to cover himself with the fronds, but he knows she sees him.

She does not give him away. Instead, she lets the demon place her inside the iron box. Schahriar watches as the demon closes the lid, and notes with a dreamer's joy and a waking man's foreboding that the demon, in his exhaustion, forgets to lock the lid.

The demon immediately lies down, his head pillowed on the sand near the box. The thud from his movement nearly shakes Schahriar from the tree, but he holds on to the branches tightly. The demon sighs in obvious pleasure, and instantly his breathing is deep and regular.

The demon is asleep.

Schahriar knows this is the moment when he must leave. He does not know why. He tells himself it is so that he can escape the demon, but he does not know which demon he is referring to—the one in the sand or the one in the box.

He climbs down from the tree carefully, making certain he sets his bare feet on shaded sand. Behind him, he hears the groan of a door and tells himself it is nothing. But when he turns, he sees the dancer leaning against a tree and smiling at him.

Her presence startles him and yet does not. Her smile is not warm, but she places a hand on her supple hip, reminding him of the dance. He feels an attraction to her, even more now that she is closer.

"Thank you for not telling your friend the demon that you saw me," Schahriar says.

The dancer turns her head slightly so that Schahriar can barely see her amusement. "He's not my friend," she says as she takes a step closer. "He is my husband. He keeps me in the box because he's so jealous."

Schahriar's breath catches in his throat. He does not want the woman this close, but he cannot send her away. She looks like someone. Someone he once loved.

But she is not. He knows she is not.

"I saved you from him," she says. That cunning look is on her face again. Schahriar finds the look hard to ignore.

The dancer sits before him and stretches out her long legs. He sees that supple skin, that marvelous belly, and remembers the urge he had to place his fingers around her waist.

"Now you must make love to me," she says, "while my husband sleeps."

This is the moment, Schahriar thinks. The moment on which it all turns. He must walk away. If he does, he will keep his sanity. If he does not, he will lose himself forever.

"If you don't," the dancer says, all the beauty gone from her face, "I'll wake him up and he'll rip your head off."

Schahriar slowly crouches before her. She has a mole, a delicate mole, just above her mobile mouth. He wonders what it will be like to kiss her.

But he cannot.

"After we've made love, you'll tell him," Schahriar says, "and he'll kill me then."

The dancer smiles. "How did you guess?"

Schahriar stares at that mouth, at that mole, and he reaches for her. He is going to take her shoulders, but instead his hands find her throat. The skin is as soft as he imagined, and as supple. He digs his thumbs into that softness and his fingers tighten.

Her look of pleasure vanishes and her face is blank for

a moment before she realizes what he is going to do.
Then she tries to scream, but she does not have enough
air.

He squeezes and squeezes and then he wakes up: . . .

This time, the scream trapped in his throat escaped,
echoing in his large bedchamber. His fingers were
wrapped around a pillow so tightly that had it been a
woman's neck, it would have snapped. His eyes focused
on the white mattress, the pillows sprawled from his
restless night, the red bed curtains and the wall of windows
sending in morning light.

He could not believe he had done it again.

He threw the pillow away from him. It soared past the
columns toward the door just as Giafar stepped in.

"Oh, no," he said calmly. "Not again, Sayiddi."

Giafar bent and picked up the pillow. It wasn't even
damaged.

Schahriar buried himself in his mattress, unable to face
the brightness of the room, the brightness of the day.
"Yes, Giafar, I had that dream again. The demon's wife
planned to kill me, so I killed her."

Giafar sighed. He set the pillow on the bed, then walked
to the table a servant must have brought in while Schahriar
was dreaming. He grabbed the silver pitcher and a matching silver cup.

"You've had that dream now for five years," Giafar
said as he poured Schahriar a glass of water. "Ever since
your wife conspired with your brother to do the same
thing."

Schahriar was bathed in sweat, as if he had really been
in the desert. His hair was wet and sticking to his forehead.
"I expected that from Schahzenan, but not from my wife.
I loved her."

"You struck her down in revenge," Giafar said.

"It was an accident," Schahriar said. "I swear it."

"Allah is just," Giafar said, holding out the cup of water. "You're free of her, Sayiddi."

Schahriar couldn't bear the thought of drinking or eating. The dream was still with him. It had to have meant something. He got up and walked across the bed, startled to feel the cool sheets beneath his bare feet instead of sand.

"I'll never be free of her," he said. "She haunts me still."

He walked through the columns to the wall of arches leading to the Persian Gardens and stared out. The water in the pools was as blue as the clouds had been in his dream. But the trees were green, the trees specially planted so that he could see them every morning.

After his dream.

He could not escape it. He could not escape any of it. Giafar did not seem to understand the dilemma that Schahriar faced. Giafar always spoke of this with a vaguely sardonic tone, as if he were humoring Schahriar about a minor problem.

But it was not minor. It was his life.

"You forget, Giafar. I have to take a wife by the next full moon or the kingdom will be given to my brother, even though he is in exile. May he rot in hell." Schahriar raised his voice for that last sentence and it echoed across the quiet pools. A servant who had apparently been working there ran away as if the demon from Schahriar's dream pursued him.

"Your father wanted you to produce legitimate heirs as quickly as possible." There it was, that tolerant voice again. Why did Giafar make light of this? Giafar knew that Schahriar's father had specified only a wedding, not heirs.

"I can't take another wife," Schahriar said. "You know

she'll try to kill me too. They all will. Just as with the demon and the dancer in my dream.''

''I'll call the Royal Soothsayers, again, Sayiddi,'' Giafar said.

Schahriar whirled away from the pools. The Royal Soothsayers had done nothing in the past. They had seemed afraid to interpret his dreams.

But he could. It was clear to him, and had been clear for some time. He had simply been afraid to face it.

''Even the demon was betrayed by his wife.'' Schahriar walked toward the column. He touched it, needing its smoothness, its coolness, to remind him that he was in his palace and not at the base of a palm tree in the demon's desert. ''The dream tells me that all wives are treacherous.''

''No, no.'' Giafar was following him. ''You've just had a bad experience, Sayiddi.''

Babble and blather. Giafar had not had the dream.

''There's only one way to deal with wives,'' Schahriar said, looking at his messy bed. ''They have to be executed.''

''I'm sure we've all felt like that, Your Majesty.''

But what Giafar said no longer mattered. Schahriar walked to the next column and hugged it as if it were a lover. ''The dream has shown me the way. I will marry, there will be a wedding—and a wedding night. But in the morning I will have her executed before she kills me.''

He sighed. The relief was greater than he could imagine. Finally he knew how he would deal with this. Finally, he had a path that he could follow. He would meet his father's conditions, the kingdom would not go to his brother, and he would not be saddled with a betraying woman.

''Sayiddi.'' Giafar sounded panicked now.

Schahriar looked at him. Giafar had a frown in the

middle of his craggy face. His beard looked tangled, as if he had been pulling on it, and his red turban had slid forward.

Then Schahriar understood why Giafar looked so upset. There was a flaw to the plan.

"She can't be a princess of the blood," Schahriar said. "Her death would cause problems."

What an awful complication, and just when he thought he had the answer. Then a solution came to him. He leaned his head against the column and looked at Giafar. "Pick me a woman from the harem, Giafar."

Giafar's frown grew deeper. "Someone bright and happy, with no thought for the future?"

Sardonic. But it did not matter. He would have to carry out Schahriar's orders.

"Do it in secret," Schahriar said. It was perfect. It was right. Of course he would have the dream until he understood what it meant. He would have the dream until he acted upon its message and regained control of his life.

Five years. Five long, miserable years.

Giafar was watching him.

"Now," Schahriar said, "send for the Chief Executioner."

He would go through with the plan. And no one would be the wiser—except those he trusted the most.

Chapter Two

"... and so the Physician Douban finally cured the Grecian King of his mysterious illness, and he was loaded with riches and honors," the Storyteller said, "but that wasn't the end of the story."

The words sent a thrill through Scheherazade. She loved the Storyteller's tales. They were filled with great characters and incredible twists.

She stretched out her legs on the carpet, nearly hitting the men beside her. The crowd was large today. The sand beneath the carpet was uncomfortable and the sun was hot. But those were just distractions. The story was what mattered.

"Courtiers at the palace were jealous of Douban. They spread rumors that he wanted to kill the King—kings are always suspicious—and Douban was condemned to death."

The crowd around Scheherazade gasped, but she did not. She had been expecting something to go wrong. There would be no story if it didn't.

The Storyteller's green eyes met hers. He was an older man with a gray beard that needed trimming. He wore the same brown turban every day, and the same gray robes. He sat in front of his tent, a small place made from rugs, and he had two assistants who stood beside him while he worked.

He sat cross-legged, clutching his knees as he spoke— rarely did he use his hands to illustrate his stories—and he watched his audience.

Mostly, on this day, he watched her.

Scheherazade pulled her blue veil tighter across her nose and mouth, leaving only her eyes visible. She knew he recognized her—she saw him so often and had spoken to him privately—but so far he had said nothing.

"Douban intrigued the ungrateful King by telling him that even after his death he would speak from the grave, provided the King turned to a certain page in the Physician's Book of Magic."

Two camels walked by, nearly drowning out the Storyteller's deep voice. Usually the sounds of the bazaar did not interfere with his tales. Every once in a while, though, they grew too loud and seemed overwhelming, the shouts of the merchants, the laughter of the crowd near the belly dancer, or—like now—the bellow of a cranky camel.

Scheherazade wished she could once have the Storyteller all to herself. She would ask him to tell her every tale he had ever heard, and she would remember each one. She had already heard a lot of them, and she had learned the beauty of his craft.

He never told the same tale twice.

"After Douban was beheaded," the Storyteller said, "the King licked his fingers and turned to the page in the dead man's book to find these words: *You too have been executed.*"

The crowd tensed around her. The man beside the Storyteller looked at him in surprise.

The Storyteller's eyes twinkled. He knew he had them now.

"The King stared at the words, then slumped forward dead." This time, the Storyteller slumped ever so slightly. He held the position for a moment, and then slowly rose.

The audience was waiting—Scheherazade was waiting—to find out how the Physician Douban had killed the King from the grave.

The Storyteller knew that his audience waited, and he paused just long enough to add to the suspense. Then his eyebrows rose and he intoned, "The pages of the book had been poisoned so that the King, when wetting his finger, *had executed himself.*"

The audience sighed as one, the revelation perfect as always. Scheherazade smiled beneath her veil. Just once, she would like to tell a story as perfect as this.

There was a lot to the telling. Not just having the right story, but reciting it correctly, with enough drama to keep the interest, but not too much to overwhelm the simplicity of the tale.

The Storyteller's assistants rose as the story ended and held out small wooden bowls. The listeners placed coins in them. An assistant passed before Scheherazade, and she put a coin in too.

As she did, the Storyteller smiled at her. "Here again, mistress?" he asked. "That's the sixth time this week."

So he had noticed her after all. Of course, she was hard to miss, sitting in front as she usually did.

She returned his smile and let her veil drop. "Seven."

He inclined his head toward her, as if she would know which of the numbers was correct. His gaze moved away from her toward his assistants, but she wasn't going to let this moment pass so easily.

She wanted to ask him her question, but she had to approach it delicately. "These people sit for hours, just listening. It's a miracle."

She had his attention again. He looked as if he were about to deny her last sentence, so she spoke quickly, to get her question out. "What is the secret, Master Teller?"

His expression softened. He wasn't offended at all, as she had thought he would be.

"People need stories more than bread itself," he said. "Stories tell us how to live—and why."

Her breath caught in her throat. She had not thought of that, yet it seemed so simple. Clearly she felt that way about stories or she would not come here day after day. She had a need for them, one she had not questioned— nor entirely understood.

All she knew was that she had learned more about herself through stories than any other way. The events of her own life became clear when she heard a story about something similar. Stories enriched her.

She wondered if the others in the crowd felt the same way.

An assistant tapped the Storyteller on the shoulder and showed him the contents of one of the bowls. The Storyteller took it and, as he frowned at it, Scheherazade knew she was forgotten.

She put her veil back over her face, thanked him softly, and stood. He nodded curtly at her and turned back to his bowl. She moved away with the crowd into the market itself.

It was an amazing place, made more amazing by the fact that so much happened all at the same time. Merchants sat on their rugs, their wares beautifully displayed. Scheherazade was always most taken with the fruits, from the dried figs to the sumptuous melons. She could have done without the nuts and the seed pods, but she looked at them anyway every time she passed.

She walked between the rugs, carefully placed so that there was a dirt path around everything. Riders led their horses and camels out of courtesy for the merchants, and people shopped, although not everyone bought. The bazaar was a social place as well, a place where people came for conversation and for company.

Scheherazade came for stories.

She walked past the snake charmer, a beautiful young woman whose braided hair was not properly covered. She sat with her feet outstretched, and a large snake glided across them, following the commands she gave it with her arms. Scheherazade shook her head and continued. If the snake charmer left, Scheherazade would not miss her. Such a thing was interesting once, but after that it became little more than a gimmick.

It took her almost as long to leave the market as it did to walk the rest of the way home. She had to go through the white walls of the city, past lovely stonework and high columns. Mostly, she kept her head down and she held her veil in place. She walked with people she didn't know—other shoppers, merchants, and strangers who had found the city, which was an oasis in the desert.

Sometimes she wondered if they thought it a mirage when they first came upon it, all white against the golden sands, the shallow river running outside the city's walls, but no real trees or plants to speak of until one came inside. She had never asked, but she was always curious. Every once in a while, when she could get away with it, she looked into the faces of people she did not know and tried to imagine how they saw the world. She knew it had to be very different from the way she did. She, who was the trusted child of the Sultan's most intimate advisor.

There were no shadows on the street. She glanced up at the blue sky. The sun was higher in the heavens than she had expected.

She was late.

She hurried through the palace gates and through the arches that led to her father's quarters. She pushed open the large mahogany doors, hoping her father was not yet home, but as she stepped into the cool darkness, she saw him talking with a man who looked vaguely familiar.

At first she thought the man a relative of the Storyteller, but his beard was too neatly trimmed, his clothing too rich. After a moment, she recognized him. The palace physician.

Something was happening, then, something she wasn't sure she should be part of.

As she stepped inside, she said, "Sorry I'm late, Father," more as a warning so that he could tell her to leave rather than a greeting.

Her father beckoned her toward him. The two men stood in the center of his study, papers and maps strewn about the desks. But her father blocked the physician's view of the important papers.

Scheherazade frowned. This meeting was definitely not normal, and the fact that it took place here instead of the physician's quarters had her worried. That, and her father's expression.

He was looking quite serious, dressed in his red palace robes, his turban slightly askew. When she saw him like this, she could see the weight of his office: Giafar, the Sultan's Grand Vizier, the most important man in the palace.

"This is my daughter, Scheherazade," her father said to the palace physician. "She's my strong right arm. Speak freely in front of her. How is His Majesty?"

Scheherazade felt her breath catch in her throat. Something was wrong with Schahriar?

The physician looked rather intrigued by it all. He rubbed his hands together as if he were gossiping instead of talking about the Sultan.

"The Sultan is being eaten by the worms of madness." The physician caught Scheherazade's eye and leaned toward her, as if he were speaking to her privately. Men had been doing that to her a lot since she had returned to the city. It irritated her. Her father, when she had mentioned it to him, had laughed and said that it was merely a compliment to her beauty.

"It reminds me a little of the case of Gilgamesh, the King of Uruk," the physician was saying, "when his friend the grand warrior Enhidn died. He wandered in darkness so thick that he could see nothing ahead or behind him but his own fears."

Scheherazade resisted the urge to step backward. The physician was too intense for her.

"What did King Gilgamesh do?" her father asked.

The physician turned to him as if he had forgotten that Giafar was there.

"Raged like a lion," the physician said. "Tore his hair, traveled the wilderness, wandered the Earth, slaughtered anyone in his path because he was afraid of death."

Scheherazade felt a shudder run down her back. This did not sound like Schahriar at all, at least not the boy she remembered.

"Can you cure the Sultan?" her father asked.

The physician stood up, as if the question brought him back to the present. "No," he said. "Only Allah can do that."

"How was Gilgamesh cured?" Scheherazade asked.

Her father shot her a warning look, but she could not take back the question. She wasn't quite sure why he didn't want to hear the answer. Perhaps he already knew it.

The physician shook his head. "It was a young woman who did it. No one knows how. A complete amateur. Beginner's luck."

Her father turned his face so that the physician could not see him, and rolled his eyes.

The physician leaned toward Scheherazade again as if he were speaking to her in complete confidence. "That sort of thing could be very, very distressing for an experienced professional like myself.''

But he didn't sound distressed. Only amused. Scheherazade took another step away from him.

"When did Schahriar become so ill?" she asked. "When I played with him as a child in the palace, he was always so happy. Everybody loved him."

"Madness creeps in unseen and floods the soul," the physician said.

"You're no help," Giafar said, disgusted.

"Patients often say that, but what do they know?"

"Should I get a second opinion?" Giafar asked.

"Why not?" the physician said. "I can come back tomorrow."

Then he placed a hand over his heart and bowed his head before taking his leave. As he did so, her father turned away, making a small sound of disgust.

Scheherazade did not move. Schahriar had been such a warm and witty companion, more fun than anyone she had known. She couldn't imagine him as a madman. He had had too much joy in him.

What had changed that? Was the physician right? Was madness something which could grip the brightest soul and dim it forever?

The heavy door clicked shut. The physician was gone.

"I didn't know Schahriar was ill," Scheherazade said to her father.

He walked past her and sat on his favorite red rug. "I've tried to keep it from everybody."

He seemed very tired. She hadn't looked at him for a long time, not closely anyway. How could she have missed this? It was clearly a great burden on him.

She sat beside him and put her arm around him. "You look terrible, Father."

"It's only natural," he said. "I have to deal with the worst kind of madman. A madman with power."

* * *

The Persian Gardens, deep in the heart of the palace, made the Chief Executioner nervous. He hated the fragile beauty of the place, designed to soothe a Sultan's soul. The wall of arches leading to the Sultan's bedchamber were behind them, and there were other entrances here as well, all of them forbidden except by invitation.

The Chief Executioner had only been here once before, but the Gardens had remained impressed in his memory. Blue pools everywhere. Greenery and flowers, smelling sweet. This was not a place to think of death, yet it did not seem to stop the Sultan.

When Schahriar had become Sultan, the Chief Executioner had finally thought he would work for a reasonable man. In those days, the Chief Executioner would never have believed that the Sultan would become the man he saw before him now.

In those days, in fact, the Chief Executioner had despaired of ever getting the chance to do his job. He had thought Schahriar too good-hearted to have anyone executed.

But this man before him, this Schahriar, was different.

The Sultan still wore his nightclothes, a gold robe over white silk. He was barefoot, and his hair was slicked back as if with sweat. His eyes were sunken into his head, and he had a wild look about him, an intensity that the Chief Executioner found disconcerting.

The Sultan leaned against a column in the Persian Gardens and insisted that the Chief Executioner stand behind him. The Sultan had given him the instructions in a soft voice, insisting that they both watch for others who might listen.

The Chief Executioner was not shocked—he had heard worse in his life—but he was surprised. He rubbed a hand over his bald head, then tugged on his long black mustache. He had no real response to what the Sultan had just told him.

"You understand what's needed?" the Sultan whispered, apparently impatient with the Chief Executioner's silence.

The Chief Executioner suppressed a sigh. "I know my job, Sayiddi," he said. "You want your bride executed on the morning after the wedding."

"Early." The Sultan's voice was husky, urgent.

But the Chief Executioner could not be rushed. Even if the Sultan gave him the order, that did not mean they could ignore the rules. And there were many rules.

"There are certain procedural problems, Sayiddi," the Chief Executioner said.

"What are they?" the Sultan asked.

"As I am executing her after the wedding, it means she'll be the Sultana, who by tradition cannot be hanged or beheaded."

"Details, details."

The Chief Executioner stepped back and tried to make eye contact with the Sultan, but the Sultan's eyes were roving over the Gardens as if he saw a thousand enemies behind each plant.

"Never fear, Sayiddi," the Chief Executioner said, not showing his discomfort. There was clearly something wrong with the Sultan. But it was not his business to do anything about it. His job was to do the Sultan's bidding. "Where there's a will, there's a way. I can strangle her."

"That's what I want." The Sultan pushed himself against the post as if he were guarding his own back.

"But I can't use hemp rope, not on a royal throat."

The Sultan closed those crazy eyes. "Must I be crossed at every turn?"

The Chief Executioner stayed close, speaking as calmly and sincerely as he would to a sane monarch. "There would be no objection to silk. A silk rope would fulfill all the legal requirements.''

The Sultan finally looked at him. His eyes were like deep, dark pools that never saw sunlight. The Chief Executioner had to work to hold his gaze.

''Rely on me, Sayiddi.''

He left before the Sultan could answer. He wasn't sure he wanted to know what else the Sultan would say.

The harem rooms in the palace seemed darker than usual. Heart's Delight sat in the center of half a dozen harem girls, whispering. The rumors were terrible, but not everyone seemed to have heard them yet. There were still girls swimming in the nearby pool, girls working on their clothing, girls giving each other makeup tips in the corners of the large main room.

The windows were small and high up so that no unauthorized person could see in. Usually the light that flowed through them was enough for Heart's Delight, but on this day she longed for sunlight and the freedom to walk the streets.

The freedom to leave this place.

They had been talking about the Sultan's plan all afternoon, whispering. Occasionally some of the other girls would look at the little group, but so far none had joined them. Perhaps the fear in their tones had kept the other girls away.

Heart's Delight slipped her free arm through Fair Face's. Fair Face had pale skin and auburn hair that always caught the eye. She was like a lily amongst the dark roses, and stood out that way. Fair Face was trembling, although she was not cold. She did not look at Heart's Delight.

The others were watching her, though, as if they expected her to do something.

She could think of very little to do. It was impossible

for them to leave. It was their job to submit to the Sultan's bidding.

She turned to Coral Lips, who looked magnificent in green. But her stunning clothing could not hide the worry lines on her face.

"Do you think Scheherazade can help us?" Heart's Delight asked.

"She's the Grand Vizier's daughter," Coral Lips said. "She's done it before."

"And she's a friend of the Sultan," Fair Face said.

"No, no," Coral Lips said. "That was when they were children. She's been away, and they haven't seen each other for years."

Heart's Delight put a hand to her throat. Scheherazade had been her only hope. She opened her mouth to say something, when she felt a hand on her back. Madame Zouche, the Mistress of the Harem, stood behind her.

"That's enough, girls!" Madame Zouche said.

Heart's Delight winced. Madame Zouche, with her skin painted white, her thick perfume, and the jewelry that jingled as she moved, frightened Heart's Delight. She kept her head down so that Madame Zouche would say no more to her.

At that moment, the doors to the harem opened. Scheherazade hurried in, her stride long and mannish. Everything about Scheherazade spoke of her freedom, from the way she dressed to the way she moved about so easily.

Heart's Delight hadn't realized she envied that until now.

Coral Lips ran toward Scheherazade, and the other girls followed. Heart's Delight had to hurry to keep up. She didn't want to stay behind with Madame Zouche.

When the others reached Scheherazade, they stopped in front of her, but Scheherazade waited for Heart's Delight. As Heart's Delight approached, Scheherazade held out her hand.

Heart's Delight took it. Scheherazade's fingers were warm and dry. Comforting.

Still, Heart's Delight couldn't stop the fluttering in her stomach. "The Sultan's going to kill us."

Scheherazade squeezed Heart's Delight's fingers. "Who told you that?"

"My mother," Coral Lips said before Heart's Delight could answer. "She got it from the cook, who got it straight from the Chief Executioner's assistant. It's a secret."

"Her mother is never wrong," Fair Face said. She leaned toward Scheherazade, as if to press upon her how important this was. "I heard it from one of the hand-maidens, who heard it from one of the guards."

Madame Zouche approached and, as usual, stood behind Heart's Delight. Heart's Delight started to move away, but Scheherazade held her in place. Besides, Madame Zouche did not say anything. She merely listened.

"He's going to marry one of us and have his bride executed in the morning after the wedding," Coral Lips said.

Scheherazade was gripping the hand of Heart's Delight tightly now. But Scheherazade wasn't panicked—why would she be? She wasn't part of the harem—but she did seem baffled.

"Why would he do that?"

"He's mad, isn't he?" Madame Zouche said.

Scheherazade's mouth opened slightly. She didn't seem shocked, though. It was as if she already knew something of the Sultan's madness.

But she didn't seem to realize how horrible this could be. Heart's Delight pulled her closer.

"And it won't stop there," she said. "He'll get a taste for it and kill us all."

Scheherazade did not deny it as Heart's Delight hoped

she would. Instead, the fear that filled the rest of them reflected in her eyes. She looked at all of their faces.

"Don't worry," she said. "I'll talk to my father."

That was the best thing Scheherazade could do, yet Heart's Delight let out a small sigh. She worried that a talk would not be enough.

Chapter Three

The fear in the harem infected her. Scheherazade was not afraid for herself, but she felt a sense of urgency that she hadn't before. She had to find her father, and she had to find him quickly.

If the rumors were right, she had hardly any time at all.

She probably wouldn't have believed Heart's Delight and the other girls if she hadn't seen the palace physician with her father, seen the way her father's face collapsed in on itself, and heard the way her father referred to Schahriar.

A madman.

Only a madman would marry a woman and kill her the next day. Something was wrong with Schahriar, something fundamental.

Or, perhaps, something that no one else understood. Perhaps no one had found a way to find the source of Schahriar's madness. The physician was certainly no help, not with his talk of worms and his belief that only Allah could cure the Sultan.

Her father had said that the Royal Soothsayers had been of no help either, that Schahriar was having dreams that were plaguing his sleep—a sign, her father said, of his tortured mind.

Or of a tortured soul.

Something had to have harmed Schahriar, something awful. An evil man did not grow from a boy like the one she remembered. An evil man did not have that capacity for love.

Scheherazade hurried through the palace corridors. The place was so huge that she could go for days without seeing anyone if she wished. Right now, she wished the palace were smaller. She had to find her father, and she had a hunch she knew where he was.

He wouldn't like it when she barged in on him.

Fortunately, there would be no one who could stop her.

She dipped beneath an arch toward the baths and saw her father's robes on the pressing table, one of the servants lovingly cleaning them. Her father's turban had been unwrapped and was being cleaned as well.

The servants were working on other clothing too.

Scheherazade straightened her spine. Her father wouldn't like this.

He wouldn't like it at all.

She waited until the servants weren't looking, then slipped through the closed doors. She wandered down another corridor, this one hot and smelling of steam. Tendrils of steam, like a gray mist, filled the corridor, and toward the end of it, the steam was so thick that it looked like fog.

She walked through it, keeping her head high. Servants were sitting near the main entrance—she hadn't expected that—and they stood as she passed, apparently realizing—belatedly—that she was a woman.

A blush built on her cheeks, or perhaps it was a reaction to the uncomfortably humid air.

But she was here now and she would get in trouble no matter what. She had best do what she came for.

It took a moment for her eyes to adjust. She had never been inside the men's steam room. An attendant threw cold water on hot rocks, just as in the women's steam area. Only this attendant was male, and barely dressed.

Her father sat on the tile near a pile of hot rocks. Four men sat around him, but they were not having a conversation. They were resting, as if they didn't even know the others were there. They all wore white towels around their heads and waists, and their chests were slick with steam and sweat.

Scheherazade resisted the urge to turn her face away.

Instead, she said, "Father, I must talk with you."

Her father looked up in surprise. When he recognized her, he moved backward until one of the stone steps interrupted him. "What are you doing here, child?"

"Put some clothes on, Father." She bent down to help him up. "This is urgent."

"I blame your late lamented mother for your lack of propriety," he said, not so much to Scheherazade but to the men, who were beginning to chuckle. "It's all her fault."

Scheherazade pulled him to his feet and put a hand on his back to hurry him out.

"Please be quick, Father," she said softly. "Or they'll say you're meeting women in the steam room."

He growled at her under his breath, but let her lead him away. They hurried through the baths, and it wasn't until they were in the corridor that led to her father's quarters that Scheherazade realized they had left his clothing behind.

Her father realized it too, for as he pushed open the

double doors that led to his study, he said, "I haven't had time to dry off."

He went to the carved wardrobe, opened it, and pulled out a white robe that her mother had given him to wear to the baths. He slipped it on, then rubbed his arms. Apparently the warmth from the steam bath hadn't stayed with him. The quick trip through the palace corridor had left him chilled.

Scheherazade made certain the doors were closed, then turned to her father. He was watching her as if she were the one who had gone mad.

"Is the Sultan going to marry and then execute his bride the morning after the wedding?"

Her father's mouth opened, and he put a hand to his chest. She had surprised him. It had been a long time since she had done that.

"How did you know that?" he demanded. "It's supposed to be a secret."

"A secret here in the palace?" Scheherazade shook her head. "Everyone in the harem already knows."

Her father let his hand drop. He closed the door to the wardrobe and leaned on it. That same look crossed his face, the one she had seen earlier, when he had called Schahriar a madman.

"How am I going to pick a bride now?" her father said. "I'll have to drag her to the altar."

Scheherazade froze. She hadn't expected her father to be so deeply involved. She hadn't thought it through— of course the Grand Vizier was involved—and now she understood why he was so disturbed. The Sultan had commanded him to chose a woman who would be put to death.

Her father was not the kind of man who could do that and live with himself afterward. Not an innocent woman who had done nothing to harm anyone.

Scheherazade made her way to the small table that sat

beside her father's favorite rug. A servant had placed a fresh pot of Turkish coffee there and two small glasses. Her father liked coffee after his steam bath.

Scheherazade poured some for him with a shaking hand. He took it and looked at her.

She didn't meet his gaze. An idea was forming in her mind, from something the physician had said. And from something she had learned in the stories she had listened to. Sometimes it took the right person to save someone else.

She had to know the extent of Schahriar's madness, however. She said, "The women in the harem are frightened that it won't stop at one girl. The Sultan may get a taste for killing them."

Her father started to pace. "If Schahriar wasn't the Sultan, he'd be locked away until the madness passed."

That wasn't quite the answer she had been looking for. She wanted reassurance that Schahriar's madness wouldn't go that far. Apparently her father couldn't give that. No one could.

"He was such a loving boy," Scheherazade said. She couldn't seem to convey to anyone how wonderful he had been, back in the days when they were young enough to be friends, when a friendship between a boy and a girl was innocent.

She felt she had gotten to know him then. The essential person couldn't be that different. A boy held the blueprint to the man. She knew, deep in her heart, that Schahriar, however mad, had to be the person she remembered.

Her father was watching her. She smiled at him, lost in memory. "We used to climb his favorite peach tree. One day I fell and cut myself."

She could see Schahriar there, in her mind's eye. The way he had scrambled down the tree to reach her side. She had been crying—the pain had been sharp and sudden and she was still young enough to cry when surprised—

and he had pulled her against him. He dried her tears and rocked her, and she had felt safe against him.

But she couldn't quite explain that to her father. Still, she had to try.

"Schahriar bound up the wound," she said, and looked at her father, who was still pacing. He hadn't heard a word she had said. She sighed and stood. "What is it, Father?"

He clutched the glass she had given him earlier. She was afraid he might break it between his hands. "What am I going to do, child? I'll never be able to go through with this. I can't pick a poor harem girl, knowing I'm condemning her to death."

That was the man she had known, the man who had raised her with wisdom and compassion.

This decision had to be tearing him apart.

And the Sultan had complete control of this. The girls in the harem knew it. They would be terrified, and they would have no chance to make it through the night. No woman, no matter how beautiful, could entice a stranger in a single evening. Not a mad stranger who intended to kill her.

But a woman who knew him, knew who he had been, knew how he loved, how he felt, a woman who shared his memories and had once shared his deepest self—she might be able to survive the night.

And if she did, she might help him survive as well.

What had the physician said when she asked him how Gilgamesh was cured? He had said, *It was a young woman who did it. No one knows how. A complete amateur. Beginner's luck.*

Beginner's luck.

Or perhaps the woman knew more about Gilgamesh than all the learned scholars and healers combined. Was there anyone who really knew Schahriar? Knew the boy he had been? Knew someone other than the Sultan?

Her father knew the man, the tortured man. But Scheherazade knew the loving boy. She could still remember how strong he had felt when he held her, how much he had cared, and how gently he had rocked her that day so long ago.

"I may have a way out for you, Father." She walked away from him, knowing he would not like what she had to say.

She paused and looked out the window. The day was still beautiful. The clouds were fluffy, the sky blue. Nothing had changed. Except her.

She took a deep breath and turned. "I'll marry Sultan Schahriar myself."

Her father spilled his coffee. It splattered his white towels and stained the robe he had had for years. A beloved robe.

He set the cup down, as if he were trying to gather himself. But when he stood, she could see the anguish on his face. "I won't let you sacrifice yourself for me."

She nodded. She had known that would be his response. And now it was time to be honest with him. Time to let him know what had been in her heart from the moment she first laid eyes on Schahriar.

He had been so mischievous then. He always smiled. His dark eyes had twinkled whenever he saw her. She could still remember how she felt whenever he winked at her or took her hand.

She had never told anyone of the time he had held her. They had almost been too old for it to be allowed. But she cherished the memory—took it out and turned it over in her mind almost every day.

"I'm not doing this for you, Father," she said slowly. "I'm not even doing it to save the girls in the harem. I'm doing it for Schahriar and myself. I love him."

"No," her father said, "you love the boy he was, not the man he is."

She started. Her father's words were too close to her own thoughts. "That boy is still there, in him."

"You'd have to dig very, very deep to find him," Her father said. "He's changed completely. It's not just the betrayal by his wife and brother. No, absolute power has eaten his soul. I know him. You think you can save him, but you can't. No one can."

"I don't believe that," she said.

Her father took her shoulders. His eyes were wild. She hadn't seen him like this since . . .

. . . since her mother died.

"Scheherazade, listen to me. You're all I have. I beg you, don't do it."

She leaned her cheek against her father's hand. He was trembling.

"I can save him from himself," she said. "I don't know how, but I've made up my mind. I know I can do it."

"Whenever your mother said that, I knew she was going to do something disastrous."

"You loved her, Father," Scheherazade said fondly.

"Yes." Her father's voice was cold. It sent a shiver through Scheherazade. "But she's dead, child. As you will be if you go through with this."

Chapter Four

All day the crowds in the street had grown. Early in the morning, Scheherazade watched them gather, coming from all over the country to see their Sultan wed. Each person was wearing festive clothing in colors from red to blue to green to yellow. Scheherazade hadn't seen so much beauty in years.

Some of the colors came from the brightly colored dye powders people were throwing at each other to celebrate the wedding. Scheherazade remembered that from the Sultan's last wedding. She had stood in the crowd below and looked up at the balcony where Schahriar and his wife stood, small figures, untouchable figures. Her own eyes had teared that day, although she had never known if it was the from the dye powder that had stained her face and clothes, or from something else entirely.

Then, the festive mood had escaped her, and on this day, the day of the Sultan's second wedding, the festive mood was escaping her as well.

Scheherazade wondered what the crowd would think

if they knew Schahriar's plan for his bride. Would they be shocked and appalled, frightened like the girls in the harem? Or would they think it another oddity that separated the Sultan from his subjects? Would they bow to his wisdom, deciding perhaps that the treacherous woman deserved her fate? Or would they turn on him?

She hoped she would never find out.

Scheherazade let out a small sigh. She was standing before a mirror in her dressing room. She could hear the music from the street performers filtering through the open window. She could also hear the shouts and laughter from the crowd itself. Street performers, from magicians to acrobats, were keeping the crowd entertained.

Her handmaidens were making the final adjustments on her wedding dress, pulling the left seam tight, adjusting the right sleeve. When Scheherazade first saw the dress, she had thought it the most beautiful gown in the world. Staring at it in the mirror, she realized how perfect it was.

Its green silk accented her eyes. The embroidery, swirls that looked vaguely like climbing vines, made the dress seem a part of her. The gold belt around her waist and the gold headdress that covered the top of her head gave her features an unfamiliar cast.

She stood with her arms out, studying herself. The music from the street grew louder and harder to ignore.

The woman before her had a smooth, innocent face and wide eyes that held no joy. Somehow, when she had imagined marriage to Schahriar—and she had, first as a child, then as a young woman, and again when she learned he was a widower—she had always thought she would wear a dress as elegant as this one, a headdress as suited to her as the one she now wore. But she had also imagined squirming with uncontainable joy. Sometimes, in the story she told herself about her marriage to Schahriar, she would argue with the handmaidens to finish quickly so that she could join her future husband on the balcony, so that she could stand at his side as he greeted his subjects below.

They would be so stunned that he had chosen such a perfect wife, and he would turn to her, extend his hand, a smile on his gentle face, and look at her with complete, unquestioning love.

Scheherazade closed her eyes against the image. That story had turned dark. That dream would never come true. She hadn't even seen the man she was to marry. All of the agreements had been made without her presence. Somehow she had expected Schahriar to come to her father's quarters, to talk with her, to speak of the friendship they had once had.

Instead, he let her father plan the wedding, and her father had looked more and more distraught.

The door to her dressing room opened, and Scheherazade sighed again. She opened her eyes in time to see her father enter. He looked resplendent in his red robes, but he had grown thinner in the last few days, as if his concern for her had eaten him from within.

She met his gaze. She knew what he was going to say, and she wished he wouldn't. As he'd pleaded with her over the last few days, her resolve had grown, just the way it used to when she was a child. Her mother used to call her a contrary girl, and perhaps she was.

Or perhaps she was just stubborn enough to bring Schahriar back to the world of the sane.

Outside, laughter rose, followed by applause. The handmaiden to Scheherazade's left turned toward the window, but the other continued to fuss with her hair.

Her father walked toward her. He took a deep breath to calm himself, as he always did when he tried not to show his emotions.

"Daughter," he said, "when you walk out onto that balcony, you will be married ..."

She recognized the tone. He was trying to reason with

her, trying to use logic. She didn't move. She didn't dare. She had been sewn into the dress, and the handmaidens weren't quite finished with her yet.

". . . and you will have signed your own death warrant."

The woman in the mirror did not look concerned by his words. Scheherazade was, but she was not willing to turn back now. She could help Schahriar. She knew it.

Even though she still wasn't sure how.

Her father crossed before her, blocking her view of herself in the mirror. He dropped all pretense at calm.

"If you love me," he said, "please, please, please, *please* don't do this."

She raised her gaze to his. His eyes were sunken and nearly black from lack of sleep. He was terrified, and he was letting it show.

He had never, in all her life, used her love for him as a weapon. He had never begged before.

His shoulders were hunched forward. She had never seen him like this.

This was her moment—her last moment—to turn back. She could picture it. In her mind's eye, she leaned her head forward onto her father's shoulder, her jewels jingling, and let him hold her. The dress pulled—perhaps it even ripped—as she sank into the hug.

Of course, Father, she would say. *What was I thinking?*

And he would hold her as if he would never let her go.

Just as Schahriar had done the day she fell from the tree.

She would not turn back. For if she did, Schahriar would have to face his future alone, and she knew, deep within herself, that she was his last and only hope.

"I know what I'm doing, Father," she said.

His eyes narrowed and she thought she saw his lower

lip tremble. Her father, in defeat. Something she had never thought she would see.

"No," he said, "you don't. You have no idea what you're doing."

There was nothing she could say to change his mind, nothing she could say that would reassure him, so she stepped forward and kissed his cheek. He caressed her hand and then backed away.

As he did, Scheherazade saw herself in the mirror once more. Her handmaiden placed the wedding veil on top of Scheherazade's headdress, making the costume complete.

Schahriar's new bride stood facing her, a stranger who might not live to see another day.

Schahriar's bride was beautiful—he would give her that. He had not expected the daughter of Giafar to be so very lovely. She was slight, with delicate features and eyebrows so thin, so expressive, that they moved even when the rest of her face did not.

Schahriar had watched her during the ceremony. She had been solemn and sincere, an innocent who did not know the fate that awaited her.

And so he had been, the first time.

Schahriar led her toward the balcony. She had looked at his hand as if she had wanted him to take hers—in fact, she had looked at him all day as if she expected something, something he would not give.

What was it that one of his old advisors had once said? A woman's wedding day was the happiest of her life, and it all went down from there.

At least, for Giafar's daughter, the ending would come quickly.

Schahriar felt a burst of irritation. He was feeling pity for the girl, and she did not deserve it. All women were tricksters. His dreams had told him that.

His first wife had told him that.

It was a lesson he shouldn't have to learn twice.

Giafar had watched the entire ceremony as if Schahriar had ripped out his heart and was proceeding to eat it. The wily old man was up to something. Otherwise he would not have let his only daughter marry Schahriar.

Unless he knew she was evil.

Unless he knew she had to die.

Schahriar shook the thought from his head. He walked onto the balcony, the girl—his bride—following him and her father somewhere behind them. Servants and lesser nobles were already lining the back of the balcony, looking more solemn than the occasion deserved.

Surely no one else knew of his plan. Why weren't these imbeciles smiling with joy?

Perhaps because he was not. He could not force himself to enjoy the charade. He was marrying because he had to, because his dead father's decree dictated it, but that did not mean he had to enjoy it.

He did not enjoy seeing the face of the woman he was about to put to death, a woman who was more beautiful than he had expected.

As he became visible to the crowd below, a roar went up. People—his subjects—shouted for him. There was the joy that had been missing in the day. His people felt it for him. His people were happy that their Sultan had taken a wife.

To them, all was finally right with the world.

The poor fools.

He walked to the edge of the balcony and placed his hands on the wooden railing. His bride trailed him like a wraith. She seemed to feel no joy either. But then, how could she, with her father looking as if the world had ended and her new husband glowering at her as if she were the ugliest creature he had ever seen?

Which she most decidedly was not.

Why hadn't he thought of that? Why hadn't he realized that her face would haunt him too, as his first wife's did, when she turned, her eyes already glazing over . . .

The crowd was cheering, cheering her death.

He narrowed his eyes, yanked himself back to the present. Packets of dye floated across the breeze like yellow, orange, and blue clouds. The people stood in the street below, their faces upturned so that they could see him, so that they could see his new bride.

One glimpse. The only glimpse. And after today, no one would see her again.

They seemed pleased by her features, by her very presence.

They would hate to hear of her death.

He leaned forward slightly, felt the warmth of her at his shoulder. He would have to find a way to break her death to his people, a way that did not seem suspicious. And then, of course, he would have to go through some sort of mourning. Would they know that this was a marriage of convenience and not a love match?

Would they care?

Or would they expect some sort of ritual sadness out of him, the sadness a man felt when his wife died, so very tragically?

Like his first wife.

Perhaps they would say he was cursed.

Perhaps he was.

"Sayiddi."

Schahriar did not realize that Giafar had approached him until the man spoke in his ear. Schahriar turned slightly, enough to see that the old man was standing between him and his daughter, as if he were trying to protect her.

You should have protected her sooner, old man, Schahriar thought. *You should have kept her from marrying me.*

"Sayiddi," Giafar was saying, "your brother wishes to offer his blessings."

It took a moment for the words to register. Schahriar did not move anything except his eyes. His entire body had gone rigid. He had not seen Schahzenan since the night his wife died.

Standing in the dark, his arms around her, her voice echoing across the Persian Gardens—

Schahzenan, kill him!

Kill him—Schahriar, the man who loved her.

"Sayiddi," Giafar said again. "Your brother—"

Wishes to offer his blessings. Schahriar had heard the first time. "May they choke him," he said.

He felt the woman start beside him, but she did not move away. She had more courage than he expected, that one. Most people cringed when he used that tone.

But Giafar did not either, and never had.

"He wants to be reconciled," Giafar said. He did not sound like himself. A bit more solemn, perhaps, a bit more cautious. As if he were speaking to a man whom he no longer knew. "It would look good, Sayiddi."

Especially since your bride will die in the morning. Perhaps that wasn't the sentence Giafar was going to say, but it hung between them, the secret that excluded the woman, the innocent, the one who had to pay for his first wife's crimes.

For his crimes.

"Do it," Giafar said, "for peace."

For peace. With his brother. So that there would not be war. There were already stirrings of it. Word of Schahriar's unpredictability had spread. He knew it. And he knew that many saw this wedding as a way to calm him down.

But the wedding would end on the morrow. Perhaps he should face his brother this time. This one time.

If he were strong enough.

Schahriar took a deep breath. He did not trust his brother, or himself. "He may approach," he said, "but I want my guards watching."

Giafar started to nod.

Schahriar caught his hand, preventing him from leaving. "I said *watching,* at all times."

"As you wish, Sayiddi."

Giafar backed away. The woman did not move. She continued to stare at the crowd. She was quite contained, that one. Schahriar watched her from the corner of his eye, as he gazed at the people below. So happy. When was the last time he had been that happy?

He pretended he didn't know the answer, but he did.

It had been on his wedding day.

His first wedding day.

Then Giafar returned with Schahzenan. Schahzenan stood toward the entrance to the balcony where the crowds could not see him. He was smaller than Schahriar remembered him. In his memory, Schahzenan loomed large, his arms around Schahriar's wife, kissing her, holding her, looking at Schahriar with accusing eyes.

On this day, Schahzenan's eyes were mocking, but the rest of him seemed sincere. He wore black—appropriate somehow, when the rest of the world seemed to be decked out in the most beautiful colors.

Schahriar's new bride moved away from him, leaving him alone with his brother, who did not even look at her. Instead Schahzenan watched Schahriar, as if he expected him to do something, anything, to destroy the day.

The day had been destroyed with the dawn. Schahriar had had the dream again, and, when he awoke, he remembered that this was his wedding day.

It had never been a good day.

His brother held out his arms, and a wave of loathing ran through Schahriar. Reconcile? To what purpose? Schahriar should kill him now where he stood.

But his brother stepped forward and the crowd saw him. They cheered.

Bile rose in Schahriar's throat. Traitors. All of them. Just like his brother.

Traitor! His own voice echoed in his mind, and his hand clenched, as it once had around his knife.

Giafar approached. He gave Schahriar a warning look. "Think of the people," he said in that strange tone. Was this his way of getting revenge for his daughter? Or was he playing another game?

Were they all tormenting him?

Giafar said, "Show them you're brothers again."

Schahriar stared down at his brother, who smiled ever so slightly. He obviously remembered that night too, the way he had kissed Schahriar's wife while the assassins came down the wall . . .

Schahriar moved forward, arms outstretched. He could wrap his hands around Schahzenan's throat, as he did to the dancer in the dream, strangle the life out of him before Schahzenan even realized what Schahriar was doing.

Schahriar owed him. For his wife. For his sanity. For it all.

Instead, his brother stepped forward slightly, and Schahriar's arms went around him. Schahriar felt his brother's solid body, honed by years of soldiering, the body his wife had felt when she died.

His wife . . .

He had awakened alone in their bed, the scent of her on the pillow beside him. There were voices in the Persian Gardens, laughter, his wife's laughter, mixed with that of his brother.

For a moment, Schahriar thought he was dreaming. His wife loved him. She belonged beside him.

He slipped out of bed and heard another sound—light thudding against the walls, as if someone were rapping on them. But it was full dark. There would be no servants outside.

Just his wife, laughing.

He stepped into the archway and saw her with a man wearing black. The wide sleeves of her gown flared as she wrapped her arms around him and kissed him passionately.

She had never kissed Schahriar passionately. He had been gentle with her, knowing that she was young and new to this. Knowing that she had much to learn and time to learn it.

She seemed to know it now.

The thuds from the wall sounded again, and this time he looked toward the sound. Three men were coming down the wall, gliding silently down ropes. The thuds he had heard were the ropes hitting the tile, the men's feet as they pushed off the wall.

His wife turned at the sound also, and saw Schahriar. She screamed, only not for him.

Schahzenan! *she cried, looking at Schahriar.* Kill him!

Schahzenan. That was the dark man. How had Schahriar not recognized his own brother?

Because he had not wanted to.

Schahzenan pushed Schahriar's wife out of the way, and they watched the assassins cross the Persian Gardens. It seemed to take forever, but it only took a moment.

And in that moment, Schahriar's world had shattered.

Still, he had enough presence of mind to reach the small table beside the arch and pull his sword out of its scabbard. He raised it just in time to block a blow from the first assassin's sword.

The man wore a hood, his face unrecognizable. But his movements were those of an experienced swordsman. He brought the blade back, gripped it with both hands, and Schahriar took advantage of the opening, slicing him across the belly.

The assassin fell aside and the second one took his place. Only he looked no different from the first, dressed all in black, his face hidden. It was as if the same man had reappeared after Schahriar had struck him down.

Schahriar's blade met his and then, with a small movement, he pushed the assassin's arm back. Schahriar stabbed him, and the assassin fell back.

Oh, my love, *his wife said, and Schahriar looked for her. But she was still holding his brother, not even watching as her husband fought for his life.*

She was his wife. He loved her. His brother did not. He could not.

Then the third assassin reached him, pulling his sword out as he moved. Schahriar knocked it free, then hit the assassin in the face with the hilt of his sword. The man collapsed, and as he fell out of Schahriar's view, Schahriar saw his brother again, making love to Schahriar's wife.

Traitor! *Schahriar shouted as he threw his sword at his brother.*

Only at the last minute his brother turned—had he seen Schahriar's action? Schahriar was never sure—and the sword landed with a thunk.

In his wife's back.

Schahzenan looked up at Schahriar, his face an accusation, Schahriar's wife clutched his chest.

She was dead.

Suddenly there were more assassins—they had to have come down the ropes—and Schahriar ran for his life.

Guards! *he shouted.* Guards . . .

"Guards!" the crowd was screaming. "Guards!"

Schahriar blinked, and saw his new wife, her head bent slightly, nearly—but not completely—hiding the expression of concern on her face. He was still holding his brother—how long had he been doing that?—and the crowd was cheering.

They weren't yelling, "Guards!" They were calling his name. And Schahzenan's name. As usual, Giafar was right. They approved of his reconciliation.

They were the only thing that kept Schahriar from pulling out his ceremonial knife and stabbing Schahzenan in the heart.

Schahriar started to pull away, but Schahzenan held him tightly.

"I hope you have better luck this time, brother," he whispered in Schahriar's ear. "Your late wife loved me, remember?"

Oh, my love, she had said, just before she died.

My love.

She had never said that to him.

Schahriar's gaze met his new wife's, and he remembered the dancer. *Now you must make love to me,* she had said, *while my husband sleeps.*

Women were all the same.

He had to remember that.

They were all the same.

Chapter Five

The Sultan's bedchamber was large and strangely shaped, with archways that opened onto a garden and doors that closed on the corridors. Servants had placed bowls with oil and a burning wick all over inside the room, making it nearly as light as day—only the light flickered ominously.

Scheherazade had never been in a room that large. It dwarfed her, making her feel as if the whole strange day had been a mistake. Surely the man who slept in this room was nothing like the boy she had known.

Even the bed was bigger than any room in her father's quarters. A silk curtain attached to the ceiling fell onto the head of the bed like a wall, and the satin coverlet was so fine and so large that Scheherazade wasn't sure she should touch it.

Still, she sat on its edge, wearing the beautiful night-dress that the dressmakers had made for her. Her hair fell loosely down her back, but pulled away from her face with large combs. They had been put in too tightly and they tugged at her skin.

The discomfort kept her awake, though. She had been sitting alone for what seemed like hours.

Here, in the privacy of this huge room, she could barely hear the sound of the revelry still going on in the streets. Great fires had been lit on the grounds, and crowds of people were drinking and dancing to music that echoed all over the city.

The people were celebrating her marriage.

She was not.

The room had clearly been decorated for a wedding night. Servants had placed two wine goblets next to a jug of wine on a small table. They had also placed a variety of foods around the room—grapes and biscuits and sweets—so much that the happy couple could stay here, undisturbed, for days if they so desired.

Even though she had scarcely eaten, the food did not tempt her. Her gaze kept wandering to the hourglass in a corner near one of the arches. Someone had turned it over just before she arrived in the room. The sands had piled in the bottom, making a base.

Perhaps, when the upper part of the glass emptied, she would die.

She placed her hands on the side of the bed, feeling the smoothness of satin beneath her fingers. All her life she had wanted this. All her life she had wanted to be Schahriar's wife. And now she was. Not that it mattered to him. He seemed to have vanished.

Would she not even get a chance to talk with him? Her entire plan revolved around spending the night with him. She needed to see him, to talk with him.

She knew that once he remembered who she was, he would not harm her. He couldn't harm her. He had cared for her too much.

A clicking sound caught her attention. At first she

thought it part of the music because it was so soft and
faint. Then she realized it was coming from one of the
archways.

Schahriar stood there, in the shadows. She had no idea
how long he had been standing there.

The flickering light hid his features from her and
accented the strength of his magnificent body. He held a
beaded necklace. He had been hitting it lightly against
one of his palms.

Scheherazade swallowed. She was nervous. She hadn't
expected to be. But her father had been right. The boy
she remembered was not present in this man. Not even
his eyes—the eyes she had watched so closely in the
ceremony—held any trace of that gentle child. Instead
they were sunken and dark, filled with an intensity that
had flared into hatred when he held his brother in his
arms.

What had happened to her Schahriar?

She turned toward him. The necklace swung like an
empty noose from his fingers.

This might be her only chance. She swallowed again
and resisted the urge to clear her throat.

"Sayiddi." Her voice sounded reed thin in the large
room. "Do you remember me?"

He froze, as if he had forgotten she was there, and her
soft words startled him. "Remember you? Of course I
remember you. We were just married."

It was not the answer she wanted. He had watched her
all day, stared at her as if she were more to him than a
pawn to be killed in the morning. She had thought that
he might have been trying to place her, trying to remember
how he knew her.

She inclined her head toward him, careful not to be
too coquettish. He did not need a flirtatious woman. She

had reminded herself of that from the beginning. She had to be as beautiful as possible, of course, but she was not as beautiful as some of the women in the harem. And he, as Sultan, could have any woman in the kingdom.

She had to show him that there was more to her than beauty. The best thing she had—the only thing she had—was their childhood friendship.

That was what would save him.

He was still staring at her, leaning against the arch as if it—and the shadows there—protected him.

"From when we were children," she said. "We played together in the palace. Then I went away."

He moved quickly, just enough that his face came into the light. His eyes were even darker than they had been before.

"I don't remember anything about my childhood," he snapped. "What's to remember? I was a child. Why should I remember?"

Her breath caught in her throat. The complete dismissal, the harshness with which he spoke, made her realize that this would not be as easy as she thought. The relationship she had cherished meant nothing to him.

Nothing at all.

He had left the shadows altogether. He was walking toward her, swinging the necklace. His movements were slow and studied, his gaze upon her face.

She watched him out of the corner of her eye, watching the necklace swaying, the clicking like the sound of death beetles. When he came up beside her, she realized how tall he was, and how very strong.

Her father said the Sultan had been dreaming of killing women. Strangling a dancer. With his bare hands.

Schahriar touched her neck. Scheherazade jumped in spite of herself. He brushed her hair away from her shoulder. His thumb traced the line of her cheek, then slowly, gently, caressed her lower lip.

The necklace fell against her neck.

The beads were as cold as death.

The joyful music did not drown out the noise from the crowd. The white roses in a vase beside him did little to drown out the odors of the bacchanal. The air was thick with the scent of smoke and wine. Occasionally his assistant would look toward the door with longing, but the Chief Executioner had no desire to join the revelry. Even if the marriage had been a true one, he would not have joined the party.

Celebrating was not something he enjoyed.

The lengths of silk cord, spread out on the rug before him, brought him more enjoyment than any party ever could.

Four lengths, folded in half, all perfectly cut, and four different shades. White, gold, pink, and brown. They shone in the light from the lamps burning around the room.

He touched one, then another. The braided silk was smooth beneath his fingers. Amazing how much power there was in a single length of rope.

He had watched her, the new Sultana. She was lovely. The headdress she wore accented her long neck. Her long, slender neck.

"How will we know when the Sultan is ready?" his assistant asked.

The Chief Executioner had forgotten the other man was there, hovering, his nerves grating on the Executioner's. A man should not be nervous about an execution, especially when it was his vocation, his love.

The assistant was watching him, dark eyes intense. He wanted an answer.

"He'll call," the Executioner said.

The answer did not seem to satisfy his assistant. His assistant wanted everything spelled out. If he could avoid this execution, he probably would. Not everyone could assassinate a new Sultana.

That long, slender neck, those wide eyes and delicate features. He had to kill her in such a way as to preserve that beauty.

Death did not destroy beauty, merely altered it.

The Chief Executioner closed his eyes for just a moment, imagining the lengths of rope against the pale skin of her neck. Gold would clash. White would be too harsh.

He needed something that would accent the freshness he saw in her, the youth that added a blush to her skin.

"I think pink will suit the Sultana." He picked up the pink length. Yes, pink would enhance the flush that fear would bring to her cheeks.

"You've such good taste, Chief," his assistant said.

"Hmm," the Executioner said dismissively. He studied the length of rope with a single knot in it. The knot was tight and it held well. He tugged the rope, felt its strength. It seemed perfect, but he did not know for certain, not until he tested it.

He wished he could test it on his assistant. But even if he were allowed to practice on a living subject, he did not want to stain the rope. It had to be pure for the Sultana.

Instead, he reached toward the vase and removed one of the white roses. He handed it to his assistant, who studied it for a moment.

The Executioner tugged the rope even harder. Would he have to explain to this imbecile what he wanted?

Then the assistant knelt before him, holding the rose upright. It had a long stem, delicate, like the Sultana's neck. The petals were as soft as her skin and just as rare.

The Chief Executioner wrapped the rope around the rose, careful not to touch the blossom. His movement was gentle, loving. His job was not to bruise or maim, but to end a life. To transform the bloom of youth to the paleness of death.

The silk rope did not touch the stem. The rope wrapped upon itself like a miniature noose.

He twisted the rope around his fingers, careful not to let it brush the rose. He moved the ends without moving the middle at all.

Execution was a fine art for nimble fingers. His assistant wouldn't be able to do any of this. He was a crude man with even cruder hands. It took decades to learn movements of such precision.

The Chief Executioner waited until his assistant shifted slightly, uncomfortable with the amount of time the Chief was taking.

Then, without warning, the Chief Executioner pulled the rope taut.

It severed the stem in an instant, and the rose itself flew through the air, cascading down. As it hit, its petals broke off, leaving only a small bud to rest against the tiled floor.

The Chief Executioner smiled.

He had his assistant move the stem. It was useless now. But the rose was still lovely, its petals covering the other lengths of rope.

Transformed, in death.

With a twist of his fingers, he had created a new kind of beauty.

Just as he would do with the Sultana.

The sounds of revelry had faded. Instead of music, Scheherazade could hear crickets and other creatures of the night. The lamps had burned low, and the shadows were growing.

Schahriar was still studying her. Perhaps she had lost her chance already. All he had to do was call, and the executioner would come.

She would not be able to talk her way out of it.

She wasn't able to now.

If only he remembered his childhood. If only he remembered *her*.

But he did not. He did not, and her only chance had died with that.

Her father had tried to warn her, but she hadn't listened.

Still, Schahriar had done nothing to harm her. The touch of his fingers on her cheek had been gentle. He had studied her as if he had never seen anything like her before.

She turned toward him, and her gaze met his intense one. Such sadness in him, such despair.

He blinked, then threw himself across the bed. The movement bounced her, making the comb in her hair slide loose. She reached up and twisted it, trying to secure it.

Perhaps, if she couldn't revive his memory, she could show him the love she had felt for him all these years. He was the wounded one now, and she had to soothe him.

It would take time.

Schahriar sighed.

"What is it, Sayiddi?" she asked in her gentlest voice.

He gripped the covers, pulling them near his face. "I was remembering another wedding night."

A shiver ran through her. His first wife. Had he loved her?

He twisted the covers in his hands. "It was bad . . ."

As he clearly expected this one to be. As it would be, if his plan were carried out.

His eyes closed, and he seemed to sleep.

She stood, unable to sit near him for a moment. She

had to think. She only had a few hours to hold him, to capture his attention, and get him to spare her life.

This was not like a story. In a story, she would be witty and clever. She would charm him, remind him of who she had been, and he would grab her as if she were a lifeline, the only person who could understand him, the only person who could save him.

But she was not witty and clever, and he was impossible to charm.

She stepped behind the silk curtain and her comb fell farther. She caught it with one hand. It was made of jade, long, like a dagger, and jeweled on top. She twisted it so that it was in the proper position, then grabbed the loosened strands of hair and tucked them in.

Then she raised the comb to hold the hair in place—

And the Sultan pulled the curtain back, his face angry and raw. He stared at the comb in her hand and she wondered, for a brief instant, if he saw it as a comb or as a dagger. She brought it down carefully, then twisted a length of hair in her fingers as a silent way of showing him what the comb was for.

His expression changed. The anger left him, but there was still an intensity to him, an intensity that made her heart pound hard.

"I don't trust you," he said.

She felt her shoulders sag. Her survival depended on his learning to trust her, and learning quickly.

His gaze hadn't left hers. "There's something going on I don't know about. You're Giafar's daughter, yet he lets you—marry me." He looked away, and then, in that slight shake of his head, she saw someone familiar, the boy she had known.

But before she could respond to him, he closed his eyes and collapsed on the bed again. His despair was almost palpable, and she wasn't sure of the cause.

"I dream too much," he said, as if he heard her unspoken question. "Forty nights I can't sleep, so I dream."

This she could help. Her father often suffered from insomnia, and she had learned how to ease his mind so that he could sleep.

She walked toward one of the tables. Schahriar watched her every move, as if he expected her to suddenly attack him.

She spoke quietly, almost as if she were talking to a child. "My father always takes a glass of wine and a biscuit before going to bed."

She picked up one of the trays and put some biscuits on it, little round, flat ones with seeds. Then she poured some wine into a glass and placed it on the tray as well.

"This isn't a night when a man is supposed to go to sleep," he said. It sounded like a protest.

She smiled softly. Did he actually desire her? She couldn't tell. "Don't worry about that, my love," she said. "We'll have many others."

He stared at her as if she had bitten him; then he pushed himself up on one elbow and grabbed a biscuit. She nodded encouragingly. If she could get him to let her take care of him, then she would be of some use to him. If he knew she felt some compassion for him, she might become indispensable.

Suddenly he threw the biscuit onto the tray. It landed with a clink.

She swallowed hard. Nothing was going to be easy with him. Nothing at all.

But she managed to keep her voice calm as she asked, "Is something the matter?"

"That biscuit has sesame seeds," Schahriar said. "I don't like sesame seeds."

The petulant way he said it brought to mind the threads of a story she had heard the Storyteller tell several weeks ago. His strong voice echoed in her mind.

Open, says Nee.

The first time he had said it, she thought he had said, *Open sesame.*

She smiled, and wondered if she would ever hear him tell a story again.

"Did I say something funny?"

"No," Scheherazade said. "It's just that 'sesame seeds' reminded me of a wonderful story. Would you like to hear it?"

She couldn't remember the story that the words had come from, but she was willing to try to tell a new story. Remembering the Storyteller reminded her of what he had said the last time she saw him.

People need stories more than bread itself. Stories tell us how to live—and why.

"I don't like stories," Schahriar said.

"You will like this one," Scheherazade said, pressing on. "It's about Ali Baba and the Forty Thieves."

Schahriar raised his head. Somehow she had gotten his attention.

"Forty thieves," he repeated. "Forty nights of dreaming and now forty thieves. Strange."

"Yes." Scheherazade leaned toward him. "But no stranger than the story itself."

Schahriar was staring at her. Now she had to come through. She had listened to enough stories. She knew she could tell one.

"You see," she said, "Ali Baba was a poor young man who lived outside Damascus. His best friend had a hump, four legs, and very big teeth. Saffron was one of the wisest camels in all Syria. Ali Baba's only family was an older brother, Cassian . . ."

* * *

First came the camel stench, followed by the familiar double grunt. Saffron stood outside the door. Fortunately, the door was too small to allow him entry.

Ali Baba poked his head out of the covers. His small hut was still cool, but the day held the promise of heat. Saffron grunted again, and Ali Baba sighed.

"I know, Saffron, I know."

The camel looked at him as if Ali Baba were the laziest creature Saffron had ever seen. Of course, he wasn't. Cassian was. Ali Baba sat up and looked across the dirt floor at his brother.

Cassian was wrapped in a pink blanket, his back to Ali Baba, snoring.

Ali Baba picked up his boot and threw it at his brother. It hit Cassian in the back. He sputtered and rolled over, his thick beard and hair so tousled that Ali Baba couldn't see his face.

"Cassian!" Ali Baba said. "It's time to get up."

"... Cassian was so lazy, he—"

Schahriar sat up so quickly that Scheherazade thought he was going to hurt her. "I told you," he growled. "I don't like stories."

She glanced at the hourglass. There was twice as much sand in the bottom as there was in the top. She was running out of time.

And ideas.

Her stomach was fluttering, but Schahriar continued to stare at her as if he expected something more from her.

He had been quiet during the opening of the story, but he had started to stir when she got to the part about waking Cassian. Perhaps she had done something wrong. She had never stirred while listening to the Storyteller.

She licked her lips. "A master storyteller once told me

that the audience must be hooked in the first moments; otherwise you've lost them.''

"I'm lost," Schahriar said.

She looked at him. He wasn't talking about the story. And this time, she clearly saw the boy she remembered, buried under the anger, the sadness, and the complete despair.

For the first time since he had come into the room, she wanted to touch him, to cradle him against her and soothe him. But she didn't dare—not yet. He had to come to her first.

She had to come up with something, and she clearly didn't have time to take it slowly.

A beetle scurried across the floor, its shiny black back reflecting the candlelight.

"That's because," she said, improvising as she went, "I haven't told you about Black ... Black Coda.''

"Who's he?" Schahriar was interested again. For all his supposed dislike of storytelling, he was a willing listener.

Black Coda. He. What an intriguing concept. When she said the words, she hadn't thought of Black Coda as a person at all.

"At the time," she said, letting the story create itself, "the kingdom was being ravaged by savage gangs. Black Coda led the most murderous of them."

Schahriar's gaze held hers now, but his eyes saw something else. Black Coda, perhaps?

"A monster," Schahriar said softly. "Black Coda."

"No one was safe," she said. She relaxed slightly on the bed. She would have to work to keep his attention, but she knew she could do it, as long as she put action in the story.

"But what does he have to do with Ali Baba?" Schahriar asked.

Scheherazade smiled. She had Schahriar now. He had forgotten all about his troubles, all about her.

All about the execution.

"Why," she said, "Black Coda made Ali Baba rich and famous. . . ."

Chapter Six

No caravan could travel without fear. They never knew when or where Black Coda would strike next. He was a master of disguise.

On this particular day, a caravan traveled not far from Ali Baba's home. The caravan wound through the hills in the desert sand, single file. The camels' packs were filled, and the travelers were obviously wealthy.

In the center of the caravan was a man wearing bright yellow. His turban was pulled low over his eyes, and he wore his scarves high across his nose and mouth. The other travelers thought him squeamish, unable to endure the wind that sometimes carried sand on it, but they said nothing.

Caravans often mixed unlikely people, people who were traveling together across dangerous countryside like this one. Of course, everyone had heard of Black Coda and his murderous gang, and of course they were taking precautions. Were not all of the travelers armed? Were they not constantly watching the hills for shadows, movement?

They feared thieves on horseback who could outrun them and circle the camels. And as they approached Damascus, they knew they would run into Black Coda.

The question was when.

As the caravan wound around the last hill, the man in yellow recognized the area. He pulled a sword from his robes and sped his camel forward until he caught the youngest, strongest man in the caravan—the only man who could be a real threat.

He grabbed the man from behind and slit his throat. The body dropped to the sand as, all around the caravan, the sand moved.

Black Coda's men burst out of the sand. They had been buried beneath it, in shallow holes, and they sped forward, shouting and brandishing swords.

The caravan did not stand a chance. The thieves attacked—determined to have the great wealth the caravan carried with it.

Black Coda, who was the man in yellow, split open the packs. Silver and jewels fell out, more money than the thieves had seen in weeks. The riches spurred them on, and they slaughtered the travelers, sometimes quickly, sometimes slowly.

As the sound of the melee carried over the hills, the rest of Black Coda's thieves joined the fight. They were on horseback—their mission to stop the handful of travelers who escaped. First they encircled them, and then they killed them, one by one.

The scene was devastating—forty thieves taking on a handful of travelers. It was all over in moments. Black Coda took silver plates and pearls and gold coins, so many that he had to steal the camels' packs along with filling his own.

His gang was practiced. They scooped the loot up quickly and were gone before the vultures descended upon the bodies, before the blood could sink into the sand.

Meanwhile, Ali Baba was collecting firewood to sell in the local market. He was far enough away from the murdered travelers that he did not see the circling vultures. Not that he was looking up. He was examining the ground for sticks, picking up all that he saw, putting the good ones in a pouch on Saffron's back and flinging the rest away. All around him were rocky cliff faces topped by scraggly trees and open caves. This was a part of the desert he did not normally come to, and he regretted this day's journey already.

"This is a slow way to make a fortune," Ali Baba said to Saffron. "And I've got so many good ideas for making money. Like my scheme for watering plum trees with alcohol to grow stewed plums."

Behind him, he heard the camel hawk and then something wet hit his back. Ali Baba turned around. Saffron had spat on him.

Ali Baba looked at his camel, who had expressed this opinion on other matters before. And usually, Saffron was right.

"I don't care what you say, Saffron," Ali Baba said. "I think it's a good idea."

He kept walking. There weren't many trees here, and the midday sun was hot. Still, it was more effort to turn around than it was to keep going. Perhaps he would get lucky. Perhaps he would find something.

Saffron snorted, and then hawed a warning. Ali Baba turned as Saffron ran past him, bell clanging.

There were black-robed men on the hillside, coming down the path.

"You think that's trouble, Saffron?" Ali Baba asked, but Saffron was already far from him, hiding in some scrub brushes.

The men were hurrying toward Ali Baba. They couldn't see him yet. He hurried after Saffron and crouched beside him in the bushes. . . .

* * *

"Saffron's warning saved Ali Baba's life," Scheherazade said.

She was still sitting on the edge of the bed, but the Sultan was stretched out before her, his hands clasped behind his head, his eyes studying her face. He was completely absorbed by the story.

"Animals," Scheherazade said, "can be cleverer than their masters."

A small, sad smile crossed Schahriar's face. "And you can trust them," he said.

The horsemen pulled up right on the spot where Ali Baba had been standing. They dismounted, and a tall man with the air of command walked toward Ali Baba's hiding place.

Ali Baba held his breath. Not breathing this close to a camel was a blessing, even if there were other, more pressing reasons for it. But Saffron, too, was holding his breath. They both seemed to know the importance of staying as hidden as possible.

The man before them had a fierce face, made fiercer by the helmet he wore. Ali Baba had never seen anything like it. Metal ran around the edge, and down the nose, giving the man's face an inhuman cast. His lower jaw was set, and his eyes were steely.

He surveyed the rocks before him as if he were looking for an intruder.

Ali Baba froze. A single movement would draw the man's attention to him.

The man, of course, was Black Coda and, unbeknownst to Ali Baba, this was his lair.

Black Coda stretched out his hand and turned it, the way a genie would. As he did, he said, "Open sesame!"

* * *

Schahriar let out a small sigh as he caught the reference that had given Scheherazade the inspiration. She smiled to herself in acknowledgment, but did not lose the thread of her story, for fear of losing him.

A great rumbling sound echoed throughout the area. A stone door, invisible until Black Coda had spoken, started moving of its own accord. It was as if the rocks shifted of their own power. Sand fell, and the ground shook.

Ali Baba looked behind him, making certain the earth was not opening up around him. Even Saffron made a small grunting noise—fortunately hidden by the rumbling of the giant door.

Finally the rocks stopped moving, revealing the mouth of a cave so large that seven of Ali Baba's shacks could fit in the opening. Ali Baba let out a small sigh of relief that turned into a gasp as he saw something large leave the cave.

Two somethings large.

Dragons, long and red, with spines like those of a lizard rising like a fan in the center of their backs. Their tails whipped wildly, and their square bandy legs ended in large taloned claws. They hissed as they ran, their mouths open.

Ali Baba resisted the urge to cover his head. He did not want to see Black Coda eaten alive.

As the beasts ran toward him and rose up, about to leap on him, Black Coda lifted his arms and shouted, "Down, boys! Down!"

He flung food at them, and the dragons caught the tidbits in their mouths, begging as dogs would. Then Black Coda beckoned his men, and they walked around the beasts, eyeing them nervously.

All of the men were carrying sacks and bags. A few had jewels dripping from the openings. The men disappeared inside the cave's mouth, and after a moment, Black Coda followed them.

Ali Baba leaned forward slightly. He knew better than to leave his hiding place. He had no idea how long the men would stay inside the cave, and he really didn't want to contend with the dragons.

Still, he turned to Saffron and whispered, "What do you think of that?"

Saffron, always wiser, did not answer. He kept studying the cave's mouth, waiting for the men to emerge.

But Ali Baba couldn't be quiet. He couldn't move, and so he spoke. After all, he had to do something.

"Sesame, that's those seeds Mother used to make biscuits with, aren't they? Why would it be sesame?"

There were shouts and banging from the cave. Ali Baba bit his lower lip and watched as the men hurried out without their loot. Apparently the dragons had gone back inside and spooked them, all but Black Coda. He stayed in for a moment.

Ali Baba watched as Black Coda scratched the beasts' heads, and then he came out too. He waved an arm, and the door banged closed. The men mounted their horses and rode away as quickly as they had come.

Ali Baba sat like a man stunned. Saffron snorted beside him, as if the camel could read his thoughts. Perhaps it was obvious. Great wealth awaited him, if only he had the courage to take it.

When he could no longer see the silhouettes of the men on horseback, Ali Baba emerged from his hiding place. Saffron followed. They walked to the cliff face and stood in front of the concealed door.

Saffron grunted a warning, but he didn't spit. He was ambivalent about this move.

At least that was how Ali Baba chose to interpret Saffron's comment.

Ali Baba raised his hands, then made a fist. He was shaking. If he did this, he would cross the great Black Coda, a man with the tattoo of a beetle on his wrist, a man known for killing someone who looked at him wrong.

But if Ali Baba ignored this, he would never forgive himself. It was his chance to gain a fortune, and with it, a future.

He opened his fist and turned his hand, the way that Black Coda had.

"Open sesame!" he said, closing his eyes as if to ward off a blow.

He couldn't stand it, though. He had to see what his words had done.

The rumbling overwhelmed him. Sand fell, and the ground shook, and to Ali Baba's amazement, the door opened.

Immediately the dragons ran out, roaring and rearing. They were even more terrifying up close. Their breath was hot and smelled of sulfur.

Ali Baba fell back, his hands up to protect his face and neck. "Down, boys," he yelled. "Down!"

The dragons sat in front of him and made soft woofing sounds. They wanted a reward, a treat. He took biscuits from his pockets—his lunch, which he had not touched—and tossed them at the beasts.

They ate with relish, and their tails wagged.

Slowly, knowing that he looked just as wary as Black Coda's men had, he walked past the dragons. They followed him like trained puppies. Saffron kept a discreet distance.

If the dragons killed Ali Baba, at least Saffron would get out alive.

He found no comfort in that thought.

The stone door was a magnificent entrance that led into

an antechamber made of rock. But the cave's mouth was like the entrance to a room of miracles.

As Ali Baba stepped inside, he could not believe his eyes. Before him was more wealth than he had ever seen, more wealth than he could have imagined in his most vigorous dreams.

It was piled haphazardly, as if it had been dropped off and never sorted. Boxes of gold coins, jewels and precious silks were piled upon piles of silver bowls and expensive carved cases. Diamonds glittered from the tiled floor. A heap of emeralds that rose to his knee blocked an archway.

He stepped deeper inside, the sun beating through the door's opening, making the gold glitter tantalizingly.

Behind him, he heard a crunch and he turned. One of the dragons walked in, stepping on sapphires as if they were mere rocks. The other dragon entered as well. They stopped on opposite sides of the great room, beneath columns with frescos that had faded long ago.

Had this once been a part of a palace? The home of a mighty king, now forgotten? If so, how had Black Coda discovered it?

Ali Baba knew he might never learn the answer, but the question did not concern him greatly. He was too stunned by the wealth.

The dragons hissed, then climbed up the columns, winding their way toward the top. They clung to the sides and their tails wrapped around the base. They stuck their heads over the edge like gargoyles, and stared at him.

He allowed himself one shiver, and then reminded himself that they had not harmed him.

Not yet.

Then the earth started shaking again. The rumbling was so loud in the cave that he couldn't hear himself breathe. He whirled and saw sand falling from the ceiling as the door closed. He was too far away from it to get out.

His heart was pounding wildly. The inside of the cave

grew dark, except for a single natural light that came from so far above him, he could not see its source. It gave everything inside a bluish cast, even the dragons, which seemed to be peering down on him, their faces closer than they had been before.

He was alone in here.

Trapped.

With them.

The last thing he wanted was to be trapped in there only to be discovered when the thieves returned. They had gotten out earlier; he should be able to get out too.

It stood to reason that the same words would open the door from the inside.

He gathered fistfuls of jewels and coins and stuffed them in his pockets. He put pouches around his neck, and carried baskets in his hand, as many as he could hold. He rolled up silver platters and coffeepots into two carpets and tied them on the edges. They were heavy, but they would hold until he reached Saffron.

The dragons continued to watch, but so far did nothing. He didn't know how long that would last.

He turned, twisted his hand as he had done before, and said, with more courage than he felt, "Open sesame!"

The door rumbled open, and more dust fell. The entire floor felt as if it were unstable.

He grabbed the rugs with one hand and ran out the open door, giggling as he came.

Saffron was waiting where Ali Baba had left him, looking worried. Ali Baba's giddiness did not help the camel's disposition.

"Saffron!" Ali Baba shouted. "Saffron! We're rich! Have you ever seen anything like it? Only in your dreams!"

He looked at the camel, then laughed. "Well, not in your dreams, but in mine."

He piled his loot on Saffron's back and hurried home.

When Ali Baba arrived home, his lazy brother Cassian was still asleep. He was lying kitty-corner on his bed, with his head hanging off it, and snoring so loudly that he sounded like the rumbling door.

Ali Baba, who knew that when his brother slept this soundly he was impossible to wake up, grabbed a bucket of water and poured it on Cassian's head.

"It's raining, Mother," Cassian mumbled. "Bring in the washing."

"It isn't raining and Mother's been dead five years," Ali Baba said. "Now get up!"

"What's for breakfast?" Cassian said.

"Fresh air," Ali Baba said. "Now get up. I've got something to show you."

He walked toward the stash he had dragged inside and untied one of the carpets. Serving platters, bowls, cups, wine goblets, all made of silver, clattered on the hard ground.

His brother raised his head, his eyes brighter than Ali Baba had ever seen them. Then he rolled out of bed and helped Ali Baba sort the loot.

They were giggling like children, and Cassian played with the gold as if he had never seen the like—which, of course, he hadn't.

Slowly, Ali Baba realized what kind of noise they were making. He stood and walked to the door, his heart pounding. He had left a trail—camel prints in the sand, which should have been covered by the wind. But what if they weren't? The hut wasn't very far from the cave, after all.

"We have to move," Ali Baba said. "In case the robbers find out who's been in their cave."

Cassian stood. "But I want my share."

"Of course." Ali Baba took his brother's hand and squeezed it in a pledge. "I'm not keeping it all for myself."

"What?" Cassian asked. "Half and half?"

Ali Baba nodded. "Half and half."

Cassian did not like the idea of splitting wealth he had not had when he went to bed the night before. He let go of Ali Baba's hand. "I'm going to the cave and get my share."

"It could be dangerous," Ali Baba said.

"I can take care of myself," Cassian said.

At that Saffron hee-hawed.

"All right," Ali Baba said. "But take Saffron. He knows the way. He'll see that you don't get into any trouble. He's got a good head on his shoulders."

Cassian snorted, staring at the jewels. "Saffron is a camel."

" 'You don't think I need a camel to look after me, do you?' Cassian asked. Both Ali Baba and Saffron nodded. There was no question in their minds that Cassian needed someone to look after him."

Schahriar was sitting cross-legged on the bed. In one hand, he held the necklace. Scheherazade lay before him, absorbed in the story.

"Why was Cassian any different than Ali Baba?" Schahriar asked.

"Ali has something that Cassian never had," Scheherazade said. "A good heart. And that protected him."

"You think a good heart can protect people?"

"Have you ever known anyone with a good heart?" Scheherazade asked, and then held her breath.

"No," Schahriar said. "Sultans don't meet people like that."

"I'm sure that they don't," Scheherazade said, careful not to let her disappointment at his answer into her voice. She went back to her story. "Anyway, with Saffron's help, Cassian found the robber's cave. . . ."

* * *

Ali Baba had given Cassian two biscuits to remind him
of the password. Cassian stood outside the door where
Saffron had deposited him, and said, "Open . . . open . . ."
And then, of course, he had to pull out the biscuits to
remember.

"Oh, yes," he said. "Open sesame."

He watched in amazement as the solid rock before him
opened to reveal a door, just as Ali Baba said it would.
The earth rumbled and the sky shook, and Cassian had
never been so happy in all his life.

Until he saw the dragons, of course.

But Ali Baba had told him how to fight those as well.

"Down, Rover!" he shouted at the dragons. "Down,
boys!"

They went down and begged as they had for Ali Baba.
Cassian threw them the biscuits, which the dragons gob-
bled up. As they did, Cassian stepped past to the place
that would make him the wealthiest man in Damascus.

The cave was more magnificent than Ali Baba had said.
Cassian was so stunned by the great wealth before him
that he did not care when the dragons came inside and
climbed their columns. The door rumbled shut, and still
Cassian stood, counting and staring and planning, trying
to figure out how he could take everything with him—
or at least more than Ali Baba had carried.

"Oh, oh," Cassian said. "I must get Saffron. He's got
the pouches."

He turned, and realized then—not before—that the
door had closed. He had been so excited, he hadn't
noticed.

"How do I open it?" he said out loud, staring to panic.

He felt his pockets, but the biscuits were gone. He had
nothing to remind him except his own feeble memory.

"What do I say? I know! Open wheat!"

He waited. The door remained closed.

"No, no, that's not it. Open barley!"

Still, the door was closed.

"Open rice! Open corn!"

But the door did not open.

And, outside, he heard voices. This was precisely what Ali Baba had feared would happen.

Then he heard a voice say, "Open sesame."

Cassian grabbed a scimitar and, as the doors opened, ran out quicker than the dragons. They weren't even off their columns by the time he got out the door.

Outside were forty men, dressed all in black, and more fearsome than Ali Baba had described. Cassian's only hope was to get through them to Saffron and get away.

As he ran, he shed jewels and coins and silver. He swung his scimitar. The thieves ran toward him and he sliced at them, screaming like a demented demon.

The robbers screamed back, frightened by the man who had come running out of the cave.

But Black Coda was not frightened. He stood his ground, waiting for the intruder to reach him. When Cassian was in front of him, Black Coda stabbed him through the heart.

Cassian fell to his knees, his eyes glazing. "Open sesame," he said to himself as he died. "That was it. Open sesame."

Chapter Seven

The oil lamps were burning lower. Not even the cicadas made any sound anymore. The entire palace slept, except for Schahriar and Scheherazade.

Scheherazade drank water as she talked, afraid she would lose her voice. Sipping occasionally gave her a chance to pause and think. She was not telling any story she had heard from the Storyteller—she didn't recall them in enough detail. She was making this one up as she went, and she didn't want it to show.

If Schahriar suspected that she was not in command of the story she told, he would kill her.

At the moment, however, he still sat cross-legged before her, clutching the necklace, his eyes bright and interested. She had gotten his mind off the darkness and, for a short time at least, he was thinking of something else.

"Meanwhile," Scheherazade said, "while Cassian was getting himself killed, Ali Baba had hired himself a young serving girl named Morgiana to help him now that he had money."

"What was this Morgiana like?" Schahriar asked.

"Some said she was beautiful," Scheherazade said. "But certainly she was clever, and very independent."

Schahriar looked at her, his eyes softer than they had been. "She sounds like you. Beautiful, clever, independent." Scheherazade suppressed a shiver. She did not want Schahriar to think of her as clever or independent. Not yet.

"Like me?" Scheherazade said. "Oh, no. She wasn't like me. Not like me at all!"

Morgiana finished tying the last of Ali Baba's meager possessions to the wagon. It amazed him how quickly a household could be packed.

Or perhaps more time had passed than he had thought. Shouldn't Cassian have been home by now? Or had his brother gotten so caught up in his greed that he had lost track of time?

Ali Baba walked to the edge of the road that led to his small shack and stared at the hills.

"That's everything, sir," Morgiana said.

But Ali Baba was staring at the road below. He saw movement. When he squinted, he realized what he saw. Saffron.

Alone.

"Saffron!" Ali Baba shouted, running to the camel. "Where's my brother? Where's Cassian?"

The camel only hung its head.

"We must go," Ali Baba said to Morgiana. "Quickly."

She hurried toward him, and together they got on Saffron. Saffron took them to the cave, but they were too late.

They found Cassian's body, tied to a tree.

You see, while Saffron escaped and went to Ali Baba, Black Coda had hung Cassian there.

"That should scare off anyone nosing about," Black Coda had said.

One of the thieves, who had just finished tying Cassian to the tree, asked, "Do you think he was with anyone else?"

"No," Black Coda said. "They would have still been with him." He turned away from the body and headed toward his horse. But before he left, he waved a hand at another of the thieves. "And get rid of those two dragons. They're useless!"

So Cassian had become a warning, a warning to all to stay away. But Ali Baba did not see him that way. All he saw was his dead brother's body, defiled by the people who had killed him.

"Poor Cassian," Ali Baba said. He was trembling, tears running down his cheeks.

Saffron was kneeling behind him, head down, as if he too had failed. Saffron had never had much use for Cassian, but Saffron knew that Ali Baba loved his brother, and so Saffron mourned too.

Morgiana put a hand on Ali Baba's shoulder. She was appalled at the sight, and part of her wondered what she had gotten into.

"What a terrible thing," she said.

"I should have tried harder to stop him," Ali Baba said. It was all his fault.

"Don't blame yourself." Morgiana looked around. She understood that Cassian had been hung there as a warning, even if she didn't understand exactly why. But then, her mind was not clouded by sadness and loss. "I think we should leave as soon as possible."

"No." Ali Baba wrenched himself away from her and walked toward the body. "We must take him with us."

"Is that wise?" Morgiana hadn't moved. "When the robbers come back and see the body's gone, they'll know

Cassian had friends or family. They might try to find you and do to you what they did to your brother."

"I know you're right, Morgiana," Ali Baba said as he approached the tree. "But he must have a decent burial." He started to climb. Cassian looked even more pathetic up close. "I just can't leave him like that, for the carrion to pick his bones. He's my brother."

Ali Baba took out his knife and proceeded to cut his brother down.

Cassian had a wonderful funeral. It was the talk of the city for weeks after.

A large group of mourners gathered around his grave. They were dressed all in black, and their wails were so loud, they echoed off the hills around Damascus.

"Cassian must have been very popular," Morgiana whispered to Ali Baba. "He had so many friends."

Ali Baba did not answer her. Instead, he walked down the path, away from his brother's grave. The cries of the mourners faded behind him.

"I hope we gave complete satisfaction."

Ali Baba turned around. An elderly mourner stood behind him. When he saw Ali Baba's face, he bowed his head slightly.

"A good show, sir," Ali Baba said, handing the man a sack of coin. "A hundred pieces, I believe."

Then he started to walk away again.

But the old man continued to follow him. "The Damascus Mourners Association has a reputation second to none! Did you see how Mustafa threw himself into the grave?"

Ali Baba hurried faster, but he could not shake the old man.

"You only get that with the Damascus Mourners. We not only provide funeral arrangements but the weeping and gnashing of teeth too! Remember us if you have any more deaths in the family."

Ali Baba only nodded. There was no more family.

He was alone now.

How alone, he did not realize until later. For now, though, he did not think things could get much worse.

He was wrong.

Black Coda had returned to his secret cave to stash more loot, and immediately noticed that Cassian's body was gone.

"Someone else knows," one of the thieves said. His arms were laden with sacks from the most recent theft.

"I make a mistake." Black Coda stared at the empty tree. Only the ropes remained, swinging in the breeze. "The thing to do now is correct it."

As he spoke, several of his men hurried out of the cave. They looked frightened—as anyone would be in their shoes. For they had to give bad news to Black Coda.

"We've been robbed, Chief!" One of the robbers yelled, staying a good distance away from Black Coda. "Jewels and gold coins are missing. What should we do?"

Black Coda was somehow not surprised. The body had disappeared. Someone had to have taken it. Perhaps the person who had discovered the cave in the first place. "How much is missing?"

"No more than a couple of sackfuls."

"Good," Black Coda said. "That means there were only two or three thieves at most. We'll search for them in Damascus."

"Where do we look?" one of his men asked.

Black Coda glanced at the empty tree. "They took the body down for burial. So we find out who's come into money recently and could afford a rich funeral."

"That's very clever, Chief," said his main henchman. "I would have never thought of that."

"Nor me," said the first robber.

"Nor me," the others said in chorus.

Black Coda looked at them all as if they had grown

second heads. "Spare me your nor-me's," Black Coda said. "We go into the city in ones and twos and in disguise, or they'll hang us on sight."

Black Coda's men drifted inconspicuously into the city. They searched high and low, asked questions of rich and poor, trying to find the thieves who had stolen their loot.

Robbers find nothing wrong with robbery, except when it happens to them.

Finally, two of Black Coda's men passed the Damascus Mourners Association. The elderly man who had been at Cassian's funeral approached them, thinking they were potential customers.

He did not know that they had brought him his most recent customer, but he was just about to find out.

On a street nearby, Ali Baba was in the courtyard of his new home, eating figs. The courtyard was larger than his shack had been. Saffron sat behind him, eating the leaves off the palm trees, and Morgiana was cleaning the steps that led into the spacious house.

Ali Baba was a rich man now, and he had a rich man's home, with more rooms than he had furniture. More rooms than he had friends.

"I'm sad," Ali Baba said.

Morgiana looked up from her sweeping. She knew how sad Ali Baba was, and she was sorry that she could not improve his mood. She was trying, by cooking him good food, and making certain that the house, already beautiful, shone like newly minted gold coins.

"Don't you like your new house?" she asked.

"Of course I like it," Ali Baba said. "I'm just sad my brother isn't here to enjoy it with me. I miss him."

"He was your brother," Morgiana said. "It's only natural."

Ali Baba sighed. "Everyone should have good fortune, but it's much better if you can share it with somebody."

Morgiana stopped sweeping. She stared at him for a long moment, wishing that he understood how much she cared for him, and then she resumed her work.

Sometimes a man does not understand the sacrifices women make for love.

It took Black Coda's men most of the day to confirm the story of the elderly man who worked for the Damascus Mourners Association. They dug up Cassian's grave to make sure they had the right corpse. Then they hurried back to Black Coda.

Even though they moved quickly, darkness had fallen when they arrived.

Black Coda was sitting before a campfire with his guards, drinking wine. The men hurried toward him. One of them clutched the colorful scarf that Cassian had worn, and brought it to Black Coda.

"This belonged to the late Cassian," the man said, holding the scarf in front of Black Coda, "the brother of Ali Baba, who's just come into money."

Black Coda recognized the scarf. It belonged to the man who had robbed him. "You know where this Ali Baba lives?"

"An expensive villa on a hill overlooking the city park," the second man said. "I'd say a particularly desirable residence, with a view of—"

"I don't want to buy it!" Black Coda snapped. "Just kill him and everyone else in the house."

"How many of us do you want for the job?"

"All of us," Black Coda said. "We don't know how many we'll have to kill."

"How're forty of us going to get past the city guards?" the first man asked.

"I know how to do it," Black Coda said, dismissing his men's concerns. "I just want Ali Baba and his brood slaughtered by this time tomorrow night!"

* * *

"And so the evil Black Coda drove up to the city gates," Scheherazade said, her throat so raw that her voice was hoarse, "ready to slaughter Ali Baba and everyone in his house."

Sunlight was pouring into the bedroom. It was dawn. Scheherazade had not realized until that moment what a beautiful room she was in.

She sighed. She had made it through the night. For a moment, she had lost track of the story. She was so very tired.

Schahriar sat up. "What's the matter?"

"Nothing, Sayiddi." She yawned. Outside, a cock crowed.

Schahriar was frowning. "What happened next?"

He looked like a little boy denied candy. She tried not to smile. He was involved. This was her Schahriar, the one she had thought lost to her.

"What happened to Ali and Morgiana? Did Black Coda kill them?" He paused and his eyes narrowed. "Or don't you know?"

She smiled, even though she no longer felt like it. Suspicion was back in his tone, and with that suspicion came the threat of execution.

"Of course I know," she said. "But I'm tired." She nodded toward the Persian Gardens. "It's already morning."

"Morning?" Schahriar turned around in shock and then stumbled off the bed. "It can't be. Morning never comes for me. It's always night."

He stopped near the archways, still clutching the necklace. "I lost track of time."

He was silent for a long moment. Scheherazade felt herself relax. He had not made it easily through the night in a long time. She had helped him with that.

It was a first step.

Schahriar had turned around. He was glowering at her. "So," he said, "you won't go on?"

"Forgive me, Sayiddi," Scheherazade said. "I'm tired."

And she was. More tired than she had ever been in her life. She couldn't remember the last time she had stayed up all night—and she had certainly never been up all night talking.

"You can finish the story later today?" There was an edge to his voice now, a petulance that was more than childish. It felt as if he were on the verge of losing control of himself, as if, in denying him, she was hurting him somehow.

"Yes, of course, I can finish later today," Scheherazade said. "But storytelling is best done at night, at least for me. I mean, it's hard to create the right atmosphere with the sun shining."

He stared at her. Not as he had stared at her all night, not with that rapt warm attention, but with blank eyes.

"Don't you think?" she whispered.

Slowly he crossed back to the bed, then walked across it. She rolled back despite herself, unable to be close to the anger distorting his face.

He bent over her.

"It's a trick!" he shouted. "A trick to trick me!"

Then he grabbed her arm and yanked her off the bed. There was such power in his grasp that she couldn't even think of getting away. He was dragging her beside him, forcing her toward the door.

"What are you doing, Sayiddi?" she asked as she dug her bare feet against the cold tiles.

He moved ahead of her, still pulling her along. "I want you," he said, tugging hard, "to meet someone."

His voice was low and cold, the same voice he had used the night before when he told her he did not remember his childhood, that there was no point in it.

She wasn't sure what she had done. If she had continued with the story, it would have ended, and then he would have had no reason at all to keep her around.

Even though she was pretty sure he wasn't going to now.

He flung open the antechamber door. Two men stood there, one of them small and nondescript. The other was taller and wore no turban. His bald head shone in the morning light. He had a long mustache and eyes that were much too bright.

Behind them stood a vase of drooping white roses.

After a moment, she recognized the Chief Executioner. She had failed.

Schahriar flung her out the door. She stopped just in front of him, remaining as close to him as she could. She didn't want to get close to the men.

She turned toward her husband. She had to pretend she had no idea of what he was about to do. It was the only way.

"What is it, Sayiddi?" Scheherazade asked. "What's the matter? Who are these men?"

"Friends, Sultana." The Chief Executioner walked toward her. "Just stay calm."

"Stay back," she ordered him. She reached for Schahriar's hand. Her fingers brushed his, but he moved away from her. "Sayiddi!"

She turned toward him, but he would not look at her.

"Stay calm," the Chief Executioner said again.

She backed even farther from him. "Sayiddi!"

She was begging now. She did not want to die. She had been so arrogant. She had thought she could help him, and it had cost her life, just as her father had feared it would.

The Chief Executioner looked over her shoulder. His pale gaze met Schahriar's. She turned and watched her new husband's face. She would stare at him as he ordered her death. At least he could remember that.

Then Schahriar let out a great sigh and walked away. As he did, he said, "You will finish the story of Ali Baba tonight!"

Scheherazade leaned against the antechamber door. The Chief Executioner froze in place. He studied her for a moment, his hand reaching toward her throat.

Then he clenched his fingers into a fist.

She felt the movement as if he had snapped her neck.

"Later," he said softly and, summoning his assistant, left the antechamber.

Scheherazade was alone.

And still alive.

Chapter Eight

Scheherazade snuck out of the palace. She did not wear her usual garments. Instead, she covered herself from head to toe in a black robe. She held a black veil over her mouth and nose, and kept her head down so that no one could see her eyes.

She was Sultana now, and was not supposed to go anywhere without an escort. Sultana for only twenty-four hours, and already she was breaking one of the most important rules.

But she could not let word get back to Schahriar of what she was doing. And she was desperate.

All she had managed to give Schahriar the night before was a story. Fortunately, it had been good enough to keep him interested. But she was a novice at this, and she knew—as anyone who had heard stories knew—that if she made one misstep, she would lose her audience.

And her life.

She hurried down the filthy streets. They were full, as they had been the week before, but everything seemed different now, darker, more threatening. She imagined that people were watching her, whispering, wondering who she was.

It was better than having them wonder why the Sultana had left the palace the day after her wedding. Especially to come to the market.

She went underneath some arches to the Storyteller's tent. She had been inside it once, the first time she had asked him questions about storytelling. She hoped he would be there now.

The Storyteller was not in his usual spot outside his tent. She was relieved to see that. She didn't have to interrupt him or wait for him to finish. She hadn't been certain she had time for that anyway.

She crossed a wide street, passing a camel and a man on a donkey. A group of men were haggling over the price of a goblet, and a group of women stood toward the edge of the market, discussing Scheherazade's wedding. She didn't hear much of that conversation, just enough to know that they had been below the balcony and thought the Sultan had looked very happy.

Fortunately, the women had been too far away to see his glower.

She pulled the hood tighter over her face and bowed her head even more.

The Storyteller's tent was just past the women. It wasn't a traditional tent—not like the ones the soldiers used. It was a series of blankets spread across pieces of wood. When the Storyteller was ready to greet the day, he flung back the rug that served as the doorway. When he slept or left the tent, he pulled the rug down, hiding the door.

The rug was up.

Scheherazade slipped inside, leaving her hood up. "Forgive me, sir," she said, "but have you time to answer a few questions?"

The Storyteller looked up at her. He did not recognize

her. "I am a simple storyteller, not a man who answers questions."

"But they are questions about stories," she said, letting her hood drop. "And they may save my life."

That caught his attention. His expression softened when he realized whom he was talking with. He patted the rug across from him. "Sit down, child."

She sat down and pulled her veil back.

"You have been gone for a few days," he said.

She nodded. "May I tell you something in confidence?"

He smiled slightly. "You mean, you do not want me to turn your tale into a story?"

She sighed. "If I die, you may. If you care to risk it."

His eyes sparkled. She had intrigued him. "You have my word," he said. "I shall say nothing of your visit."

So Scheherazade told him of the Sultan's vow, and of her decision to marry him anyway. The Storyteller was as good a listener as he was a tale spinner. He listened to everything—the way she had thought the relationship would save her, and when she learned that it hadn't, how she had started telling a story, a story she did not know the ending to.

She also told him about the way the Sultan had dragged her to the Chief Executioner that morning, and how it was only the Sultan's desire to hear what would happen next in the story that had saved her life.

When she was through, she paused. Her voice was tired from the night before.

The Storyteller leaned forward, as intrigued by her life's story as Schahriar had been by Ali Baba's.

"I just sit in the bazaar, telling stories, and if the audience isn't interested in what I'm saying, it walks away," the Storyteller said. "But if your audience isn't interested, you're dead."

Scheherazade nodded. "I thought storytelling would be easy. But it isn't. I almost lost it before I got started."

"I've told you before," he said, "the first moments are vital."

She had remembered that after she started. It had been what had saved her. That, the beetle, and Black Coda. "I paused at a good point," she said, "with the thieves sneaking into Damascus to kill Ali Baba."

"Sneaking in how?" the Storyteller asked. "In what?"

"A wagon."

He shook his head. "Too ordinary. It has to be something more exotic." He frowned at her. "You're starting the story *again*. You have to hook the audience *again*."

She hadn't thought of that. She hadn't realized that tonight she would have to start all over again. It had been difficult to hook Schahriar the first time. She didn't know how to do it this time, when he already knew half the story. "How?"

The Storyteller smiled a small, secret smile. "I was walking last night past the Great Mosque in the Street of Sighs, exactly an hour after sundown, when I came face-to-face with Death."

"Had he come for you?" she asked, worried.

The Storyteller paused for a long moment; then he grinned. "You see?" he said. "You're hooked."

Such a small example, and so very clear. She could do that.

She believed, for the first time since dawn, that she would make it through another night.

When she arrived back at the palace, she found her father waiting for her.

"Let's walk," he said softly.

He took her arm and led her down a dark corridor. She had never seen her father like this. He was frantic. She had heard from one of the servants that half the palace had heard her voice that morning when she had demanded

to know who the Chief Executioner was. They had heard
her fear and had been waiting to hear of her death.

Among the guards there were wagers as to whether she
would survive another night.

Her father gripped her arm tightly and did not speak
until they were far from prying ears.

"He's still mad," her father whispered, "and he'll kill
you. I've made arrangements for you to escape."

Her poor dear father. He had been more right than
wrong. She should have listened to him before. But she
had no choice now. She had already made her decision.

"It's too late," she whispered back. "If I fled, he'd
punish you, and then pick one of the poor girls in the
harem."

"So you'll stay and risk your life?" Her father sounded
appalled.

"I promised I'd help." She did not meet her father's
gaze. She was happy that he hadn't asked her where she
had been. She didn't want to tell him she was seeking
advice in the market. "If I can make him listen to my
stories, maybe he'll change."

"You don't sound as certain as you were," her father
said.

She closed her eyes. "I'm not."

The day passed swiftly. Too swiftly. She managed a
nap, but it was not long, and she was plagued with horrible
dreams. In them, the Chief Executioner had used a pink
rope to sever the stems of a dozen white roses. Then he
had looked at her and said, "I do this because of you,
Sultana. Because of you."

She had awakened with her heart pounding, unable to
return to sleep. But she had lain in her room until her
handmaidens arrived to dress her for the night ahead.

Her clothes as Sultana were beautiful, more beautiful

than she could ever have imagined. Schahriar, or perhaps her father, had gone to great expense to provide the proper garments for her. If it had been Schahriar, it was another sign of his madness—plotting to kill his new wife, yet providing a wardrobe's full of clothing for her.

Or perhaps it was shrewd. It would show no evil intent, after all. In fact, it showed that he planned to live a long life with her. Only that, somehow, she had proven unsuitable. All of his hopes, then, would have been for naught.

While her hair was taken out of its combs and was being brushed a hundred times, she went over the story's opening in her mind. She planned two alternative openings in case the first one did not catch him. Other parts of the story had flashed through her all day, ways she could twist it to hold his interest, but she was not willing to plan too far ahead.

She had become superstitious. Planning had not gotten her very far the night before. Making up the story as she went had worked best for her. She would continue to do that this night.

Finally, she was dressed in a new silken nightgown. Her hair, trailing down her back, shone in the light. She was perfumed and polished and ready to face the man who would be her death or her salvation.

Her apartments adjoined his, of course, and when she was summoned, she came through her dressing room door. The servant vanished almost instantly.

At first, she didn't see Schahriar. The bedroom looked subtly different. There were no lamps all over as there had been the night before, although someone had thoughtfully laid out food again.

The sharp, sweet smell of a hookah pipe filled the room, and finally she saw Schahriar, sitting in a chair near one of the archways leading to the Gardens. The stem of the hookah pipe was long and made of silver and crystal. The pipe itself, which Schahriar smoked, was carved from wood and ivory.

He raised his dark eyes when he saw her, but did not greet her. She felt her heart pound. Did he expect her to begin the story as if nothing had happened? As if they did not know each other?

She walked to the nearest column. Schahriar continued to smoke, watching her approach. She leaned against the column. Its marble was cool against her skin. He stared at her, expectantly.

She had seen that look in the market, on the faces of the Storyteller's audience. *Entertain me,* the look said. *Entertain me now.*

She took a deep breath, and began.

"As I was saying," she started, and paused just enough so that he could interrupt if he needed to. Apparently he did not, for he said nothing, just continued to smoke and stare while he waited. "Black Coda brought his whole gang into Damascus, in a wagon, to murder Ali Baba."

She took a deep breath, watching the Sultan closely. His expression had not changed.

"But it was no ordinary wagon," she said. "It carried forty life-sized stone jars in the back of the specially built wagon. And Black Coda, a master of disguise, was the old man driving."

Schahriar stopped smoking. He tilted his head slightly. "The wagon was carrying his men in stone jars?"

She felt her breath catch in her throat. She couldn't tell if he had noticed the change and didn't like it or if he was hooked.

"How did Black Coda explain the jars?" Schahriar asked.

Scheherazade let out a small sigh of relief. He was hooked.

"Well," she said, "Black Coda was very shrewd. . . ."

* * *

Black Coda hunched over his walking stick. He wore a cloak so old and so large that his body seemed lost in it. The only thing that was visible were his hands and they, he knew, looked very old—damaged from the outdoors and scarred from sword fights he had been in.

The wagon was behind him, his men hidden in the jars. Fortunately his men were well trained. They often hid under sand at an attack point. They knew how to be quiet and motionless.

So, when the guard at the Damascus gate stopped him, Black Coda was prepared.

"What's this, old man?" the guard asked.

Black Coda coughed and wheezed. He tried to speak, coughed again, and fought for breath before saying, "Forty jars of lamp oil for the royal palace."

Schahriar chuckled, and Scheherazade stopped speaking in surprise. She hadn't heard him laugh since they were children. The sound was different, older, but still had the edge of that wild, unfettered laughter they used to enjoy as children.

She leaned against the column, watching him.

"Forty jars of oil," Schahriar said, pleased. "That's clever. Very clever. Obviously Black Coda had a black heart, but a bright brain."

And Schahriar was in the story, at least for this night. Scheherazade felt herself relax as she picked up the threads of the tale.

The guard waved Black Coda and his wagon through. As it trundled down the deserted street, Black Coda turned around and whispered, "All clear."

One of the lids rose. Black Coda saw a bit of hair, a flash of eyes, but not enough to recognize which of his men hid inside. Always, a different man popped out of a hiding place first.

"I'm glad that's over," the man said.

As if it were a cue, the other robbers popped their heads out of the jars to get fresh air. They surveyed the street in all its silence. Black Coda continued to walk with the wagon, letting it rattle in the darkness.

The men who had initially found Ali Baba's house were up front. When Black Coda stopped at a fork in the road, one of the men whispered, "Turn right to get to Ali Baba's."

Black Coda turned right, and the wagon followed. Anyone who looked would have seen the funny but sinister sight of forty heads poking out of forty jars.

But fortunately for Black Coda, no one looked.

Meanwhile, Ali Baba had no idea of the danger he was in. He didn't tremble, but he should have trembled.

Life in his new house went on as it had for the past few days. Since it was now night, Morgiana was fulfilling her duty as the housekeeper and locking the courtyard gate.

Saffron lay in his usual spot beneath the palm tree. Ali Baba was inside.

Morgiana knew how perceptive Saffron was, even though he was just a camel. She also knew that Saffron was Ali Baba's best friend.

So she talked with him as if he could give her advice.

"How are we going to protect him, Saffron?" she asked. "He's a dreamer."

Saffron nodded. Apparently, Ali Baba's tendency to dream large dreams worried the camel as well.

Morgiana wiped her hands on her skirt as she approached Saffron. "The robbers will try and find him. He should have never taken his brother's body down."

Saffron sighed.

"And what about all those schemes for making money?"

Saffron spat in disgust.

Morgiana put her hand on Saffron's head and crouched beside him. "He needs someone to look after him."

Saffron nudged her hand with his snout.

"Yes, I do love him," Morgiana said. "But does he love me?"

Saffron nodded vigorously.

Morgiana's eyes narrowed in suspicion. "You're a camel. What do you know about love?"

Saffron's eyebrows arched upward. He looked very indignant—even for a camel.

"Sorry, sorry," she said. "I'm sure you know about everything, Saffron. You're a very wise camel."

And Saffron was, too. He saw things as clearly as Morgiana did, more clearly than Ali Baba did. Neither Saffron nor Morgiana foresaw that an attack would come that night.

But Black Coda was just outside the gate. He had stopped the wagon, unhitched the horses, and put wooden blocks beneath the wheels to keep it from rolling back down the hill.

As he worked, one of Ali Baba's servants walked over to him. Black Coda played his old man role to perfection.

He bowed his head so that they could not see his face and said in his raspy, old man voice, "Praise be to Allah. Would your master mind if I left my wagon in the street while I feed and water the horses?"

"What are you carrying, old man?" the servant asked.

"Lamp oil for the palace." Black Coda reached into the pocket of his robe and removed some coins. "It'd be worth four gold pieces if you could keep an eye on them."

The servant took the coins so quickly that his fingernails

scraped Black Coda's palm. "Your goods are safe here, old man. Never fear."

Black Coda worked on the wagon until the servant disappeared into the house. Then he whispered, "I'm going to feed and water the horses. It'll look suspicious if I stay here."

He grabbed the horses' reins with one hand and added, "I'll be back in two hours, when it's quiet. Then we'll kill everyone in the house."

Chapter Nine

Schahriar had put down his hookah pipe. He was stretched out on the chair, his legs extended before him. He looked very comfortable.

Scheherazade was thirsty. She had been talking a long while now, but she did not want to break the spell of the tale that she was telling. So, as she moved to the next section, she mimicked Morgiana's actions.

She gathered up a tray and brought it to Schahriar.

"I thought you might like a hot lemon and nutmeg, sir." Morgiana set the tray beside Ali Baba. He was in his study, working on papers.

"Thank you, Morgiana." Ali Baba smiled. "I think it's time you called me Ali."

* * *

Scheherazade poured coffee into small cups and handed one to Schahriar. He took it almost as if he didn't realize what he had done. He still seemed lost in the story.

So she continued.

"I've been thinking of money-making schemes," Ali Baba said.

Morgiana frowned. "But why think up such schemes, Ali? You're rich."

"That's luck," he said. "I may not be lucky all my life."

Morgiana heard a sound from outside. She drew back the silk curtain and saw a wagon parked in the street.

"I want to know if I can survive," Ali Baba was saying, "if my luck turns."

Morgiana wondered if Ali Baba's luck had turned. The wagon made her very uneasy. She had to find out where it had come from.

She went back into the kitchen. The servants were eating their supper.

"There's a wagon parked in the street outside," Morgiana said. "Whose is it?"

"It's a merchant, lady, with jars of oil for the palace," said the servant who had spoken to Black Coda. "He asked permission to leave his wagon there for a few hours."

"Did you check him closely?" Morgiana asked.

"Yes, lady."

Her eyes narrowed. She did not trust this servant. Ali Baba had hired him, and Ali seemed to trust too easily.

"How much did he give you?" she asked.

"Nothing, lady. Nothing."

The other servant turned her head toward Morgiana and rolled her eyes. Morgiana had the same feeling, but could do nothing about it. After all, the first servant had denied taking a bribe. Unless she wanted a scene, she would not confront him—at least until morning.

She peeked into Ali Baba's study. He was still working, trying to come up with some scheme that would make him rich all over again. Morgiana shook her head fondly and went to bed.

As she sat in her small bedroom brushing her hair, her oil lamp flickered. She frowned at it, noted that the oil was low, and was about to get up when the lamp went out.

She picked up the lamp and went back into the kitchen. The servants were clearing away their plates. She went to the store cupboard where the drum of oil was kept, but it was empty.

"Is there any more oil in the house?" she asked.

"We have to buy some tomorrow," the male servant said.

She did not want to wait. She did not know how long Ali Baba would be awake, and he might need more oil. "Hasn't that merchant some jars of oil in the wagon?"

The servant looked surprised. He had clearly forgotten that. "Yes."

"He won't mind us taking a little for the night," she said. "We'll pay him in the morning."

Morgiana and the servant went out into the darkness. He carried small containers so that they could get some oil. As they approached the wagon, Morgiana heard a voice, speaking softly.

"I'm stiff as a board," the voice said.

It seemed to be coming from one of the jars.

"Praise be to Allah," said another voice from a different jar. "It can't be long before the killing starts."

Killing! Morgiana felt herself grow cold. Black Coda's men had found them, then, and planned nothing but bad for them all.

She put a finger to her lips so that the servant would

say nothing. She got them quietly away from the wagon. Once she was back in the house, she ran to Ali Baba.

He was still in his study, hard at work.

"Morgiana," he said, "this man's got a marvelous scheme for breeding termites with wooden legs. I think I should invest."

"They've come, Ali!" Morgiana said.

"Who?"

"The murderers you stole the money from," she said.

Ali Baba stood so quickly that he knocked the papers over. He did not seem frightened, but he was alarmed. He followed Morgiana out of the house. As they went through the courtyard, Morgiana whispered, "I've sent one of the servants for the authorities," she said.

Saffron lifted his head and made an inquiring honk. Ali Baba put a finger to his lips. Saffron nodded.

Ali Baba peered through the door. He saw the wagon below. "We can't wait for the authorities," he said. "Those murderers might jump out of their jars at any moment."

"I've got an idea." Morgiana whispered it to Ali Baba, who chuckled.

"Good, good," he said. "Listen to this, Saffron."

He whispered to Saffron, who nodded his approval.

For some reason, both Ali Baba and Morgiana were relieved that Saffron thought the plan a good idea.

They immediately went into action. They took the servant with them and walked to the street. As they approached the wagon cautiously, Morgiana whispered instructions to the servant. He tiptoed to the back of the wagon.

Ali Baba and Morgiana made their way to the front. Morgiana got there first. He was halfway there when the servant lost his footing and bumped into the side of the wagon, rocking it.

"Chief?" a voice from a jar said.

Ali Baba, Morgiana, the servant, and Saffron froze.

"Chief?" the voice asked again. "Is that you?"

Ali Baba looked toward Morgiana, who nodded cautiously.

Ali Baba licked his lips and said in a disguised voice, "Any moment now."

"Hear that, men?" the voice said. "Any moment now."

A whispered chorus of "Good, good" echoed hollowly through the other jars. The sound unnerved the three people and the camel outside. They had known the jars were filled with forty thieves, but to hear forty whispered voices brought it all home.

When Ali Baba reached the front of the wagon, he looked around it and signaled his servant, who untied the gate at the wagon's back. Then Ali Baba and Morgiana lifted the wagon shafts, tilting it backward.

The jars began to slid off the wagon. When they hit the street, they spun for a moment, and then they landed on their sides. They rolled down the hill, going faster and faster until they were a complete blur. A few rolled out of sight, but most rolled until they hit a building at the spot where the hill turned a corner.

The jars shattered, revealing very sick, very dizzy robbers inside. A few tried to stand, but they could not. A couple reached for each other, missed, and fell down all over again.

The sound of forty smashing jars brought people out of their beds and into the street. Ali Baba and Morgiana ran down the hill toward the mess as people surrounded the dizzy robbers.

At that moment, the authorities showed up. Dozens upon dozens of armed troops, happy to catch Black Coda's gang, fell upon the men and arrested them. Ali Baba saw a few men getting away, and he pointed them out to the authorities, who caught them with no effort at all.

It is not difficult for anyone to catch a dizzy man, especially if that man is trying to run.

Within moments, Black Coda's evil gang was captured. The entire town started to celebrate, but Ali Baba and Morgiana were the first. They hugged each other, then looked at each other in surprise.

They hadn't meant to do that. But it had felt good, better even than Morgiana had thought a hug from Ali Baba would feel.

Their hug was not private, though. From an alley just up the hill, Black Coda watched. He snarled at the sight of Ali Baba's celebration, and then Black Coda slipped away into the night.

"The next day," Scheherazade said, "Black Coda's men hung like ripe fruit. It was all over."

Schahriar frowned at Scheherazade. He, apparently, was not ready for the story to end.

She smiled at him. "Well, not quite over."

Ali Baba threw a magnificent party to celebrate the defeat of Black Coda and his gang. The townspeople filled Ali Baba's house, grateful that he had rescued them from Black Coda.

Morgiana was one of the guests of honor. She, after all, had come up with the plan to defeat Black Coda, and Ali Baba wanted that known. She dressed in a silken garment made mostly of scarves. Ali Baba realized she was more beautiful than he had ever given her credit for.

When it came time to make the toast, Ali Baba lifted his glass. He was not much for speeches, but he was willing to make a try.

"We're celebrating today," Ali Baba said, "because

Black Coda and his gang have been squashed like— beetles, thanks to the advice of my friend Morgiana.''

The crowd cheered and waved their fists in approval. Saffron, in the corner, took a moment away from the bale of hay he was eating his way through to trumpet his approval. Some of the guests looked at the camel, startled.

''We are most lucky to have as our special guest tonight,'' Ali Baba said, ''that most famous wit and entertainer in all of Islam, Mullah Nasrudin!''

An elderly man with a huge white beard that stuck out as far as his arm, stepped forward. He wore a striped turban and a matching cloak—all of it gaudy, as an entertainer's clothing should be.

''How old are you, Mullah?'' one guest asked.

''Forty,'' he said, smiling.

''You've been saying that for at least ten years,'' the guest said, laughing.

''I always stand by what I say.'' Nasrudin's voice was golden. The words flowed off his tongue, as sweet as honey. ''But I want to tell you about my greatest moment. It happened when the Sultan actually spoke to me. I was standing outside the palace when he shouted loudly, so everyone could hear. 'You lout, you're standing in my sunlight. Get out of the way!' he said.

There was much laughter and applause, even though Ali Baba thought Nasrudin's performance was not quite what Ali had paid for. Some of his disappointment must have shown in his face, for the man next to him nudged him.

''Ask if Morgiana will dance for us,'' he said. ''She's a beautiful dancer.''

''I didn't know that,'' Ali said, turning to her.

She was sitting against the wall, beneath some of the ribbons he had strung up. She did not look surprised at the request.

In fact, all around them, people started shouting

Morgiana's name. Several men held out their hands to her so that she could take them and stand up. She smiled at all of them, but got up on her own.

She walked toward Ali Baba. He was still surprised that the woman who had run his household had this secret talent.

"I can't dance a step," Ali Baba said.

She raised her eyebrows, then lifted her skirts and stepped onto the makeshift stage. "I'll show you how it's done."

The musicians played a dance melody, and Morgiana began her dance slowly, sensually. She circled the room enticingly . . .

". . . like this," Scheherazade said.

And for the first time in her life, she danced for a man, using the steps she had seen in the bazaar and practiced secretly in her room.

She started across the room and snaked her way toward Schahriar.

He lay on the bed, the hookah pipe forgotten, and watched her with astonishment and longing.

Scheherazade felt the dance grow more sensual. She had never felt more beautiful. She danced her way toward the bed until she stood right in front of Schahriar.

She danced until she could not stand the pressure of his gaze, and then she continued her story.

The music ended, and Morgiana bowed. The guests applauded long and happily. Ali Baba could not stop looking at her. It was as if she had been transformed before his eyes into a different woman, one he should have seen from the beginning, one he desired more than any he had ever met.

The musicians began playing another piece of music, drums only, and Morgiana walked across the stage with a dancer's sense of purpose. She approached a male guest and pulled his sword from its scabbard, holding it above her head by the hilt.

The sword caught the light of a hundred hanging lamps. She whirled like a dervish, always in time to the music, woman and drums and sword like one. She moved across the stage until she reached Nasrudin.

And then, without warning . . .

". . . she savagely plunged the sword into his chest," said Scheherazade as she pretended to stick an imaginary sword into Schahriar.

Schahriar fell back against the pillows with a cry of surprise.

"Nasrudin stared in astonishment at the sword sticking in his chest," Scheherazade said. " 'That's not funny,' Nasrudin mumbled. 'Not funny at all.' And then he pitched forward. Dead."

Schahriar sat up, his expression bleak. "They all kill. Women are born to kill. Root 'em out. They kill without reason."

Scheherazade let her arm drop. Schahriar's vehemence startled her. She hadn't realized she had been so deep into the story. She must have frightened him by miming the stabbing.

Her own heart was pounding. Perhaps she had made a mistake.

Schahriar looked as if his most horrible nightmares had come to life.

"She had her reasons for killing," Scheherazade said, trying to push on.

"Everybody has their reasons," Schahriar said. "That's the terrible thing."

"Everyone was shocked, Sayiddi," Scheherazade said. "Even Ali Baba cried out . . ."

"Morgiana! What have you done?"

Morgiana was shaking. She leaned down and grabbed Nasrudin's beard and pulled it off, revealing the face of Black Coda.

"I saw the tattoo when I was sitting next to him," she said, her voice shaking as badly as she was. She had never killed anyone before.

The guests gathered round to look at the evil Black Coda. Even dead, he looked frightening, as terrible as they had imagined.

And he had been among them, had tried to entertain them. The man who had baited him during his act wondered if the great entertainer Nasrudin had always been Black Coda, and if people had laughed at a murderer's jokes for more than a decade.

Ali Baba pulled Morgiana against him and stroked her arm to calm her. Slowly, she stopped shivering.

"What would I do without you, Morgiana?" Ali Baba said, and as he spoke, he realized that he loved her, that he had loved her from the moment he met her.

She put her arms around him. Ali Baba would get credit for defeating forty thieves, would become famous for ridding Damascus of Black Coda, but that was not the greatest thing he did.

The greatest thing Ali Baba did was to find Morgiana and learn to trust her. For without her, he would have been dead forty times over.

Without her, he would not have lived long enough to enjoy the fortune that had cost him so much.

Chapter Ten

After Scheherazade finished telling of the death of Black Coda, she turned to Schahriar. He hadn't moved from the position he had gotten into when she had startled him with her pantomime.

Schahriar looked down at himself, apparently a bit startled that he still seemed on guard, and then stood. "I need to relax," he said.

He walked through the arches to the Persian Gardens. Scheherazade watched him, uncertain what to do. Should she follow him or leave him in peace? He gave her no clue.

When he reached the white stone, he stopped. "Well?" he said. "Come on."

She followed and then wished she hadn't when she realized where he was going.

He was going to the hot baths at the very edge of the Gardens. He slipped off his robe and laid it across a table, as if he had done that many times before. He was naked, and the perfection of him took Scheherazade's breath away.

He did not seem embarrassed by his nakedness. He did not even seem conscious of her watching him. As he stepped into the large bath, steam rising from it, Scheherazade looked away.

Water splashed as he slipped beneath it, then came up sputtering. He put his arms on the tiles around the edge and stared at her.

"Join me."

She did not know which man spoke to her—the gentle one she knew lived within him or the unpredictable one she had seen for the last two days. She bowed her head, though, and said, as meekly as she could, "Yes, Sayiddi."

Then she waited for him to turn away so that she could disrobe.

He did not. His eyes sparkled in the lamplight. "You cannot get in wearing that."

"I know, Sayiddi." With shaking fingers, she reached for the buttons and proceeded to undo them. He watched her with the same intensity he had shown when she danced for him. But that hadn't felt like her. That had felt as if she were being Morgiana instead of Scheherazade.

Here, she was just Scheherazade, undressing before her unpredictable new husband.

Before Schahriar.

She let the nightgown slip off her shoulders. Schahriar made a small sound, rather like a gasp. She walked across the tiles as if she had walked naked before a man her entire life.

There were stairs at the edge of the pool, and as she went down them, she noted how hot the water was. It was nearly to the point of being uncomfortable, and yet, after a moment, it felt good.

She slipped beneath its surface, careful not to dunk her head all the way. The warmth had a strange effect on her muscles; they felt as if they were melting. The knots that had been part of her since she decided to marry Schahriar were slipping away.

No wonder he liked this place. It worked like magic on tension, easing it. She moved her arms in the water, careful to keep herself from getting too relaxed.

If she got too relaxed, she would make mistakes, and she couldn't afford to. Schahriar seemed better this evening than last, but his reaction to her pantomimed sword fight had reminded her that he was as volatile as ever.

Schahriar had moved away from the edge of the pool. He was now sitting on one of the underwater benches, leaning against the wall of the bath.

Scheherazade continued to move her arms, watching him out of the corner of her eye. He was still staring at her, that intensity enveloping her as if he were physically touching her.

"What happened to Ali Baba and Morgiana?" Schahriar asked.

Scheherazade tilted her head slightly. Had that intensity come from his desire to hear more of the story?

"Ali Baba finally had one good idea," she said, knowing that this was where she had to take a risk. "He married Morgiana."

"He wasn't clever, but he was lucky," Schahriar said. His reaction wasn't at all what she had expected. She had thought he would rail at the idea of marriage. Instead, he spoke calmly, as if he were still caught in the story. "He needed someone like Morgiana to make sure he made the most of his luck."

He had distanced himself from Ali Baba by calling him lucky. She hadn't wanted that. "Something like that."

"It could've been a man who befriended him," Schahriar said, musing.

"Yes," Scheherazade said, knowing she didn't dare disagree. But she had to bring Schahriar back to the story she had told. She had ended the tale when Ali Baba realized what a treasure he'd had in Morgiana, the woman he had ultimately married. Scheherazade couldn't get caught in a discussion of whether or not a man might have been a better friend to Ali Baba.

So Scheherazade added, although she knew she was treading on dangerous ground, "She proved a very good wife, Sayiddi."

"I suppose it can happen," Schahriar said calmly. "But not likely."

"Just because you had a bad experience once, Sayiddi—"

"Bad?" His voice shook, and then rose. "Bad?" He turned in on himself. The open way he sat was gone. He huddled against the side of the pool. "Do you know what she tried to do to me? And I loved her."

"Do you still love her?"

He huddled even more, his face hidden by his arms. He spoke so softly that, if it weren't for the echo of the pool, Scheherazade would not have heard him. "She rots. Deep down. Six feet down."

"Death doesn't change it," Scheherazade said, softly.

"She tried to kill me!"

"That doesn't matter," Scheherazade said. "If you love somebody enough, you can forgive them anything."

His arm dropped and she saw his face again. He frowned at her, as if he didn't quite understand what she had said.

Her breath was coming in shallow gasps. He had startled her with his quick emotional shift, and she didn't want him to see that. So she sank deeper into the water and continued moving her arms.

Schahriar sat up again on the bench and watched her.

She had no idea how long they remained in silence like that, him watching her, her moving as gently as she could. Eventually, the water eased the tension his outburst had brought—and reminded her how tired she was.

Except for her nap, she had had no sleep for nearly two nights now. Her eyes kept closing of her own accord. If she fell asleep in here, she might conveniently drown. Then Schahriar wouldn't need the services of his Chief Executioner. The Sultana's death would be ruled an accident—and she supposed it would be. She would have drowned and Schahriar would not have lifted a hand to help her.

Another story that she told herself. She had no idea if it were true, and she didn't really want to test it. So, without asking Schahriar's permission, she got out of the water and slipped on a robe that hung beside the bath. Then she stretched out near the steps.

Schahriar watched her, but said nothing. His eyes were narrowed, as if he were thinking about what she had said. She hoped he was thinking about trust and good wives instead of picking flaws in her story. She hoped he was softening toward her. She had no way to really know.

But the only way she could teach him to trust her was to trust him first. And that meant sleeping in front of him, so near to the water, where all it would take was a quick movement, a dunk of the head into the hot bath . . .

Somehow she slept. Her body left her no other choice. One moment she was awake and worrying about what Schahriar might do, and the next she heard his voice, speaking to her as if from a great distance.

"Is that the end of the story?" Schahriar asked.

Of course it was. And it ended happily. But she didn't dare quit.

"No," she said, sitting up. There was a servant behind her, holding a pitcher of wine. How long had the servant been there?

How long had Scheherazade been asleep?

"No," she said again.

Schahriar was looking at her. She had to come up with

something. "Faisal," she said, "and his wife ... Safil, from ... Constantinople, were at Ali Baba's wedding."

She hoped Schahriar didn't realize that the pauses she put in were because she was making this up as she went.

"Faisal," she said, "had designed Morgiana's wedding dress."

Schahriar stood up, revealing his naked chest. He watched her closely, but the intensity was gone. He seemed like a man who wanted entertainment and nothing more.

"Faisal was one of the best tailors in the East, but both he and his wife always looked as if they'd been stuffed by a good taxidermist."

She smiled at that description, but Schahriar did not. He got out of the water. As he started up the stairs, Scheherazade looked away. She found herself suddenly quiet shy.

Beside her, she saw two more servants come out of the shadows. Had they been there the entire time? She blushed to think of it.

"At the wedding," she said, feeling that her silence had gone on too long, "they met an extraordinary friend they hadn't seen in years."

"Who?" Schahriar held up his arms as his servants wrapped him with a towel.

Scheherazade saw their shadow across the pool. The shadows were distorted. One of the attendants looked small and squashed and twisted.

"Oh," Scheherazade said, "a hunchback. His name was ... Bacbac."

"Good name, Bacbac," Schahriar said.

Schahriar seemed a more willing audience this time. He wasn't in as big a hurry to be caught by the story. It seemed as if he already were hooked.

Hadn't she felt that way about the Storyteller? Because

she knew he would tell her a good tale, she would give him some time to develop it.

But she knew that while the time was longer in the second story, it still wasn't very long at all.

"Bacbac liked his name too," Scheherazade said. "In fact, Bacbac liked most things about himself—even his hump, for without it he might not have become the Sultan's favorite Jester."

She glanced at Schahriar. His attendants were tying his robe about his waist. He looked less vulnerable in his nightclothes. She stretched her feet into the warm pool. Some of her tiredness was gone, and she was ready to tell the new story.

"Anyway," she said, letting the tale take her away, "back in Constantinople, Faisal invited Bacbac to supper. And Bacbac never turned down a free meal. . . ."

Faisal's large dining room smelled of his wife's spectacular fish soup. Candles were lit in the center of the table. Faisal and his wife sat at one end and Bacbac at the other.

Bacbac was always a good dinner companion. There was no need to entertain him. He would rather do the entertaining. Faisal liked guests who talked a lot. It allowed him to play host and enjoy the wonderful meals his wife always made for guests.

Bacbac was in the middle of his fifth story of the evening. Already Faisal had laughed so hard that his sides ached.

"Prince Hinbad is so ugly, even starvation can't look him in the face," Bacbac was saying. "What a sight. No tide would bring him in. His mouth is so big, he can eat a banana sideways."

Then he grabbed the edges of his mouth and pulled them wide, banana-shaped. Faisal and his wife laughed.

"And his wife!" Bacbac said. "Her face is all dried

and wrinkled like a prune. She's the kind of woman you have to look at twice. The first time you don't believe it! At her wedding, everyone kissed the groom.''

Faisal laughed so hard that his stomach hurt. His wife was clapping her hands together and howling with laughter. Bacbac threw his head back and bellowed. Then he sputtered and gasped and wheezed.

All part of the show. Such a funny fellow. Faisal wondered if Bacbac was ever serious.

Bacbac continued to hack and wheeze, sticking his tongue out as far as it would go. It was so funny that Faisal's wife laughed louder than she had before. Any other time, she would be offended at the rudeness of the guest.

Bacbac made a choking, sputtering sound, and then fell face-first in his bowl.

Fish soup splattered everywhere, including the back of his bald head. Faisal laughed all the harder. So did his wife.

Bacbac didn't move.

That was strange. Usually Bacbac joined in the laughter.

Faisal's wife had stopped laughing too. She got up as Faisal said, ''Bacbac? Are you all right? Bacbac!''

Bacbac did not answer. Safil went to him and lifted his head out of the soup. His face was covered with fish broth, and his eyes stared blindly ahead.

Safil let him fall back into the plate, spilling more soup. This time, Faisal did not laugh.

''I think he's dead,'' Safil said.

''Dead!'' Faisal said. ''He can't be dead. You're fooling us, aren't you, Bacbac? Another one of your jokes?''

''He must have suffocated,'' Safil said. ''Probably a fish bone got stuck in his throat. Poor Bacbac. We must tell the authorities.''

''They'll blame us.''

Faisal stood. He saw the ruin of everything they had

done. How could they prove that they hadn't done this deliberately? Everyone knew that Bacbac talked too much. It was a small stretch to think that they had given him bony fish soup, knowing he would inhale as he spoke, and choke.

"It was an accident," Safil insisted.

"They'll still blame us," Faisal said. "He was the Sultan's favorite. They'll point the finger. Can't you just hear them? 'There they go, the people who killed poor little Bacbac.'"

Safil gasped. "We'll lose all our customers."

"Reputation shattered," Faisal said. "Credit destroyed, income lost, no money."

They held each other and looked at Bacbac who, a few moments ago, had been an entertaining guest, and who was now about to cause them complete ruin.

"What are we going to do?" Faisal asked.

"We could take him to the old physician next door," Safil said.

"It's too late for a physician," Faisal said, disgusted. "He needs an undertaker."

"I mean we could leave him there," Safil said.

Faisal felt his breath catch. What a suggestion!

"Dump him," Safil said, still trying to convince him. "So long as the body is not found here, he isn't our responsibility."

Faisal nodded. "Let someone else take the blame," he said. "That sounds good."

So they had a plan. They would take Bacbac to the physician's, and then they would come back and clean up the house as if he had never been there.

First, though, they had to get him across the street.

The shortest route was through the front of the house, which served as the tailor's shop, then across a dark alley and up a flight of stairs. Safil went out the door first to see if anyone was around.

An older couple passed on the street. She waited until they were gone before she motioned to Faisal.

Faisal came out, carrying Bacbac on his back. Bacbac was heavier than he looked and hard to hold. Faisal grunted as he walked, glad that he didn't have to take Bacbac far, or it would ruin his back.

Safil followed Faisal through the dark alley, keeping to the shadows. She constantly looked over her shoulder to make certain no one saw them.

Then Faisal started up the staircase, groaning as he went. Safil looked at the sign posted along the wall to make certain that the doctor was still there.

The sign was there and everything was written in several languages. She read: *Ezra ben Ezra—Physician to Princes.*

Faisal had trouble on the stairs. He was breathing hard, and after each step, he swayed. Safil finally had to put her hands on his back, bracing him. So she had her hands on his back which bore the burden of Bacbac to keep them all from falling back.

It was a difficult task.

But they finally made it to the first landing. Faisal turned and set Bacbac down gently, leaning him against the railing.

"We'll leave him here," Faisal whispered.

"Good," Safil said, making sure that Bacbac did not slide over. When she was satisfied that he would stay as they had left him, she started down the stairs. "Let's go."

Faisal followed her. They were halfway down the stairs when a woman's voice asked, "Who's that?"

It was Dr. Ezra's wife, Miriam, who came to the door. They had often been plagued with nonpaying customers dropping off an extremely ill and extremely destitute person. Dr. Ezra would do what he could, of course, and they would get no money for helping.

Miriam hated this, and over time, she and Dr. Ezra

agreed that she would answer the door. She would be less tempted to help the sick person on the landing than he would.

This time she was faced with a familiar scene. An unconscious man on the landing and people sneaking away so they wouldn't have to pay for his care. She crossed her arms and asked in her most sarcastic tone, "Can I help you?"

"We came to see Dr. Ezra," Faisal said. "For our friend. If it's not too late?"

Miriam did not answer him. She would make no judgments without help.

Faisal extended his hand. In it, he held two gold pieces. Miriam took them and smiled.

"It's never too late with Dr. Ezra," she said.

"Want to bet?" Safil whispered to Faisal.

"I'll get him," Miriam said. She glanced down at Bacbac. His skin had turned a pasty white and he still had fish guts on his face. "Your friend doesn't look too good."

As she disappeared into the house, Faisal and Safil ran away. Miriam did not notice. Even if she had, she would not have been surprised. After all her years as a doctor's wife, nothing surprised her any more.

She went up the stairs to their apartment. Ezra was in the study, using a magnifying glass to examine a thick manuscript.

"Ezra," Miriam said. "We've a customer."

Ezra didn't even bother to set down his magnifying glass. "Another penniless vagrant?"

"No," Miriam said. "He's paid."

Ezra looked up. He hadn't heard those words in a while. Miriam showed him the gold coins. Ezra got up quickly.

"He's outside on the landing," Miriam said.

"Show him to me, my dear," Ezra said as he followed her out. "Before he gets away."

She followed him down the stairs to the landing. Bacbac

remained as she had left him—white face, fish guts, and all, looking more and more like the corpse he was. But Dr. Ezra couldn't see him. Dr. Ezra couldn't see much. He opened the door, stepped through it, and tripped on Bacbac.

Miriam reached for him, but was not quick enough. She had to watch the two men as they rolled down the stairs and landed at the bottom with a large crash.

"Ezra? Ezra, speak to me!" she shouted. She ran down the stairs herself—careful to hold the railing. Ezra was on top of the pile of limbs and robes.

"You must wear your glasses, Ezra," she said when she reached him. He was moaning and holding his head. "How do you feel?"

"I don't know," he said, sitting up.

"You don't know?" Marian asked. "You're a physician."

"So I'm a physician," he said, disgusted. "So what else you want you should tell me?"

If her husband could snap at her, he was feeling all right. Miriam turned her attention to Bacbac.

"Sir," she said as Ezra bent over Bacbac. "Your friends said you don't feel well. I'm sure my husband can help."

"No, he can't," Ezra said, his head pressed to Bacbac's chest.

"Of course you can," she said.

"No, I don't think so." Ezra sat up. "He's dead."

Miriam looked at Bacbac and saw that his head was twisted at an unnatural angle. She didn't know why she hadn't noticed it before. "The fall down the stairs?"

"A terrible accident," Ezra said.

"It's worse than that," Miriam said. "He comes here for medical help and he ends up dead. What will that do for your reputation, Ezra?"

Ezra didn't want to think about that. He peered at the body. "He looks familiar."

Miriam looked at him too, then raised a hand to her neck. "Oh, it's Bacbac, the Sultan's Jester!"

"Alas, poor Bacbac, I knew him well."

"We're doomed," Miriam sobbed. "We'll be blamed. We're foreigners."

"Help me carry him upstairs," the doctor said. "Quick."

They picked up Bacbac and carried him up the stairs. . . .

"It's amazing how quickly people can improvise when they have to," Scheherazade said, as the assistants bundled her in a warm robe, another new one that she had not seen before.

Schahriar had been watching the entire procedure, never taking his eyes off her. She had felt flushed, but had gone on with the story. He was still watching her, waiting for more.

"The Ezras had to take a gamble," she said, tightening the robe's belt herself. "Forgetting that gambling is only a way of getting nothing for something . . ."

The Ezras were in better shape than poor Faisal. They carried Bacbac to the roof of their building. The flat roof overlooked domes and minarets under a brilliant, starry sky.

"All we have to do is find the right chimney to drop him down," Ezra said.

They carried Bacbac between them. For a short man, he was extremely heavy. Dead men are always heavier than living men. Miriam thought the torture of carrying him around on the roof was almost more than she could bear.

Although she could bear losing her reputation less.

The chimneys around them were capped—all except one. It looked as if the top had been broken off in a storm and never repaired.

Ezra and Miriam saw it together and hurried toward it, as if their minds were working in perfect unison.

"Push his arms up so he'll slide down easier," Ezra said.

As Miriam levered Bacbac's arms over his head, his body fell on top of Ezra. Ezra let out a moan as Bacbac's skull hit the biggest bump on Ezra's.

"It's as if he doesn't like what we're doing," Ezra said.

"Nonsense," Miriam said. "He'd see the funny side of it."

She grabbed Bacbac by the waist and pulled him up. Getting Bacbac off his head seemed to improve the doctor's mood.

"You're right," Ezra said. "He was a professional funny man."

He peered into the chimney.

"No fire," Ezra said. "That's good. Stuff him down."

They levered Bacbac into position, and this time he stayed. They let go of his arms and he slid down the chimney as if he were coal going down a chute.

They didn't stay to hear him land. By the time Bacbac hit bottom, Dr. Ezra and his wife were gone.

Chapter Eleven

"You do not like doctors much," Schahriar said with some amusement.

They were back in his bedchamber. He was standing before the arches, staring into the Persian Gardens. Scheherazade was sitting on the bed. She had poured herself some water a few moments ago and thought she saw someone watching her from one of the grills on the far wall.

The idea that she and Schahriar were not alone sent a shiver through her. She glanced at the grill again, but the face was gone. It must have belonged to one of the servants who were constantly on call to do Schahriar's bidding.

"You could just as easily say that I don't like tailors," Scheherazade said.

Schahriar's hand clenched into a fist. Scheherazade felt herself go still. She had said the wrong thing. His comment about doctors was important to him.

"But it is just a story, Sayiddi," she said, "and the doctor and the tailor are characters."

"So there is no truth in it?" he asked.

"The truth is not always obvious truth," she said.

He was silent.

"As for doctors," she said. "I think there are times when they do not understand their patients."

"I think you are right." His hand slowly relaxed.

She took a deep breath. "I haven't finished the story of Bacbac."

"No," Schahriar said. "You left him in a chimney."

Scheherazade smiled. "And not just any chimney. You see, the chimney belonged to an herbalist named Hi-Ching. . . ."

Hi-Ching was not in the room when the Ezras first tried to stuff Bacbac down the chimney. He did not see the soot falling in his empty fireplace. He entered not long after, carrying an oil lamp.

His room was very different from any other in the city. It had papers with writings hanging from the wall. A statue of Buddha sat in the middle of a dresser, with incense burning all around it. Chinese herbs and remedies were scattered on every surface.

Hi-Ching was not a happy man. He was a stranger in Constantinople and quite lonely. While the Ezras were getting Bacbac into position, Hi-Ching poured himself a drink and looked at his statute.

"Ah, Buddha, send me a sign," he said. "Say I'm not forsaken in a foreign land."

He raised the glass to his lips and was about to take a drink when he heard a horrible rumbling in the chimney. As he whirled, he saw Bacbac crash into the empty fireplace.

"Robbers!" Hi-Ching shouted. "Thieves!"

Bacbac's head wobbled on his neck. Hi-Ching took

that for defiance. He ran forward and kicked Bacbac's chest. Then he karate chopped Bacbac in the neck.

Bacbac sprawled on the floor. He landed face up, but his skin was so covered with soot that Hi-Ching could not see his features.

Hi-Ching stood over him. "My hands are lethal," he warned.

But Bacbac, of course, did not respond. Hi-Ching stared at him for a long moment, then squinted. Were the robber's eyes open? he wondered. He leaned forward and cautiously touched the robber's filthy neck.

"Dead." Hi-Ching said, and drew back in disgust. Then he shook a finger at the corpse. "I warned you about my hands."

He settled back on his haunches and got a better view of the body.

"I know you," he said. "You're the famous Bacbac, the Sultan's Jester!"

He backed away from the body in shock. "Why did you come down my chimney?"

But of course, Bacbac did not answer. There seemed to be no clues at all. The Sultan's Jester had no reason to rob anyone. Why would he come?

Then Hi-Ching figured it out, and he didn't like what he thought. "It's a joke to set the whole town laughing. We Buddhists are always being laughed at. Well, the laugh's on you, Jester Bacbac."

Hi-Ching's voice echoed in the small room. "No," he said to himself. "The laugh's on me. They'll say I murdered you. I'll be hanged!"

He paced, trying to think of something to do to get himself out of the situation. He couldn't come up with much. All he could imagine was trying to hide the body. At least a karate chop did not show as the manner of death.

Hi-Ching put a hand to his face in contemplation. A karate chop did not show. Hmmm. . . .

That allowed him to hide the body in plain sight.

But he would have to act quickly. If he hid it near his house, people could assume that Bacbac never made it up to the roof or down his chimney. Yes! That was what would work.

Hi-Ching opened his front door and looked down the street. He saw no one. So he went back inside and hoisted Bacbac onto his back. Bacbac was not as light as he looked. A twinge went through the small of Hi-Ching's back, irritating an old wound. When this was over, Hi-Ching would have to find an acupuncturist to take some of the pain away.

He hurried down the street as fast as his legs—and Bacbac's weight—would allow him to go. When he reached the first door, he was disappointed to see that it wasn't dark. Someone had placed a torch above it.

So he moved on to the next. He could hear singing far away. His heart pounded, and he wondered if it would burst. He had never been so frightened in all his life.

He found a dark alcove and shoved Bacbac in it, making sure the body was upright. It looked as if the jester were standing in the shadows, waiting to jump out and surprise someone.

Hi-Ching shivered a little, then ran down the street back to his house. The singing followed him like a curse, growing louder and louder.

As Hi-Ching disappeared into his own door, a drunken English merchant, Jerome Gribbin, lurched out of the dark. He was the source of the singing, out of tune and nonsensical. Even if Hi-Ching had spoken English, he wouldn't have understood the words, but he would have understood the type of song.

It was a drinking song, one Jerome Gribbin had heard his fellows in England sing a hundred times. But no one knew the song in Constantinople, and he was sorry for that.

He was so drunk that he staggered into walls. He almost fell into the alcove, used a hand to steady himself, and knocked Bacbac loose. Bacbac's body fell out of the alcove and draped itself over Gribbin's shoulders.

Gribbin immediately panicked. "I'm being attacked!" he shouted, whirling around. "You'll get no money from me!"

He tried to shake Bacbac off, but couldn't. Bacbac had somehow become entangled in Gribbin's coat. Gribbin thought Bacbac had his hand in Gribbin's pocket, and he panicked all the more.

He shoved Bacbac against the nearest wall and bashed him until Bacbac fell. Gribbin leaned on the wall and screamed for help.

"Guards! Guards!"

Two of the Sultan's guards were in the streets and came running. As they got closer, Gribbin shouted, "Seize this man! He just tried to kill me!"

One of the guards tried to calm Gribbin while the other bent over Bacbac.

"Instead, you killed him," the second guard said.

"I did?" Gribbin said, far more sober than he had been a few minutes ago. "S-splendid."

"You're drunk," said the guard closest to him, about to pass out from the stench of Gribbin's breath.

The guard looking at the body gasped. "This is Bacbac," he said. "The Sultan's Jester."

"And you killed him," said the guard nearest Gribbin.

Gribbin was beginning to understand that things looked very bad for him. "Why would I kill him? We haven't even been introduced."

"That's for the judge to decide," the first guard said, grabbing Gribbin.

"And when he has," the second guard said, "we'll hang you."

"The trial of Jerome Gribbin," Scheherazade said, "was the social event of the season."

She was still sitting on the bed. Schahriar had joined her. He was lying across it, eating grapes and listening intently. He looked better than he had at any time in the last two days. He seemed almost normal.

Scheherazade took a grape for herself, and Schahriar handed her an entire bunch. She smiled at him, but did not stop her story.

"The Judge in the case was the venerable Judge Zadic. Judge Zadic was totally incompetent, but as he was a judge, nobody had noticed. . . ."

It seemed as if the entire city were in the courtroom and, indeed, if there had been enough room, the entire city would have been there. As it was, there were peddlers selling drinks and fruits while the spectators talked and ate and occasionally paid attention to the proceedings around them.

There were only six people who heard every word of the trial: Jerome Gribbin, who sat in chains in the center of the courtroom, nursing a tremendous hangover; Faisal and Safil, who clutched each other and hid toward the back; Dr. Ezra and Miriam, who stood in the balcony and cringed at each word spoken; and Hi-Ching, who looked as if guilt might eat him alive.

Judge Zadic had listened to the cases that the attorneys brought before him with somewhat less attention than the so-called murderers of Bacbac did, but with a lot more attention than the other spectators. Still, he was unclear on one thing.

"Why did you kill him?" the Judge asked Gribbin.

"I thought he was trying to rob me," Gribbin said.

The courtroom exploded into laughter. Bacbac trying to rob someone? He was the Jester to the Sultan, a man who could have whatever he wanted. He was beloved. He had no need to rob anyone.

The only people who weren't laughing were the six who all felt as if they were on trial.

"Bacbac robbing you?" the Judge asked, when his own laughter passed. "Forty years administering justice and that's the worst excuse I've ever heard."

"I made a mistake," Gribbin said.

"You certainly did," the Judge said. "All Constantinople will miss poor Bacbac. We'll not see his like again. A fellow of infinite jest."

The Judge laughed to himself, then pointed at his clerk. "Infinite jest. That's a good one. Write it down, in case I forget it."

The clerk nodded.

"Bacbac lightened our lives. He gave us laughter, rich and overflowing laughter, straight from a heart as big as he was small."

The laughter in the courtroom died. The spectators who were not paying attention suddenly started to. They all remembered Bacbac.

"We knew him," the Judge was saying, "loved him, and laughed with him. We'll remember him all our days."

Some in the crowd started to weep. Faisal and Safil looked at each other in horror. Ezra and Miriam grabbed each other's hands. But the one who was most affected was Hi-Ching, standing alone in the back. He could not believe what he had done, and now he was letting someone else suffer for it.

He looked at his hands, his lethal hands, and clenched them.

Judge Zadic was still dealing with Gribbin. He leaned

forward to pronounce Gribbin's fate. "I sentence you to be hanged!"

Gribbin looked as if he were in the middle of a nightmare. He was about to protest when, from above, someone shouted, "No!"

Everyone turned in the direction of the voice. Hi-Ching bolted through the crowd and down the stairs, shouting, "No!" the entire way.

He came out in the center of the courtroom and stood beside Gribbin, bowing and shouting, "No!"

"Who is this Chinese person?" the Judge asked Gribbin, who was as confused as the Judge was.

"I killed the poor hunchback!" Hi-Ching was shouting. "I stuffed him in the alcove."

"No!" Dr. Ezra shouted and ran into the center of the courtroom. Miriam followed, looking a bit bewildered. "I killed poor Bacbac and dropped him down Hi-Ching's chimney!"

"No!" Faisal shouted from the back of the room. He hurried forward and joined the growing crowd in the middle of the courtroom. A tearful Safil followed.

"I killed poor Bacbac," Faisal said.

"We both did," Safil said.

All around, the spectators were murmuring to each other. They had expected a show at Bacbac's funeral, but not one as great as this.

"I don't understand," the Judge said. "Would somebody please explain?"

"I killed him," Hi-Ching said. "My hands are lethal!"

"I tripped over him in the dark," Dr. Ezra said.

"He's shortsighted," Miriam said. "You can't hang a man for that."

"It was a fishbone," Safil said.

"I'm still the best tailor in Constantinople," Faisal said.

"Not so loud," Gribbin said. "My head's splitting open."

But everyone was shouting at once. The clerk was calling for order and the Judge, bemused by it all, thought of ordering a lamb shish kebab, but figured everyone would overlook his joke in the confusion.

Suddenly, trumpets sounded and the doors in the back of the court burst open. Royal Guards marched in, followed by the Sultan, Badr Al-Din. He was a large, jovial man, who greatly missed his Jester, Bacbac.

He walked to the front of the court and faced all of the guilty parties. Everyone bowed, and the courtroom grew silent. He blocked Judge Zadic's view, but the Judge could not complain. After all, this was the first time a Sultan had graced his court.

"Who killed my funny man, Jester Bacbac?" the Sultan asked.

"I did," said Faisal, Ezra, Hi-Ching, and Gribbin. Miriam and Safil were silent, letting their husbands do the talking for once.

The Judge leaned over and said into the Sultan's ear, "But who do I hang, Sayiddi?"

The Sultan paused dramatically. No one spoke. The guilty parties held their breaths.

Then the Sultan said, "Nobody. It was clearly an accident."

The courtroom remained silent, stunned at the Sultan's decision. The judge sat down, slightly disappointed that he didn't get to hang anyone.

"Besides being my jester," the Sultan said, "Master Bacbac was my friend, and if I knew him right, he would have appreciated the manner of his death. It was his final jest. Dear Bacbac didn't have to be alive to be funny. Even dead, he made us laugh."

The courtroom burst into laughter, even Faisal, Safil, Ezra, Miriam, Hi-Ching, and Gribbin.

* * *

Even Schahriar.

He stood with his back to Scheherazade and laughed long and loud. He was clutching the necklace again—had been since the middle of the story—and as the story had neared its climax, he had moved to his favorite spot overlooking the Persian Gardens.

Scheherazade smiled too. It was good to hear Schahriar laugh. She wondered if he had done much of it these last few years.

As his laughter died down, he said, "Is that the end of the story?"

"Not quite," Scheherazade said quickly. "As the mourners were walking away from Bacbac's grave, they saw a man—"

"This is a different story." Schahriar whirled. All the laughter was gone from his face. The crazy man she had seen twice before had appeared again.

And she had no story. If she had, she would have launched into it. But all she could do was say, "It's the best one yet. Extraordinary, full of excitement and thrills."

"Don't trick me again." Schahriar clutched at the necklace, working it as if it were a braided rope. "Once you start, I want to know how it ends."

Scheherazade swallowed hard. She needed another story and quickly. Only her mind had frozen, trapped by Schahriar's anger.

He raised his hands to his head. "There's something devilish in your mind," he said. "I see demons in your eyes."

"Our Mullahs say every good story has a moral," Scheherazade said.

Schahriar's eyes narrowed. "What's the moral of Bacbac's death?"

"Faisal, Dr. Ezra, and the others should have taken responsibility for their actions," Scheherazade said. "We all should."

"But if they had, Bacbac wouldn't have fulfilled his destiny to make people laugh, even dead."

"That's true," Scheherazade said. "Stories are less simple than we think they are."

Schahriar turned away from her. He bent down.

She started into the next story. It was all she could do. "This new one, for instance—"

Schahriar rose, his sword in his hand. He headed for the bed so fast that Scheherazade could not move. He brought the sword down—

And missed her by such a thin margin that she felt the breeze from the blade. He slashed the pillow beside her. Feathers rose, covering her as he marched across the bed, slashing all the pillows.

She cringed. She could not help it. But she did not move. If she moved, she would show her fear and he could not see that. He needed her to be calm.

Feathers fell around them like rain. Schahriar stopped as suddenly as he started and sank to his knees beside her. She had never seen such anguish in a person's face before.

"What's the matter, Sayiddi?" she asked, keeping her voice level. "Is there something I can do for you?"

"I just missed killing you," the Sultan said. "And you ask if there's something you can do for me?"

"I'm concerned for you."

He whispered, "Be concerned about yourself, Scheherazade."

Her fingers clutched the satin spread. He hadn't spoken her name since their marriage. She wasn't even sure he knew it.

But he did, and if he did, he probably—deep down inside—remembered their childhood together.

"I'm concerned about you, my love," she said gently.

"Why?" he asked.

She kept her gaze on his, so that he could see the truth in her words. "I love you."

He frowned, as if she were the crazy one. "Why?"

"You need me," she said.

The Chief Executioner peered through the grill as he had done off and on all night. He hadn't been able to abide the girl's story, nor the Sultan's reaction to it.

Then, when the Sultan picked up his sword, the Executioner had watched with fascination. Now, as the feathers still fell around the Sultan's bed—and as the Sultana spoke softly, gently, to him—the Chief Executioner turned away.

"It's going badly," he said to his assistant. "The Sultan's missed another chance."

He walked toward the single white rose he kept in the room as a token.

"His brother wouldn't have," the Executioner said. "Schahzenan never hesitated. He was an executioner's friend."

His assistant said nothing. The Executioner picked up the rose and ran it through his fingers, ignoring the prickle of its thorns.

"You know," he whispered, "there's some who think the wrong brother is Sultan."

And he was beginning to agree with them.

Chapter Twelve

Scheherazade's room in the palace was not yet her own, but she felt safe there, as safe as possible under the circumstances. She had not slept—she could not sleep, not after Schahriar's latest outburst.

She hadn't been expecting it. She had thought, when he laughed, that he was finally coming round, that he was finally beginning to become the Schahriar she remembered.

And then, within a moment, he had returned to the man who had ordered her death. He had missed her by inches. When she closed her eyes, she could hear the whistle of the blade as it fell beside her.

She had done something wrong. No storyteller paid for ineptness the way she did—or the way she would if she failed again.

So after a few hours of trying to nap, she sent for the Storyteller. She could not go to him. The last time had been a horrible risk. She had managed it, but she had been lucky.

This time, she was not willing to take the risk. Schahriar might execute her without seeing her, and then she would not survive. She remembered the look in the Chief Executioner's eyes. He had looked at her as if he could imagine his hands around her throat.

She would not let him get so near to her again.

When the Storyteller arrived, sunlight was pouring in the windows of her room. Scheherazade had ordered cakes and Turkish coffee, and she had them waiting on the table in the center of the room. One of her most trusted handmaidens stood just inside the door, so that Scheherazade had a witness who would claim there was no impropriety while she was alone with the Storyteller.

But the handmaiden stood far enough away that she could not hear the conversation. No one else dared hear it, not even Scheherazade's father.

As the Storyteller entered the room, he looked bemused by the grandeur. It certainly did not match his humble robes. But he sat when Scheherazade asked him to, and he smiled at her warmly as she paced.

She had missed warmth. In the last few days, her life had grown cold and frightening.

"What am I going to do?" she asked. "I told the Sultan that my next story would be extraordinary."

The Storyteller poured himself a cup of coffee. "Anticipation is part of the storyteller's art."

Scheherazade gripped the back of her chair. "But I haven't got a story."

"Use a traditional one." His fingers lingered over the cakes. She finally extended the plate. His nervousness at being there showed only in his reluctance to take the food.

"What sort of traditional story?" she asked. "He's already had an adventure and a comedy."

"Make it different," the Storyteller said. "Tell him something with magic in it. A fantasy, but with heart. That's what they all want. Heart."

Heart. Warmth. Yes. She had just been thinking about how that was missing.

She sat down across from him. "Thank you," she said.

He nodded. She took a cake as well, so that he wouldn't eat alone.

That seemed to open him up. He ate with pleasure. She wondered if he had ever eaten such rich food before.

She poured herself some coffee and waited until he was done eating before she said, "You spoke before about meeting Death."

The Storyteller wiped off his fingers. "Oh, I didn't meet him. I passed him on the Street of Sighs. I told a close friend what had happened, and he said he'd seen Death too in the street and Death had given him a terrible look."

Scheherazade relaxed in her chair. How she had missed having someone tell her stories.

"He was so frightened," the Storyteller said, "that he was leaving for Sarmara that night. So I went to see Death to find out what was going on."

He paused. Scheherazade could not wait to hear more. "And?" she asked.

The Storyteller looked away, as if something had distracted him. "Another time, perhaps."

Scheherazade felt her disappointment keenly. The Storyteller must have seen the look on her face, for he smiled.

"You must learn," he said, "how to leave your audience in suspense."

Suspense. The word revolved around Scheherazade's mind as she tried again to take a short nap. This time she succeeded, and she awoke with the beginnings of a new story in her mind.

Not a moment too soon, because shortly after she woke up, one of the Sultan's attendants summoned her. Scheherazade did not have time to get one of her handmaidens. She chose a nightgown from her expansive closet, and over it she put the most beautiful red satin robe she had ever seen.

She knew it would accent her hair and coloring. She wanted to look as beautiful as possible that night.

When she arrived in the bedroom, the oil lamps were strewn about as they had been the first night. There were pitchers of water near the bed, and some Turkish coffee on a side table.

She did not see the sword.

Schahriar was sitting on the bed, propped up against the pillow, wearing the red pajamas he had worn the first night. The necklace lay on the bed beside him, but he did not touch it.

When he saw her, he scooted over to make room.

"So," he said as she sat down, "let's hear this extraordinary story."

"Well," Scheherazade said, pleased that he had spoken to her first, "as the crowd was leaving the courtroom, the most famous magician in Africa, Mustappa, passed by on his way to Samarkand."

Schahriar's eyes lit up. He seemed relaxed, almost pleasant.

"Mustappa," Scheherazade said, "was a charismatic man with piercing eyes, a seductive voice, and a manner that would freeze friends at twenty paces. When he came into a room, the mice jumped on chairs."

Schahriar smiled.

Scheherazade leaned back. "But he isn't the hero of this story."

Schahriar turned toward her. He was even more open than he had been before. "Who is, then?"

He had caught her. She had been thinking about him instead of the story itself.

"It's—Sinbad," she said. "No. I mean . . . Aladdin."

Aladdin was a handsome young rogue who knew how to find trouble and to avoid it. The day Mustappa came to Samarkand, Aladdin was in the bazaar, gambling on the horses.

He was standing in a crowd of gamblers. He had bet on horse number Four. His friend, Hassan, had bet on horse number Three, and they had a side bet going between them as to which of their special horses would win.

Unfortunately, neither horse was in the lead. In fact, both Three and Four were bringing up the rear. As Aladdin watched, he clutched his hat and screamed, "No!" enough times that a man standing next to him moved away.

Aladdin climbed on a barrel and balanced himself against Hassan's back. The horses galloped around the bazaar, and Four managed to make it to the middle of the pack.

But that was not far enough. Even Aladdin knew that as he watched the horses cross the finish line.

"Cheat!" Aladdin shouted. "It's all a cheat."

He got down. Hassan sighed heavily and shook his head. They had lost a lot of money between the two of them.

"That race was fixed," Aladdin said.

"No question," Hassan said. "Anyone could see that, Aladdin."

"Honest men like us go for a day at the races and get cheated blind out of our hard-earned money," Aladdin said.

"It just shows that honesty doesn't pay," Hassan said.

"We'd better get back to work," Aladdin said. The men walked in opposite directions.

Aladdin bumped hard into a well-dressed man in the crowd.

"Sorry, sir," Aladdin said, and quickly walked on.

The well-dressed man, still disconcerted from the encounter, patted his pockets. He couldn't find what he was looking for.

"My purse!" the man shouted. "I've been robbed!"

Hassan rushed to the man's side from the opposite direction. Hassan no longer looked like the disgruntled gambler, but like a concerned young man.

"What's the matter, sir?" Hassan asked.

"That young rogue," the man said. "The one who bumped into me. He picked my pocket."

"I saw which way he went," Hassan said. "Follow me."

He led the man away from Aladdin and deeper into the crowd. Hassan pointed in the general direction of several people.

"Stop, thief!" Hassan shouted, trying not to laugh.

While Hassan was making sure that no one discovered Aladdin, someone else watched the entire thing. Mustappa stood at the edge of the crowd, feeling intrigued.

He had been searching all over the world for an excellent pickpocket. He had seen many, but none with the finesse that Aladdin had.

He decided to follow Aladdin and see where the journey would lead.

The journey led to a dark corner of the bazaar. Long after the poor well-dressed man had left, still searching for the person who had picked his pocket, Hassan rejoined Aladdin and together they split the contents of the man's stolen purse.

Suddenly, there was a commotion at the other end of

the bazaar. Voices shouted, "The Caliph's guards!" and Aladdin and Hassan looked up, panicked.

It took them a moment to realize that their worst fear had *not* come true. The well-dressed man had not spotted them and put the authorities on them.

Six guards on horseback were slapping people away, opening a road down the middle of the bazaar. Behind them, a gold carriage led by a team of white horses made its way into the bazaar.

Aladdin and Hassan pocketed their newfound wealth and watched the scene before them.

"Who's in the coach?" Hassan asked.

"Let's find out," Aladdin said.

Before Hassan could stop him, Aladdin ran toward a cart full of melons. He lifted one end of the cart, dumping the melons in the road before the carriage.

The white horses reared, and the coach came to a sudden stop. The guards, who were already halfway across the bazaar, had to turn around and come back.

The embossed shutters over the coach's windows moved back, and a woman's face appeared. She had delicate features and dark eyes.

She was stunningly beautiful.

She looked around until she saw what had caused the commotion. Her gaze met Aladdin's, and he felt something he had never felt before. A spark, perhaps. An acknowledgment. And there was something about the look on her face that told him she felt the same way.

"Who's that?" he asked softly.

"Princess Zobeide, the Caliph's daughter." Hassan tugged his arm, realizing how much trouble they were in. "Come on! Let's get out of here."

But Aladdin was not willing to move. He did not want to break eye contact with Zobeide. He had, in the space of an instant, fallen in love.

She hadn't broken the gaze either. A slight smile, warm and intrigued, played across her lips.

The guards came galloping back, shouting. One of them spotted Aladdin and Hassan.

"There they are!" a guard shouted.

The guards blocked off both ends of the street, but even then, Aladdin didn't notice. He was still staring at the Caliph's daughter and she at him. The moment seemed to last forever.

"Aladdin!" Hassan yelled in a great panic.

That broke the spell. Aladdin looked, saw the guards, and in an instant realized how much trouble he was in. He looked up, saw that he could get to the roof of the arch, and started climbing.

Hassan was right behind him. They reached the gutters and climbed across the roof. The guards rode their horses to the column that Aladdin had climbed up, and stopped.

Princess Zobeide watched in fascination as the two men ran across the roof. But she didn't really see the guards or Hassan. Her gaze was for Aladdin only.

For Aladdin had been right. She too had felt something, some spark, some recognition. Only she hadn't been as fast to call it love.

Women aren't nearly as rash as young rogues.

Aladdin and Hassan climbed to the top of the highest roof. There they taunted the guards, who still hadn't moved. Aladdin took Hassan's hand and clasped it in solidarity, as they often did before a job.

Then they split up and ran in opposite directions.

Princess Zobeide smiled at their audacity. Even one of the guards laughed before the troop of them surrounded the carriage. The driver clucked at the horses, and they were all on their way again, Aladdin forgotten by everyone—except Princess Zobeide.

Aladdin jumped off one roof and onto another. There he saw a man wearing beads and a most colorful robe.

A man with a goatee and a sword larger than any Aladdin had ever seen before. A man who seemed tall and powerful. A man unlike any other in Samarkand.

It was Mustappa. He had watched everything Aladdin had done.

And he had approved.

"Where did you come from?" Aladdin asked.

"The other side of the world," Mustappa said. "Africa."

"What do you want with me?"

"Stay calm, Aladdin." Mustappa stood and walked toward Aladdin. "Do I look like I'm with the Caliph's Guards?"

Aladdin did not back away. A rogue never does. "I'm always calm," Aladdin lied. Then he frowned. "How do you know my name?"

"I was a friend of your late father." Mustappa put a hand over his heart. It was a gesture of respect.

The gesture made Aladdin suspicious. "I didn't know he had any friends."

"Very few." Mustappa grinned. "Actually, just me. He was so crooked, he could hide in the shadow of a corkscrew."

Aladdin relaxed then. "You did know him!"

Mustappa laughed and patted Aladdin's arm. Together they got off the roof and went through the bazaar. The Caliph's guards were long gone, but Aladdin was not comfortable being out in the open.

It was too soon after the well-dressed man had accused him of picking his pocket. Aladdin had to remain hidden.

Somehow Mustappa seemed to know that. He led Aladdin to a dark, narrow alley. As they walked, Mustappa said, "I watched you at work."

Aladdin tensed. He was good. Too good to be seen by someone casually watching. He wondered if Mustappa had lied, if he were, in fact, with the Caliph's guards after all.

But Mustappa said, "You remind me of me when I was young. You're not as ruthless as I was, or as cunning or as bold or daring, but in some ways you remind me of me."

The idea intrigued Aladdin. Was this how Mustappa had known his father?

Before Aladdin could ask, Mustappa said, "Do you want to become rich?"

"Yes," Aladdin said. "But quick."

"It's the best way," Mustappa said.

The crowd pressed against them, and they couldn't talk anymore, not without attracting attention.

Mustappa led Aladdin out of the alley and into another part of the bazaar. Mustappa bought Aladdin some Turkish coffee, pulling coins out of his robe. Aladdin did not see his purse, however, and was surprised to note that, until that moment, he had not even looked for it.

Aladdin found them a place to sit at the edge of the bazaar where no one could overhear them. When Mustappa brought the coffee, Aladdin said, "Tell me about getting rich."

"I might put some business your way."

That intrigued Aladdin. "Business?" he asked. "Shady business?"

"Shady, shadowy, shifty, but profitable."

"What do I have to do?" Aladdin asked.

Mustappa reached down and grabbed Aladdin's hand. "First I have to check your suitability."

From his sleeve, he pulled out a small gauge and slipped it over Aladdin's middle finger. The gauge hurt, but Aladdin did not move. Instead, he was staring at the patterned tattoo that ran across the back of Mustappa's hand.

Then Mustappa removed the gauge and stood. "Meet me at dawn outside the city gates," he said.

Aladdin wasn't sure he was gong to do this. He always had other business at dawn—sleep. There were few pockets to pick that early in the morning.

Mustappa reached into his robe and removed a purse. He slapped it into Aladdin's hand and said, "Here's a token of my good faith."

And then he walked away.

Aladdin weighed the purse in his hand, was startled at the amount of gold coins inside, and hurriedly hid it under his vest—where no pickpocket would look.

Then he too left, unable to believe his good fortune.

Chapter Thirteen

"Thieves and fortunes," Schahriar said, putting his hands behind his head and sinking deeper into the pillows. "I detect a pattern to your stories."

Scheherazade looked at him sideways. He seemed more relaxed than she had seen him. "Do you?" she asked.

"Yes. I believe I could guess where this one is going."

"You could," she said, smiling at him, "but you would be wrong."

He looked at her sideways. "You dare say the Sultan is wrong?"

"You haven't guessed yet, Sayiddi."

He smiled. "You got out of that too easily."

"More easily than Aladdin got out of his predicament," she said. "And, at the moment, he didn't even know he was in one. . . ."

Aladdin arrived home that night with the purse still safely tucked in his vest. He lived in a small hovel, with barely enough room for himself and his mother. He was lucky enough to have a roof over his head, but it was a straw roof covered with cans, and it leaked whenever there was rain.

He dreamed of being rich because it was an escape, a way to live better than even he could imagine.

When he walked in the door, he saw his mother cooking over the stone hearth. The soup she was making smelled foul, but then, her cooking always did. Her talents lay in other directions.

Aladdin made sure the door was locked before he went to the table. There he poured out the contents of his purse. The gold coins jingled as they landed on the wood.

His mother hurried over. She grabbed a coin and tested it by biting it.

"That's the first thing I did, Mother," Aladdin said.

She took the coin out of her mouth. "It never hurts to get a second opinion." She waved the coin in her hand. "They taste right."

She set the coin back down on the table, her eyes glittering at the wealth before her. She asked Aladdin how he got the money, and he told her the entire story.

"So," she said, fingering the pile, "he says he knew your father. Did you believe him?"

"No." Aladdin grinned. "I believed his money."

His mother spread the coins around, as if she couldn't keep her hands off them. "He must want something big from you. Twenty gold coins is a mighty expensive introduction. He could have four men killed for that kind of money."

She put the coins back in the purse, pulled the strings closed, handed it to Aladdin, and went back to the stove.

He smiled as he took it and, reflexively, weighed it in his hands. His smile faded. "There are only nineteen coins here."

She walked toward him, hands on her hips. "Are you accusing your poor old mother?"

"I'm accusing you of palming a piece."

She got within inches of his face. "Did you see me?"

"No," he said. "I know by the weight."

She smiled. "Thanks be," she said. "I thought my hands had lost their cunning."

She took the coin out of her mouth and laid it on his palm. He chuckled, put the coin in the purse, and then hugged her. "Your pickpocketing hands will never do that, Mother. You're still the best."

"You know how to flatter a body, you young rogue." As she eased out of the hug, her smile faded and she took his arm. "Take care tomorrow morning, when you meet Mustappa."

"Trust me, Mother."

"That's what your dear father used to say, but nobody ever did."

And so, Aladdin and Mustappa left Samarkand. Aladdin didn't trust Mustappa, but when there was money involved, Aladdin was prepared to take a few risks.

Mustappa took Aladdin on his horse, and they rode into the mountains. It was midmorning by the time they reached a mountain stream. They dismounted, and Aladdin somehow got the duty of leading Mustappa's horse. Mustappa walked ahead of them both, following the path.

Someone had built a marvelous stone bridge across the stream's chasm, and as they crossed, Aladdin made the mistake of looking down. The water churned and foamed and disappeared into the darkness below.

He looked up and saw the water tumbling at them from above, looking somewhat more benign. He learned then that it was only his perspective that made the difference.

Mustappa didn't look at all. He walked quickly, carrying his staff instead of using it for balance. Aladdin spent a great deal of that morning staring at the staff. It had a ram's horn as its top, and Aladdin wondered if it had a better purpose than a walking stick.

He hoped he would not have to find out.

Mustappa led them to a rocky cliff face that led upward. Aladdin wondered if they would see the stream's source.

Apparently Mustappa was not one to travel quietly. He started many conversations, most of them about Aladdin. Finally Aladdin asked Mustappa about himself.

"I'm a magician," Mustappa said. "A wizard."

"Are you a good one?" Aladdin asked.

"No," Mustappa said. "I practice black magic."

Aladdin was glad that he was behind Mustappa so that Mustappa could not see his reaction. For the first time in a long time, someone had startled Aladdin.

"Oh," Mustappa said, suddenly understanding, "do you mean am I good at being a magician?"

He turned toward Aladdin and grinned.

"I don't want to boast," Mustappa said, "but I haven't met anyone who can live with me in a straight fight, magic to magic."

"So what do you want *me* for?" Aladdin asked. "If you're so powerful?"

"All power has its limits," Mustappa said. "I want you to retrieve an object for me. I can't get it myself for reasons too complicated to go into."

Aladdin did not like this. That meant that Mustappa had hired Aladdin to do something dangerous or foolish or both.

"Try," Aladdin said.

"It's to do with magic rules," Mustappa said. "They're tiresome, but they have to be obeyed."

Somehow that did not ease Aladdin's mind. "Why pick me?"

"You didn't believe I was a friend of your father's?"

"Not for a moment," Aladdin said. "So why me?"

Mustappa grinned. "I saw larceny in your soul."

The path flattened, and Aladdin found himself beside the stream. Only it was wide here, and was more properly called a river. The current was strong, swirling and eddying about. The air was cooler here than it was in Samarkand, and smelled faintly of the river itself.

"What do you want me to do?" Aladdin asked Mustappa.

"Go into an old tomb," Mustappa said. "You'll find an old lamp there. I want you to bring it to me."

"What tomb?"

Mustappa climbed onto a rock and pointed across the river with his staff. "There."

Aladdin got up beside him. Across the river, he saw many trees and a bit of a darkness, but nothing else.

He was not going to let on, however, that he couldn't see where they were going.

"How much?" he asked.

"We'll discuss it when you get back," Mustappa said.

"We'll discuss it now or I don't go," Aladdin said.

"A hundred gold pieces."

"Please," Aladdin said, shaking his head in disgust. "Don't insult me and don't ask me to trust you. I don't trust my own shadow. Five hundred."

"Done," Mustappa said. He removed a purse from his robe and slapped it into Aladdin's hand. "Here's half."

Then he continued to walk forward.

Aladdin weighed the purse, reflexively. It was the heaviest purse he had ever held.

"You gave in too easily," he said, hurrying after Mustappa. "I should have asked for more."

Mustappa laughed. "You do so remind me of me when I was young."

He again reached into his robe. "Take this ring." He held an ornate silver ring out to Aladdin. "Rub it if you get into trouble."

Aladdin took the ring. "Trouble? What sort of trouble?"

"With magic," Mustappa said, "you can always expect some kind of trouble."

He crossed a series of rocks until he stood in the very center of the river. The rocks formed a man's face, rising above the water. Aladdin and Mustappa stood on the man's chin, the water swirling around them.

Mustappa put down the end of his staff. It barely touched the water's edge. "Just don't touch anything in the cave besides the lamp."

Aladdin didn't like this. He remembered his earlier thought—that Mustappa wanted him to do something dangerous or foolish or both.

"Five hundred isn't enough," Aladdin said.

"A deal is a deal," Mustappa said. "Don't try and betray me. I swear on Hector's feathers, you'll never see your wedding day if you do."

"Who's Hector?" Aladdin asked.

"My pet raven and my best friend," Mustappa said. "I like you, Aladdin, but I have a terrible temper, and in the heat of the moment a man is liable to act against his own best interests."

Aladdin was about to protest when Mustappa grabbed his left hand with his right, took the ring from it, and jammed the ring on Aladdin's finger. The ring bit into Aladdin's skin.

Aladdin tried to pull away, but he could not. Mustappa forced his hand lower. When his fingers touched the moss-covered stone, the stone started to move. It opened like a mouth, and it seemed as if the stone face's eyes moved as well.

Water dribbled in the edges of the mouth, but did not pour as it should have. It was as if something magical kept the water out.

Aladdin peered inside the mouth and saw a platform

that became a flight of stone steps leading down into the
dark. He hesitated for a moment, then remembered the
money. He would get even more when he came out.

How hard could it be to take a lamp from a tomb?

He looked at Mustappa, who nodded at him. Aladdin
swallowed, keeping his nerve, and then jumped down to
the platform below.

He landed on the stone, and as he did, the steps fanned
outward, like a puzzle come to life. He looked up. Mustappa was farther above him than he had imagined he
would be. It wouldn't be easy to get out of the tomb. . . .

Scheherazade paused for a drink of water. Schahriar
poured more into her glass. He was being quite attentive.

"Do you still think my stories are similar, Sayiddi?"
she asked.

"No," he said. "But I want you to hurry up and drink.
I want to know what's in that tomb."

She drank the cool water. So far, this evening had been
easier than the other two. No outbursts and some courtesy
from Schahriar.

Perhaps things were getting easier.

She set her glass down. Schahriar was watching her,
expectantly.

"Aladdin didn't know what kind of trouble he was
getting into," she said. "If he had, he probably wouldn't
have taken the five hundred."

Then she smiled. "On the other hand, he probably
would have. . . ."

The stone stairs were wet. The dripping water formed
a feeble waterfall. Aladdin had to be careful. If he placed
his foot incorrectly, he would slip and fall into the darkness below.

By the time he reached the bottom, his eyes were used to the thin light coming in from above. The tomb seemed to have its own luminescence, but he couldn't tell where it was coming from.

He stepped off the last stair and turned. A gray man stood before him.

Not gray, really. Stone. And not a man, then, but a statue. A statue of a soldier.

As Aladdin looked past the man, he saw rows and rows of statues. Thousands of them, lined up perfectly, as if they were about to march to war. Each one was different, as if they had been modeled on real men.

Or as if an entire army had been turned to stone centuries ago.

Aladdin's heart was pounding, and he was breathing hard. He didn't like the tomb. It was cold and damp and felt wrong somehow, as if something awful had happened there.

They all seemed to be guarding something. He couldn't quite make out what it was, in the light coming in from above. The something was too far away. But it was behind the soldiers. He had to go down a long row to see it.

Aladdin started down the row, walking carefully, remembering Mustappa's admonition not to touch anything. He brought his arms in so that he wouldn't brush the soldiers.

The air was as dry as dust, and the skin on the back of his neck prickled. He felt as if he were not alone. But he saw no one else, heard no one else. He kept walking, even though he didn't want to, thinking of the 250 gold coins that awaited him when he emerged with the lamp.

The lamp. How was he to find it in this vast place?

He had no idea. He supposed he would have to search. If he needed to leave, Mustappa would help him. He was here on Mustappa's behest, after all.

The silence was incredible. The deeper he got into the

rows of soldiers, the more lost he felt. It was as if he were walking among a sleeping army, an army of the dead that would come to life with little prompting.

If it did, he would be in trouble. Already hundreds of them were behind him, blocking off his escape.

Finally, he reached the end of the long rows of soldiers. They stood before a large tomb where a life-sized statue of an emperor lay on top of a giant stone coffin. In the emperor's hands was an old lamp.

It appeared to be loose, not part of the statue at all. It almost looked as if someone had set it there accidentally. Or it would have looked that way if the emperor's fingers didn't curl around it, protecting it.

Slowly, Aladdin climbed the stone stairs that led to the tomb. He constantly looked over his shoulder, afraid he would see someone, afraid he would get caught.

Aladdin was never afraid, but this place got to him. This place was stranger than any place he had ever been before.

When he reached the top, he looked at the statue before him. The emperor's face was as distinctive as the soldiers'. Clearly these statues were modeled upon living people, from a long time ago.

That was enough to unnerve anyone. The feeling of a presence here, and all the sand and dust, merely added to it.

Aladdin swallowed against a dry throat and reached for the lamp. He had to be very cautious because he didn't want to touch anything at all. It would be hard to remove that lamp from the fingers without touching them, but if anyone could do it, Aladdin could.

Perhaps that was why Mustappa had hired him, because Mustappa had known that taking the lamp would be like picking a pocket. It would need nimble fingers.

Carefully, Aladdin removed the lamp. As his own fingers closed around it, there was a great stamping sound and the earth rumbled. He turned. Dust was rising from the statues' feet and was filling the tomb.

He couldn't swear to it, but he believed that the entire army had just come to attention.

That was it. That was all it took to shatter his fragile nerves.

Aladdin clutched the lamp to his chest and ran down the stairs. He ran between the rows of soldiers because he had no other way to get out. Only he wasn't as cautious this time.

He brushed one, lost his balance, and fell. The lamp skittered out of his hands and landed in the dust just out of his reach. The soldier above him teetered like a drunken old man.

And then he noticed that water was dripping on the soldier's head.

The tomb was under the river. It wouldn't take much for the water to come crashing inside the emptiness.

Aladdin grabbed the lamp and got to his feet. This time, he was careful not to touch the soldiers as he went. He clutched the lamp in both hands.

But behind him, he could still hear that statue he had bumped rocking. It hadn't settled yet.

Then he heard a horrible sound, the sound of stone crashing into stone. The statue had fallen forward, and slammed into the statue before it.

Aladdin snuck a look and saw soldiers falling like dominoes. If he got caught beneath them, he would be smashed to bits.

He ran even harder, trying to stay ahead of the falling soldiers. They were spaced evenly apart and so they hit each other with unerring regularity; the sound they made was like gigantic footsteps coming after Aladdin. The steps echoed in the tomb, and the impact of their falls made the floor rumble, jarring the other statues.

If Aladdin didn't hurry, he could be buried under hundreds of statues of soldiers long dead.

He switched rows and somehow knocked another statue loose. Eerily, the first row stopped falling. The second continued where the first had left off, almost as if the statues were toppling on purpose.

Aladdin was making an odd keening sound as he hurried out of the tomb. He ran even faster, trying to stay ahead of the falling soldiers. He managed it, but the soldiers were falling just behind him. He could feel the earth vibrate beneath his feet.

It felt as if they were chasing him, as if they were going to get him. He had no idea what they would do to him if they caught him, but he knew it wouldn't be pleasant.

He finally reached the stairs and started up them just as a soldier crashed near his feet. A second soldier fell, grazing Aladdin's boots. This time he yelped.

He ran up the stairs, not caring that they were wet, his back rigid because he couldn't use his arms to keep his balance.

The stairs were folding back in on themselves, like a solved puzzle, and the space where he could put his feet was getting smaller and smaller.

Behind him, the stairs disappeared. If he failed to get to the top, he would tumble into the darkness below and be at the soldiers' mercy.

He had to leap to the top stone, and then he clung to it as the last of the steps disappeared. His heart was pounding so hard, he thought it would beat a hole in his chest. He clutched the lamp to his belly and breathed as deeply as he could.

He could taste the damp air from the surface, and nothing had ever felt so good.

"Aladdin!" Mustappa shouted.

Aladdin turned. He had forgotten the magician. It seemed as if he had been down there forever.

Mustappa was above, just as Aladdin had left him, clutching his staff and looking down. Had he heard the tumbling soldiers? The small cries of distress Aladdin was making as he ran? Had he seen the dust?

Had he cared?

"Did you get the lamp?"

Ah, yes. The reason for it all. Aladdin got to his knees and extended the lamp into the sunlight. The tarnished surface didn't even glitter. It looked worthless.

Mustappa extended his staff so that the ram's horn curled near Aladdin.

"Hand it up to me," Mustappa said. "It'll be easier for you to get out."

It would be too. But Aladdin did not trust Mustappa. What was to stop him from pushing Aladdin back into the darkness, to face that army alone?

"It's no trouble." Aladdin brought the lamp down so that it was nowhere near Mustappa. "I can get out myself."

Mustappa shoved the staff in farther. If Aladdin wanted to, he could grab the staff and pull Mustappa inside.

But then, he might never get out, and he wouldn't get his money.

"Pass it up," Mustappa said. "There's a good boy."

"I'm not a good boy," Aladdin said. Mustappa had known that when he hired him. The point was to succeed in this, and Aladdin had. Now Mustappa was trying to cheat him.

"Give it to me," Mustappa said, articulating each word, "or I'll get angry."

"I'm angry already," Aladdin said. "Do you think I'm gullible enough to fall for that old trick? You get the lamp and ride off without paying what you owe me. It's an insult to my professional integrity. You get your lamp when I get my gold."

"You think I'd ride off?" Mustappa sounded startled.

It was the same voice he had used when he told Aladdin that he had known his father.

"Yes," Aladdin said. "You've got shifty eyes."

"You. Cheap. Street. Scum!" Mustappa yelled as he pulled the staff back.

"I resent the word *cheap*!" Aladdin yelled back.

Mustappa clutched the staff with both hands and stood up. Aladdin could barely see him.

"I was going to raise you up. Now I cast you down into the depths," Mustappa shouted. "You want the lamp? Keep it, damn you!"

He made a gesture with his hands, and suddenly the mouth of the cave started closing. Aladdin jumped for the edge, but carefully, so that he did not fall into the pit below.

Of course, he missed.

He cursed Mustappa, but his invective wasn't as creative as Mustappa's.

As the mouth closed, Mustappa waved his staff and cursed Aladdin.

"Ingrate!" Mustappa shouted. "Rot in the darkness!" He made several obscene gestures, and then the mouth slammed shut.

Mustappa stood up and slapped himself on the forehead three times, calling his own name in disgust. He shouldn't have lost his temper like that. That temper was his greatest fault.

It made him lose the lamp.

"I don't care about the lamp," he said to himself. "There are plenty more wonders in the world for me to steal. I'm going home!"

And he walked away.

Of course, Aladdin knew nothing of this, but he suspected he was alone.

At least, he suspected it after he stopped cursing Mustappa less creatively from below.

The darkness was incredible. He hadn't realized how much light had come in through the mouth. And now he was alone here.

With the soldiers.

Would the stairs re-form? Would the soldiers come up and get him?

As if in answer, he heard a giant thud below. It reminded him of the first thud, the one he had heard when he was standing beside the emperor's tomb.

The soldiers were moving.

Aladdin's skin crawled. He was alone with a ghostly army.

Dust was rising all around him. Even if they didn't catch him, they might fill his lungs with dust and he would die. . . .

"This was a crisis," Scheherazade said.

Schahriar leaned close to her, hanging on her every word.

"And in a crisis," she said, "there's nothing more effective than magic."

Aladdin grabbed the ring that Mustappa had given him and rubbed it frantically. He felt ridiculous doing this, but it was his only hope.

There was a flash of light so bright that it nearly blinded Aladdin. A genie appeared across from him, spinning rapidly round and round. He landed on the platform, still vibrating, and settled down slowly, the way a ring would if it had been dropped, bouncing from one side to another.

The genie was round and small, and as he stopped moving, a puff of blue smoke came out of his pointed hat.

"Who are you?" Aladdin asked.

"Omar Khayyam," the Ring Genie said sarcastically. "I'm the Genie of the Ring—who else?"

He showed Aladdin the sole of his right foot, which was stamped with his weight and the gold symbol: *100% Pure.*

"Stamp of authenticity," the Genie said, putting his foot down. Then he leaned forward. "Before I answer any more questions, what color was my smoke?"

Aladdin had to think. The question was not what he expected, not with the advancing army below.

But apparently his silence was too much for the Genie, who asked, "Was it blue?"

Aladdin nodded. The smoke had been blue. He remembered that now.

The Genie looked distressed. "If it was blue, it means that I am melancholy, sanguine. And that means I need more *me* time."

The ground shook as the soldiers took another step forward. Aladdin had trouble keeping his balance.

The Genie looked down and frowned, as if he knew his complaints were undignified. "What do you want? I have enemies. I have a migraine."

"What do you think I want?" Aladdin shouted. The ground shook again. The soldiers were moving quicker. "I want out!"

"I! I! I!" The Genie punctuated each *I* by shaking his finger at Aladdin. "It's all about you, never about me!"

Aladdin took a step back from the crazy man before him.

The Genie let loose with a litany of complaints that he had heard from previous customers, unperturbed by Aladdin's response. " 'Get me out of here.' 'I want to go home.' 'Put me out! I'm on fire!' 'Give me ox giblet and the merguez surprise.' "

There was an even bigger thud, and then the platform

started to go down. The Genie looked over the edge. So did Aladdin.

The army completely surrounded them, and the platform was descending.

The Genie screamed. "Allah! We're going to die! I don't want to die!"

He fell on his knees before Aladdin. The platform kept going down. In a few moments they would be within reach of the soldiers.

Aladdin grabbed the Genie by his pudgy arms and tried to get up to stand up.

"Come on!" Aladdin said. "Pull yourself together."

"Spare me, please." The Genie put his hands together as if he were praying. "I'm only 718 years old."

The soldiers took another step forward, and this time Aladdin was close enough to see them do it. It was a terrifying sight.

"I was going to repent!" the Genie cried to the heavens above. "I was going to go on a diet! Oh, please!"

Aladdin grabbed the Genie's wrists. "Get us out of here!"

The Genie stood up, suddenly—frighteningly—calm. "Ever hear of the magic word *please*? You think just because I work for you, you can treat me like some sort of manservant."

The soldiers pivoted in unison. The platform was still going down. Aladdin was about an arm's length from the top of the nearest soldier's head.

"Or a slave," the Genie was saying.

The soldiers were to Aladdin's waist now.

"Or a eunuch."

The soldiers were even with him, and there was a strange chanting.

"And you can't."

The soldiers turned slightly.

"Are we understood?" the Genie asked.

Aladdin nodded. The Genie slapped his hands together—and suddenly it was very bright. So bright that Aladdin felt momentarily blind. Then he blinked.

He was standing on that stone face again, the river swirling around him. It was the middle of the afternoon, and the mountain sun was warm.

The Genie screamed again. He was standing in front of Aladdin, his eyes closed.

"Oh! The light! The light!" the Genie shouted. "I cannot see. I am blind. It is too bright!"

"Sorry," Aladdin said.

"I feel sick," the Genie said. "My bones, they ache. I'm going home to take a long rest."

Then he vibrated again, turned into a blaze of gold light, and disappeared into the ring.

Aladdin stood there for a long time. It took quite a while for his breathing to get back to normal, even longer for him to realize that the Genie was gone, and longer still to realize that there was no sign of Mustappa or the horse.

Aladdin had to walk all that distance home. And, after the experience inside the tomb, he was very glad to do it. He was glad to be outdoors.

It was full dark when he reached the house. His mother was there—it seemed she was always there these days— and, after he told her the story, she made him put the lamp on the table.

She peered at it, then poked it, while Aladdin ate his supper. Finally, she said, "I don't understand. Why did Mustappa pick the best rogue in Samarkand to get this piece of junk? It's demeaning."

"It must be worth something or he wouldn't have gone to all that trouble." Aladdin finished his dinner and set down the bowl.

His mother turned the lamp over in her hand and

frowned. "You're right, son," she said. "It's probably a priceless antique."

Aladdin took the lamp from her. It didn't look like an antique to him. It looked like a dented lamp, which had no value at all. Still, he rubbed it with his vest, trying to see if the tarnish came off.

As he did, smoke poured out of the lamp's spout. The smoke grew more and more until it shook the lamp out of Aladdin's hand. The lamp skittered across the room pouring out more smoke than a burning house.

Aladdin tried to jump out of the way. His mother clutched his arm. The smoke enveloped them entirely. Only it didn't smell like smoke. It smelled like an ocean mist.

Then the smoke coalesced into a pair of eyes.

That was too much for Aladdin and his mother. They ran from their own home, screaming.

The lamp flew out the window after them. Aladdin and his mother watched in fright as the smoke, pouring out the window, solidified into an arm. Then a head smashed through the roof, followed by a huge body and chest. Legs destroyed the walls. In an instant, Aladdin's house was a ruin that could hardly stand on its own.

But Aladdin was not looking at the destruction of his house. Instead, he was looking at the giant creature who had caused it. The creature appeared to be naked (although he was covered from the waist down by the house itself), and he was bald. He had a long goatee that hid a narrow chin.

Even after the day Aladdin had had, this creature was terrifying.

"Don't just stand there like a leaning tower of jelly," Aladdin's mother said. "Talk to him."

"Why me?" Aladdin asked.

"I'm just a poor weak widow woman," his mother

lied. And when that didn't work, she said, "It's your lamp!"

Aladdin raised a hand in greeting, wondering if it would do any good.

"Good evening, friend!" he shouted.

The creature leaned forward. The tips of his pointed ears were smoking. He had writing all over his face which, Aladdin had to admit, was more pleasant than it should have been.

"Speak up, insignificant mortal, lowly one," the creature said. His voice boomed like thunder. As he spoke, smoke rings came out of his mouth.

Aladdin shouted, "Who are you?"

"Who am I? Who am *I*?" The creature sounded stunned that Aladdin did not know him. "Have you not heard of me? I am the Lamp Genie! *The* Lamp Genie."

He extended a hand, and his fingertips smoked. "I can give you anything you wish—wealth, dreams, power, premature and violent death."

Then he put the hand to his head. "Well," he said, a bit less dramatically, "scratch the last one."

"You're like the Genie of the Ring?" Aladdin asked, trying to understand.

"Like the Genie of the Ring?" the Lamp Genie shouted. "That pusillanimous pimple on the backside of creation? Never!"

The Lamp Genie leaned forward and Aladdin and his mother took a step backward.

"He's a reject, a failure in the genie world," the Lamp Genie said. "His puny powers are nothing compared to mine."

"Are you two related?" Aladdin asked.

"No!" the Genie boomed. Then he stood up and frowned. "Well, maybe. I don't know. The tests were inconclusive."

"What can you do?" Aladdin asked.

"What can I do?" the Genie asked, laughing. "Oh, I don't know. How about *anything* for starters?"

He poked a finger toward the sky, and lightning rent the heavens.

Aladdin and his mother cringed. They had no idea what magic they faced.

Chapter Fourteen

Sunlight was pouring into the bedroom, falling across Schahriar's marvelous bed. Scheherazade sat on the edge of it, playing with a Chinese harp as she told the story of Aladdin.

Schahriar sat beside her, as close as he could get, his face intent as he listened. He still held the necklace, but he didn't seem to notice it. He appeared to be lost in the story.

Scheherazade was tired. She had finally reached a place where it felt safe to stop.

"That was the beginning of it," she said. "Aladdin, a rogue, and son of a rogue, from a family of rogues, found he could have everything he ever wanted. All he had to do was ask."

"So?" Schahriar turned to her. In his bright eyes and charming demeanor, she finally saw the man she had been looking for. "What did he ask for?"

"We can save that for tonight."

All the charm left Schahriar's face. He sprang up and

walked to the arches—a sign, Scheherazade was learning, of his madness returning.

"I want to know now!" Schahriar said like a petulant child. "Not tonight."

He came closer to her.

"It's your fault. You made the story so gripping with your wit and charm and—and your beauty."

Scheherazade was intrigued. He had never said anything of the kind to her before. "What has my beauty got to do with storytelling, Sayiddi?"

His gaze met hers. Those soft green eyes held the warmth that she had been longing for.

"Because," he said, "if I lose interest for a moment, I see your face and I can't leave. Please. Tell me what happened to Aladdin."

She stood. He put his hands on her shoulders. His touch was gentle. "Tonight," she said.

His grip tightened. "I order you!"

"It would not be the same story if I was ordered to tell it."

He let go of her, and his eyes seemed to get darker. He brought his hands to his hair in complete frustration. "It's all tricks!"

She could feel his anger building. He hadn't let it out all night. Did that mean this outburst would be worse than all the others because it built up?

She had to find a way to calm him. "Remember what happened to Mustappa when he lost his temper? He lost his wonderful lamp."

"Tell me!" Schahriar begged.

"Tonight," she said.

His hands caressed her cheek and then hovered near her neck. She felt the beads from the necklace brush against her skin. His thumb found her collarbone, and his hands began to encircle her fragile throat.

Scheherazade remained immobile. She remembered

what her father had said of Schahriar's dream, how he believed he strangled women, and she wondered if that was how she was going to die.

Then Schahriar shoved her away from him so hard that she fell on the bed.

"Chief!" Schahriar screamed. "Now!"

The grill where Scheherazade thought she had seen faces the past two nights opened to reveal a door. The Chief Executioner entered, with his assistant behind him.

Scheherazade pushed up on her elbows. She had failed. Somehow, in denying Schahriar, she had failed. She had to recapture his attention.

The Chief Executioner hurried across the floor. He looked eager—too eager. He held up a hand, and as he did, the assistant put strands of pink rope in it.

Schahriar faced the two men.

Scheherazade sat up. She couldn't even see Schahriar's face anymore. He had to look at her. He had to remember the moments they had shared just in the last few days.

The Chief Executioner snapped the rope between his hands.

Schahriar wasn't going to face her. "Take her!" he said to the Chief Executioner.

The Executioner smiled.

Scheherazade had to do something. "Just wait until tonight," she said to Schahriar, but he did not answer her.

He didn't even look at her. He didn't even acknowledge her.

"Tonight!" she said again, louder.

But Schahriar was leaving her with the Executioner, who smiled at her. Then his gaze went to her neck.

"Tonight!" Scheherazade whispered, knowing that she had lost.

Chapter Fifteen

The Chief Executioner reached the bed. He had grabbed Scheherazade's wrist when Schahriar said softly, in a tone of defeat, "No."

"Sayiddi?" the Chief Executioner had his back to Schahriar. Scheherazade saw the Executioner's look of absolute anger and frustration.

She wanted to cringe from it, but she didn't move.

"No," Schahriar said. "I've changed my mind. Leave her."

He tossed the necklace onto the bed. It landed beside her. The Chief Executioner picked it up and stretched it tight, as he had done the rope.

He glared at Scheherazade. "Your stories won't save you forever, Sultana," he whispered.

"What did you say?" Schahriar asked from across the room.

The Chief Executioner backed away from Scheherazade. "Nothing, Sayiddi."

"Your services are not needed this morning," Schahriar said. "You're free to go."

"Yes, Sayiddi."

The Executioner tossed the necklace onto the bed beside Scheherazade. The necklace had been twisted into a noose.

Then the Executioner and his assistant left.

Scheherazade let out a small sigh of relief. Schahriar walked into the Persian Gardens. He said not a word to her as he disappeared among the trees.

She was still sitting on the bed. She rubbed her wrist. It ached where the Chief Executioner had held it, and her back hurt from the way she had landed on the bed when Schahriar pushed her.

She had thought the night had gone so well. And then she told Schahriar that he would have to wait to hear the rest of the story.

His outburst had startled her more than it should have.

She stood slowly, wondering how much more of this she could take. Every time she thought she had made progress, she discovered that she had made no progress at all.

A strand of pink rope lay across the tile floor. She bent over and touched the rope's satin. It would feel so smooth against her neck—until the Chief Executioner pulled it taut.

She shuddered, picked up the rope, and put it in her pocket. She would keep it as a remembrance of what she faced, what she had nearly suffered this night.

Schahriar would not catch her by surprise again.

That day, Scheherazade did not seek out any help. She decided that sleep was the most important thing. She took a long nap, long enough that she felt refreshed when she awoke.

Refreshed, but still unsettled. Perhaps her father had been right. Perhaps Schahriar would never improve.

Perhaps she had been kidding herself all along.

Scheherazade hung the rope over her mirror and stared at it as her attendants dressed her for her next meeting with Schahriar. Again they put her in a new gown, one she had not seen before. This one was a dusty rose with beadwork, and they dressed her hair with beads as well.

Did her attendants know that she did not sleep? That she spent all night weaving stories to keep Schahriar occupied?

They probably did. There were no secrets in the palace, after all.

When Schahriar finally summoned her, it was late. The oil lamps were placed around the room as they had been before, and there was food once again on trays near the bed. Schahriar lay in the center of the bed, wearing a bright red-and-green robe, the emerald on his finger sparkling in the light.

He looked tired and sleepy for the first time since she had begun telling stories, as if he could drop off at any moment. A few days ago, she would have thought it was her stories enabling him to relax, but she had lost that hubris the night before. She had no idea what effect her stories were having on him—except that they were intriguing him enough to keep him from killing her.

She sat gingerly on the edge of the bed, as far from him as she could get. She no longer felt that bond that she had felt with him the night before.

He barely acknowledged her. As on the second night of their marriage, he seemed to wait for her to begin.

She was nervous, as nervous as she had been that first night. She could hardly remember the threads of the story.

"The Lamp Genie," she said, "was standing in the remains of Aladdin's house. He was laughing, a big robust sound that—"

"But he wasn't laughing, was he?" Schahriar said.

Scheherazade froze. Unlike those first nights, he was not going to allow her any embellishments. "No," she said softly. "That's right. He wasn't."

Schahriar did not even open his eyes. It was as if movement were too much effort for him.

"I let you live so you could complete the story of Aladdin," he said. "You should at least get it right."

He picked up the necklace. It had been sitting on the bed. She hadn't noticed it until he touched it. His fingers worried over it like a lover touching his beloved's skin.

"Now," Schahriar said, "there was a storm, wasn't there?"

"Yes, there was." She took a deep breath and continued with the story, afraid that Schahriar might interrupt again.

The rain came down hard. It poured on Aladdin and his mother so that they were soaked within an instant. Puddles became rivers and the rivers flowed around their feet. Only the Genie seemed untouched.

"You were saying?" Aladdin asked the Genie.

"I am your humble and obedient servant," the Genie mumbled.

"What?" Aladdin asked. "I didn't catch that."

"Nothing important," the Genie said. "A mere technicality. The fine print in my contract, so to speak."

"You have to obey me, don't you?" Aladdin asked, smiling.

"I? Obey you?" The Genie's voice got louder. "I should cast you into a sea of torment. I should have you trampled on—"

He looked toward the sky and sighed. The stars were out even though the rain was coming down hard. "Yes! You can have everything you ever wanted."

"What about stopping the rain?" Aladdin asked the Genie.

The Genie pulled open a drawer in his chest. From it, he removed a plumber's wrench. He reached into the sky, his hand disappearing into a rain cloud, and twisted and twisted and twisted until the rain stopped.

Then he touched his chest, removed his right nipple, and steam poured out of him. He slowly shrank, like a balloon losing its air.

"Are you sure there's not another unfulfilled wish I can grant you, Exalted Lord and Master Aladdin?" As the Genie got smaller, his voice lost its booming quality and actually became rather tinny and nasal.

Aladdin picked up the lamp and walked toward the Genie. The Genie was now the size of Aladdin and his mother. Aladdin had to peer through his ruined house door before he could see the Genie.

Even though the Genie was small, he was still smoke from the waist down.

"I'm in love with Princess Zobeide, the Caliph's daughter," Aladdin said. "I don't know her. I just saw her across a crowded street."

"It's usually across a crowded room," the Genie said, beckoning Aladdin and his mother into their own house, "strange as that may seem."

"I want her."

"I can give you things," the Genie said, holding up his charred, smoking fingers. "But when it comes to the human heart, I'm powerless."

"You can ask for anything in the world," his mother said, as she poked Aladdin in the chest and backed him against the ruined wall, "and all you can think of asking for is some young chit of a girl who isn't good enough for you."

She turned to the Genie and her voice was melodious,

wheedling. Her con voice. "Genie, you can give us things?"

"You got it in one, Mother," the Genie said.

"Not so much of the *mother*," she said. "I'm young enough to be your granddaughter! How about things like money?"

"Yes," the Genie said, the sarcasm clear in his voice. "Gee, never heard that request before. You would be the first to ever ask for something like that."

"Let's have the money." She took Aladdin's arm and shook it. "Bushels and bushels of money. With money you don't need magic."

The Genie floated toward her. "Are you sure that's the way you want to go? I mean money is good and all, but everybody asks for money. Why not ask for something new and exciting?"

"Okay," Aladdin said. "How about some sort of flying machine?"

"Come on, kid," the Genie said between laughs. "Be realistic. Some sort of flying machine? I could fly all over the world. Wait, how about this? How about someone serves you on this flying machine?"

The Genie got close to Aladdin. His smoke smelled of sulfur.

"You could have drinks and serve peanuts," the Genie said, still laughing. "Maybe a little show to keep you entertained. That's almost as funny as the guy who wanted the camelless wagon."

The Genie took a deep breath. "Okay, okay, maybe we should just stick with the money. Here we go."

He blew into the damp ashes in the fireplace. They became a giant smelting press which turned out red-hot gold coins. The light was bright orange and warm, and Aladdin's mother crowed at the wealth forming at her feet.

Aladdin was thrilled as well. For at that moment, his

life changed forever. He thought he understood how it changed, but he was wrong.

Aladdin's mother put on an extraordinarily vulgar display of wealth. But as usual, it worked.

Aladdin's mother convinced the city of Samarkand that she and Aladdin were royalty from the fictitious country of Zouman. They decided to see if Aladdin couldn't get his first wish after all. Aladdin's mother got her son an audience with the Caliph, Beder.

That day, Caliph Beder was having a trying afternoon, listening to petitions by rich supplicants. His Grand Vizier, Assad, was disposing of the petitions with brisk efficiency, and the Grand Vizier's vapid son, Gulnare, was asleep, leaning against one of the marble pillows.

Gulnare's soft snores lulled the Caliph, who wished he could sleep too. His attention wandered, and Vizier Assad noticed.

"We have more petitions, Your Majesty," Vizier Assad said. "They're important."

Caliph Beder nodded toward Gulnare. "Your son doesn't think so."

Vizier Assad backed up, holding the petitions tightly, and surreptitiously kicked his son. Gulnare woke up with such a start that he hit his head on the marble pillar.

At that moment, one of the court officials entered. He announced new visitors. "Your Exalted Majesty, His Highness, Aladdin Ebn Alcouz and his mother, the Princess Seleh Souman."

Aladdin and his mother entered. They were wearing rich clothing and fur-trimmed hoods, and Aladdin's mother wore more jewels than the Caliph had ever seen on one person in his court. They were followed by servants carrying large golden chests.

Aladdin and his mother walked to the small throne, ahead of all the other petitioners, and bowed.

"Your Majesty," Assad whispered, "these people

aren't on my list. They shouldn't be here. I don't know anything about them.''

"That must be very disturbing for you, Assad," Caliph said. He gestured for Aladdin and his mother to rise. "How did you get past my guard and into the court?"

"We had introductions," Aladdin said.

"What introductions?" Assad demanded.

"Irresistible introductions." Aladdin extended his hand toward the nearest chest. It was full of gold coins, and on top were two smaller chests.

The Caliph sat up. That much money caught even his attention.

Two servants brought the smaller chests forward and opened them. Inside were hundreds of pieces of jewelry and precious gems.

The courtiers gasped in awe. The Caliph got off his throne to examine the jewels.

"Indeed," he said, "these are introductions no courtier could resist."

Aladdin's mother handed the Caliph and Vizier Assad two jeweler's glasses. They held them to their right eyes to examine the gems.

"My mother and I have brought them from Zouman," Aladdin said.

Aladdin's mother's eyes lit up. "They meet with your approval, Majesty?"

"Flawless!" the Caliph said, unwilling to set down the jeweler's glass or the gem.

"They're yours, sire," Aladdin said.

The Caliph let the glass down and looked at Aladdin with surprise. "This is a most generous gesture, Prince. You will always be most welcome here at court. And if we can make your stay more pleasant. . . ."

Aladdin nudged his mother, who stepped forward. "My son is too shy to ask, but we heard of the beauty of your daughter, the Princess Zobeide. Prince Aladdin would formally like to ask for her hand in marriage.''

There were moans around the court.

"This is outrageous," Vizier Assad said. "Two strangers from Zouman, asking to marry the daughter of the great Caliph Beder. Humph!"

"Humph!" Gulnare echoed.

"We did not come empty-handed," Aladdin said, gesturing again at another chest. The servants opened it to reveal more coins. "Two million gold pieces."

"The Caliph doesn't need your vulgar gifts," Vizier Assad said.

But the Caliph was staring at the money as if he had never seen such wealth before.

"I wouldn't say two million was ever vulgar, Assad," the Caliph said.

Aladdin's mother said, "And as a start—"

"Your majesty," Vizier Assad interrupted. "My son! Your daughter!"

"Oh, yes, yes," the Caliph said, regretting he had ever made the match. "Hmmm. I'm afraid you came a little late, Prince. The Grand Vizier's son, Gulnare, is pledged to my daughter. Indeed, they are to be wed in three days."

Aladdin could not believe his ill luck. All of this, and he still didn't get his heart's desire.

At that moment, a gong sounded, and Princess Zobeide strode in quickly. She was carrying a Chinese harp and was being followed by courtiers. She looked purposeful.

"Father—" she started, but her father spoke over her.

"We were just talking about you, my dear," the Caliph said. "This is Prince Aladdin of Zouman. He asked for your hand in marriage."

She looked at Aladdin for the first time, and he smiled at her. That spark, that recognition, was there again, stronger this time for both of them.

"I'm too late, I fear," Aladdin said.

She frowned. His face looked as familiar to her as her own. "Haven't I seen you somewhere?"

"I've been 'somewhere,' " Aladdin said. "But I would have remembered you, Princess."

Gulnare hurried toward the Princess, but Aladdin stepped on Gulnare's robe so that he could not walk quickly. Then Aladdin smoothly brushed against him and removed his belt. Gulnare whirled, trying to hold up his pants.

"I have a marriage gift for Your Highness," Aladdin said. One of his servants gave him a magnificent pearl necklace, so long that it could have looped around the Princess twice over.

Aladdin folded it so that it hung over her robes, and then put the necklace around her neck. Her skin was warm to the touch. She looked at him, and he regretted being too late. There was something between them, and she felt it too.

"You are too generous, Prince Aladdin," the Princess said.

"Yes, I'd say that, too," Gulnare said, protesting from behind Aladdin.

Aladdin's mother pushed Gulnare aside and took her son's hand. "He has a generous heart."

The Caliph sighed. He saw how it was between his daughter and Aladdin. And, if the truth be told, he would have rather had Aladdin for a son-in-law than the hapless Gulnare. But a deal was a deal, especially when dealing with the son of the Grand Vizier.

"You may wish to withdraw these generous gifts now," the Caliph said regretfully.

"No, no, they're yours, sire," Aladdin said, bowing as he spoke.

The courtiers broke out in spontaneous applause. The entire court was startled by Aladdin's generosity.

But Aladdin did not notice. His eyes were only for the Princess—and hers for him.

Aladdin left the court with mixed emotions—joy at seeing the Princess again and realizing that she returned his affections; sorrow at the fact that she was marrying the horrible Gulnare. Aladdin's mother's emotions were less mixed. She would help her son find a way to marry the Princess, even if the girl was not worthy of him.

She suggested asking the Genie's advice.

They went home, where they found the Genie amusing himself by blowing bubbles with a pipe.

He would take straw dolls and statues and place them inside the bubbles where they would come alive. As Aladdin walked into the room, the Genie placed a straw dancer inside a bubble, and as the bubble enveloped the straw, she started to dance. Aladdin could even hear the music, thin and tinny, but audible.

"How do I stop that idiot Gulnare from marrying the Princess?" Aladdin asked.

A bubble with a live but tiny pig inside it floated past the Genie.

"Let's turn him into a pig," the Genie suggested. "Better yet, a roast pig."

Aladdin sat down and stared at the bubble, which now had a platter with a boar's head inside it. "Tempting, but it's just not me."

"What about an accident?" the Genie asked.

"Too crude," Aladdin said.

"Before you do anything," the Genie said, "find out if Princess Zobeide has feelings for you. She might be in love with that idiot Gulnare. Women often love men unworthy of them. . . ."

"The reverse is also true," Schahriar said. He was sitting up in the center of the bed, with the satin blanket over his back. In his hand he still held the necklace, but he was not playing with it, not as before. "Men often love women unworthy of them. Why is that?"

Scheherazade stepped out of her storyteller role. This was her chance.

She walked toward the bed.

"Love has nothing to do with worth," she said as she sat near him. "Love is a madness. Prince or beggar, no one knows where it will strike. We have no control."

"How do we stop loving?" Schahriar sounded so plaintive that she longed to take his hand. But she knew that would be a mistake.

"That's the wrong question," Scheherazade said. "You should ask, how do we start loving?"

Schahriar was silent for a moment. He stared at the bed as if he saw something on it that she could not. Then his gaze softened and met hers.

"You're a wise woman," Schahriar said. "I think I've found a treasure." He let the necklace drop. "But will I be able to keep it?"

Scheherazade felt her breath catch in her throat. She wasn't sure how to respond. He seemed lucid for the first time.

Then his gaze hardened. "Was it the Genie who said women often love men unworthy of them? Or was it you?"

A challenge, to see what she believed. Whether she believed he was worthy of her.

After all, she had admitted that she loved him the night before. Now he was testing that love.

Scheherazade smiled gently. "No," she said. "It was the Genie."

There was a discreet knock on the door, and then it opened. Scheherazade let out the breath she had been holding. She had reached a moment of understanding with Schahriar only to have it interrupted.

She turned. Her father entered. His gaze met hers first, and he said, "Are you all right, child?"

"Yes, Father," Scheherazade said.

Schahriar had tensed across from her. Her father seemed to notice as well.

"Sorry, Sayiddi," Giafar said. "But this is no time to stand on ceremony."

"What is it, Giafar?" Schahriar asked. He had picked up the necklace again. "This is too early for affairs of state. You put me in a bad mood."

"My news will only make it worse, sire," Giafar said. "Your brother, Schahzenan, is raising an army against you."

Scheherazade felt a chill run down her back. Was Schahriar in any condition to command an army?

As if in answer, Schahriar sat up straighter. It was as if he put on the mantle of Sultan even as Scheherazade watched.

"He's finally come into the open," Schahriar said. "How big is the army?"

"Big enough," her father said. "Big enough."

Chapter Sixteen

This business of building an army was a tedious thing. Schahzenan wiped the sweat off his forehead and dismounted. He let one of his men lead his horse away.

Thousands of men, hundreds of tents, herds of camels, and he still felt as if he had not done enough. They were half a day outside Baghdad, and Schahzenan was not yet willing to ride into the city.

His officers were growing restless. They were running more and more drills on their stallions and getting the armorers to create enough armor for everyone, even though Schahzenan had not ordered that.

Schahriar would be caught by surprise no matter when Schahzenan attacked. If Schahzenan had been Sultan, he would have slaughtered anyone who betrayed him. Schahriar should have killed his brother when he had had the chance.

Instead, he had embraced him on the day of the wedding.

That had been the hardest thing Schahzenan had ever

done. Schahriar had killed Schahzenan's one true love, and Schahzenan had yet to avenge her.

But his vengeance would be long and bloody, and his brother would pay.

Schahzenan shook off his cloak. He had inspected all of the troops that morning, even the ones farther into the desert, the new recruits who had only been with him a week. All of his men were strong and able and itching to fight.

He walked to his command tent. It was twice the size of the other tents in camp, with expensive rugs on the floor and all of his prize possessions. He had been on the run for a very long time.

Not that he needed to run. Schahriar should have captured him the day Schahzenan came into the city for the wedding. Captured, killed, and displayed him as an example.

Apparently Schahriar, lovesick fool that he was, did not want anything to spoil his wedding day.

Amazing that Schahriar was able to find another woman to love him. Amazing that Schahriar loved her back.

Although the timing had been suspicious. If it had been any other man than Schahriar, Schahzenan would have thought he married to fulfill their father's decree.

But Schahriar had always vowed a man should marry only for love, and he had done so the first time, poor fool. That had allowed Schahzenan to convince his mistress to seduce Schahriar. If she had succeeded in killing him as she had been supposed to, Schahzenan would be on the throne now instead of Schahriar.

Instead of hiding out in the desert, building an army to recapture what was rightfully his.

He strode inside his command tent, handing his cloak to his nearest aide.

"What news?" Schahzenan asked.

"There's a man to see you from Baghdad," his aide said.

Schahzenan raised his eyebrows in surprise. Baghdad? Schahriar's home? Schahriar had a traitor in his midst. "Send him in," Schahzenan said.

After a moment, a man came in alone, wearing dust-covered robes and a hood that nearly hid his face. Still, Schahzenan recognized him.

"Chief Executioner," Schahzenan said in surprise. "What are you doing here?"

The Executioner salaamed and then said, "Sayiddi, in his sickness, your brother the Sultan planned to kill his bride after the wedding."

Schahzenan started. He had thought Schahriar loved the new bride. Slowly Schahzenan let the information sink in. Then he smiled. "You see? He's mad."

Schahzenan had suspected it all along. What good news this was.

"But he can't go through with it," the Chief Executioner said. "The Sultana is still alive."

It took Schahzenan a moment to digest the news. His brother was more than mad.

"Better," Schahzenan said. "He's weak. The people will follow a madman but never a weakling."

"I'm not here to betray the Sultan, Sayiddi, but to protect my interests."

The Executioner had Schahzenan's full attention now. Schahzenan opened his arm and led the Chief Executioner deeper into the tent, where the aides could not hear.

"Go on," Schahzenan said.

"The Sultan's too soft for killing, which leaves me out of work." The Executioner sounded regretful.

Schahzenan now understood why the Executioner had come to see him.

"On the other hand," the Executioner was saying, "I

never saw you shrink from using a rope, axe, or knife. So, if you take the Sultan's place . . ."

"Never fear," Schahzenan said. "There'll be much for you to do, Chief, when I win. I see the streets of Baghdad lined with nooses. Gallows on every corner. It'll be a golden time for you, Chief, I promise."

"Thank you, Sayiddi." The Executioner bowed his head, and then left.

Schahzenan kept a smile of triumph off his face. He did not want his aides to know that he had just gotten the final piece, the part of the puzzle he had been waiting for. Now was the time to act, while Schahriar, mad and weak, was preoccupied with his new wife.

Schahzenan snapped his fingers. His main aide bowed to him. "Prepare to march on Baghdad. We'll rid the world of this weakling."

His aides left the tent to give his orders to the officers. Schahzenan did not follow.

Instead, he went deeper into the tent, to the one place no one was allowed to go but him. He pulled aside a silk curtain. The smell of scented candles wafted toward him. The light here flickered. The candles never went out.

They illuminated the face of his beloved. She looked peaceful in death, more peaceful than she ever had in life. He had made certain that the embalmers had used all their tricks to preserve her despite the great heat. Still he had to be careful with her.

He bent over her. Her face was covered with a thin netting. Her skin was unnaturally pale, and her eyes—the thing that had first attracted him—were closed.

What he wouldn't give to see her laughing, to feel her lips warm and supple upon his own.

Schahriar had robbed him of this. Schahriar, who had tried to kill them both.

Schahzenan bent down and whispered to his beloved, "We will be revenged, my love."

She did not respond. She could not any longer. He could only imagine what she would say, the way her beautiful eyes would light up when she heard his plan.

She would say it was beyond time for him to go to Baghdad. She would have wanted him to do it long ago.

Schahriar would not know what hit him.

"He always took what was mine," Schahzenan said. "I was born to rule, but it fell to him because he was born the eldest by four minutes. Four minutes that changed the world. He's not fit to be Sultan. If I'd been in his place, I'd have had me killed long ago. But he hasn't got the stomach for it. I have!"

Then he kissed her. And he could almost imagine that she kissed him back.

Schahriar stood on the balcony on the other side of his bedroom. The desert stretched before him like a vast sea. Somewhere, out there, Schahzenan had an army and was preparing to attack.

Schahriar shivered. The sun was setting and the air barely held the remains of the day's heat. Soon it would be cold, and he would be alone.

Unless Scheherazade came.

He had sent for her, although he wasn't sure why. He had spent all day planning for his brother's attack. Schahzenan would not catch him by surprise this time.

The way he had the last time.

Schahzenan! Kill him!

Why were those the last words Schahriar remembered his wife—his *first* wife—saying? Perhaps it was because her very last words, telling Schahzenan that she loved him, were too unbearable.

Or perhaps it was because her cry—*Kill him!*—showed that Schahriar acted in self-defense.

He drew his cloak around his shoulders. Behind him,

he heard a door open. He smelled the faint scent of roses: Scheherazade's perfume. He should have whirled, should have protected himself, but she had had a number of opportunities to attack him—a number of opportunities to defend herself—and she had not taken them.

Was he finally learning to trust someone? Or was he simply that much more willing to die?

Night was settling on the desert. It was cold, but Scheherazade was beside him. He could feel her warmth against his shoulder, just as he had done on their wedding day when they had stood on the balcony overlooking the city, watching his subjects celebrate.

Then he had thought Scheherazade would not make it to the following night. That she had made it this far showed her wit and charm and beauty—and her ability to weave a tale.

She looked up at him. He could see her small, dark head move, feel the question he felt every night when she arrived: Should she continue?

Of course. This night, when he had nothing to think of but his brother's past and future betrayals, he welcomed the story.

Anything to keep his mind off Schahzenan.

"You're right about women loving men unworthy of them," Aladdin said.

The Genie continued blowing bubbles, as if the affairs of mere mortals did not really interest him.

"Perhaps she loves Gulnare and not me," Aladdin said. "But we've got time to find out. They don't marry until next week."

"Wrong." His mother came in the door. She looked as if she had hurried to his side. "Gulnare and the Princess're being married tomorrow!"

Aladdin had to find a way to stop the Princess's wedding, but first, he decided to take the Genie's advice. He wanted to find out if she loved him and not Gulnare. He asked the Genie if there was a way to do so.

The Genie said yes, and Aladdin agreed before he heard the entire spell. Perhaps if he had known what the Genie was going to do, he wouldn't have consented.

Then again, it was the only way to find the answer he needed. . . .

That night, the Princess Zobeide sat in her bedroom as a handmaiden brushed out her hair. The Princess held her hand mirror and watched as her handmaiden counted out a hundred strokes.

Suddenly, the doors behind her opened, and a well-dressed monkey walked into the Princess's quarters. For a monkey, he was quite handsome.

He walked up behind her, and the Princess gasped as she saw him in her mirror.

"Where did you come from, little fellow?" she asked.

The monkey jumped onto her dressing table and picked up a powder puff. He dabbed it daintily on his chin, and the women laughed.

"He's a darling," her handmaiden said.

"Come here, little fellow," the Princess said, patting her lap.

The monkey needed no more invitation. He scampered to her and held her.

She carried him around with her for the rest of the evening. Eventually, she lay down on her bed. The monkey was beside her. She rubbed his stomach, tickling him. He oo-ooed and barked with great pleasure.

It was his pleasure that made her realize that this was the eve of her wedding. This was the last night she would spend by herself.

The Princess sighed. "I'm marrying Gulnare, the Grand Vizier's son, tomorrow, little fellow."

The monkey chattered angrily. The Princess completely

understood his reaction. If she had been allowed to have any feelings about this match, they would have been anger as well.

"It's all signed, sealed, and delivered," she said. "You wouldn't understand. Affairs of state."

The monkey made a sad sound and shook his head.

"I did meet a charming young man who—" She stopped. "Well, there's no point in thinking about him. If only—" She stopped again and stared at the monkey. "Oh, they are the saddest words in any language. If only."

She cuddled the monkey to herself and blew out the light. Within moments, she was fast asleep. But the monkey remained, eyes open and motionless, for a long time. Finally, he got up and went to the window.

The Lamp Genie materialized outside the window as the monkey scampered out. The monkey hung from the ledge.

The Lamp Genie held out his hands in case the monkey lost his balance.

"What did you find out, Master Aladdin?" the Genie asked.

A cloud of smoke formed around the monkey. When the smoke cleared, Aladdin hung in the same position the monkey had been in.

He was grinning.

"She doesn't love Gulnare," Aladdin said. "She loves me!"

The Genie took Aladdin home, and together they planned how to disrupt the wedding. Then the Genie returned to his lamp, and Aladdin caught a few hours of sleep.

Early the next morning, he told his mother what he had done.

His mother laughed. "You always were a terrible young monkey," she said.

Aladdin laughed too. It was time to get his plan under

way. He rubbed the lamp. Smoke came out and formed into the Genie.

"Genie," Aladdin said, "I was just telling Mother—"

"The Princess and Gulnare were married an hour ago in secret," the Genie said.

"No!" Aladdin shouted.

"The Grand Vizier won't let a little thing like magic monkeys stop him from making his son heir to the throne," Aladdin's mother said.

"Have they consummated the marriage yet?" Aladdin asked.

"Not yet," the Genie said, "but any moment now."

So, Aladdin thought, there was still time.

Now all he needed was a plan.

Chapter Seventeen

A cold night breeze made Schahriar shiver. Scheherazade ran her hands along her arms. It had become full dark, and he hadn't even seen the sun go down.

Her stories caught him and held him like a fish on the line.

"Let's go inside," he said and gently took her elbow. To his surprise, she did not shy away from him. She should have after all the rough treatment he had given her.

Instead she smiled at him and walked with him into the bedroom.

Once again it was set up for a wedding night, with the oil lamps lit all over the room, and the bride's feast on the tables. He had not ordered this, but he did not object. Sometimes it seemed as if the entire palace knew his plans and was trying to thwart them.

Although tonight it seemed as if his plan were very far away. In a dream, perhaps, or a nightmare that belonged to someone else.

He sat on the bed and patted the spot next to him. Scheherazade sat down.

"So," Schahriar said, "the Princess married Gulnare because she was required to."

"Yes," Scheherazade said. "And Gulnare did not know that he was not her first choice. Nor was she his. If Gulnare had his life to live over again, he'd still fall in love with himself. . . ."

While Gulnare took a long time preparing himself for bed, the Princess waited for him. Their bridal bed was large, but it felt small to her. A trap that she had not prepared herself for.

She blew out the lamps and lay back in the darkness. She wrapped the flimsy nightgown around herself and decided to think of something pleasant. The first thought that came to her mind was that young prince from Zouman—

"My love, my dove," Gulnare called out from the dressing chamber. "It's me, your husband."

"Who else?" she said to herself. Then, louder, she said, "I'm here."

There was a thump near the dressing room door. Then a moan and another thump. It seemed as if Gulnare hit every table and chair on the way to the bed. By the time he reached her, he was limping.

"Are you all right, my sweet?" the Princess asked. She rather hoped he wasn't.

He pulled the curtain back away from the bed. A ray of moonlight from a nearby window fell across the blankets. The Princess moved out of the light. She didn't want him to see her.

"My love," he said, "you look as beautiful as . . . as beautiful as . . . as—"

"That's all right," she said, unable to take any more of this. "I'll guess the rest."

She lay back down on the bed and closed her eyes, bracing herself for the inevitable.

What she didn't know was that there was a Genie outside her window, and just inside the privy Aladdin hunched, aiming the nozzle of a pipe toward the open door. The Genie held the other end of the pipe and he was sucking on it furiously.

That created an incredible force, which sucked Gulnare backward. It didn't affect the Princess, who was lying down. In fact, she didn't even feel it.

But Gulnare couldn't stop himself from going backward. He grabbed tables and chairs and walls, but the force kept pulling him.

Aladdin braced the pipe inside the privy, made sure the door would remain open, and left through the window. Gulnare was sucked through the open door and down the toilet into the filth.

The force of the suction was so strong that he was unable to move or shout. It drew his cheeks together, leaving him unable to do anything except breathe—and he wasn't sure he wanted to do that.

After a few moments, the Princess got tired of waiting. She opened her eyes. She scanned the room and even looked under the bed. But Gulnare was gone.

The next morning, the Caliph was furious. Gulnare had been found, stinking and shivering, at the bottom of the privy. The Princess was relieved, but she told no one that.

The Caliph vented his anger on Grand Vizier Assad. He called the Grand Vizier to the audience chamber, in front of the entire court, and then summoned Gulnare—without giving him time to wash.

While the Caliph waited for his smelly son-in-law, he shouted at his Grand Vizier. "It's an insult to my daughter! And worse, to me!"

"Your Majesty—" Assad started to say, but at that moment, a dirty, bedraggled Gulnare was escorted into the royal chamber by guards. The entire court shrank away from him and held their noses. A few people ran out, unable to tolerate the stench.

The Caliph whirled on Gulnare. "You stink!"

"So would you, sire," Gulnare said, "if you'd spent the whole night in a privy."

"Why did you, son?" Assad asked.

"I couldn't help myself," Gulnare said.

"He prefers a stinking privy to a beautiful young woman," the Caliph said, shaking his head. "I tell you, there's something seriously wrong with this boy, Assad. I can't have him as a son-in-law. The marriage is annulled!"

As soon as word of the annulment hit the streets, Aladdin requested an audience with the Caliph. Of course, the audience was granted.

Aladdin made an even better offer this time for the Princess's hand.

The Caliph smiled. "Three million in gold is most generous, Prince Aladdin, for my daughter's hand in marriage."

"I love her, Your Majesty," Aladdin said.

"Good," he said, nodding. "That always helps. But I can't sanction this marriage unless I know my daughter will live in the style to which she is accustomed. You haven't even got a palace."

"I'm building one," Aladdin said.

"You can marry her when I see it with my own eyes," the Caliph said.

"It'll be ready in a week's time."

"You don't know builders, my boy," the Caliph said, laughing. "My own palace took over a year to build."

"Mine will take a week," Aladdin said.

And of course, with the Genie's help, it did.

While the Genie was working on the palace, Aladdin came to visit him. The Genie sat in the middle of an empty field and worked on a loom, weaving a tapestry.

The tapestry was of a palace. As the image appeared on the tapestry, so did a real palace appear in the distance.

"Don't say it," the Genie warned. "I know it's a clumsy way of building a palace, but it's the only way I know."

"We all work differently," Aladdin said. "This is your way."

"I like you, Master Aladdin," the Genie said, working so fast that it looked as if he had five arms. "Believe it or not, I've had some two hundred odd masters in my time, and you're the noblest of them all."

Aladdin smiled. He tried to be a good master. It was nice to know he was succeeding.

"But remember," the Genie said. "I still have Solomon's curse on my face, and I'll betray you at the drop of a turban, if it suits me."

"Of course," Aladdin said. He doubted the Genie had warned any of his other masters. He felt vaguely flattered, in a way. "No hard feelings."

"I have to survive," the Genie said.

"Don't we all," Aladdin said.

"Perhaps," the Genie said. Then he nodded toward the distance. "Look!"

The palace rose against the azure sky. It was even more magnificent than the Caliph's palace.

Aladdin found his mother, and together they investigated their new home. The Lamp Genie followed them.

He waited on the balcony while they examined the courtyard. It was wide and ornately carved.

"Well, mortals," he said, "where are my compliments?"

"Magnificent!" Aladdin said.

"My best work since the Taj Mahal," the Genie agreed.

"Let's go and feed the sturgeon," Aladdin's mother said. She went toward the pond. Aladdin followed. As they disappeared through the door, the Genie added a few statues to the courtyard. He still saw the palace as a work in progress.

"Only a few days later," Scheherazade said, "the Princess and Aladdin were married. This was, perhaps, the happiest day of Aladdin's life."

Schahriar smiled and leaned back on the pillows. Scheherazade had not expected that reaction from him. She had thought he would argue with her over the marriage as he had done with Ali Baba's, but Schahriar did not.

He seemed totally involved in the story.

She leaned forward. "Aladdin should have been a little pessimistic. After all, he used to say that a pessimist is someone who knows what's really going on. . . ."

For on the day that Aladdin got married, Mustappa was in his study in Africa. The study was a marvelous sunlit room filled with books and manuscripts and musical instruments. A raven—the famous Hector—sat on one of the perches near the ceiling while Mustappa read.

"You're working too hard," Hector said. "Too hard."

"You're right, Hector." Mustappa didn't even look up. "But there's so much to learn, so much mischief to do."

Suddenly, all of Hector's feathers fell off. They rained on Mustappa's manuscript.

The raven screamed in fright. "Ahhh, I'm naked!"

He tried to cover himself with his wings, but they too were bare. He didn't look like a real live bird anymore, but like one someone was preparing for Sunday dinner.

Mustappa picked up a feather and contemplated it as

if it held as many secrets as the manuscript he had been reading.

"What's going on, Chief?" Hector asked.

"I once swore by Hector's feathers," Mustappa said, staring at his naked raven.

"Well, I want them back!" Hector screamed.

Mustappa made a slight movement of his fingers, and the feathers returned to Hector's body. The bird examined himself from all angles, very pleased. But Mustappa took no notice.

Instead he went to his makeshift harp and plucked a string.

"Tell me, harp," Mustappa said, "is that rogue Aladdin dead in the cave?"

The magic harp sang her response:

> No, he is not dead.
> On this very day
> He is to be wed.
> Losing your temper, Mustappa, didn't pay.

"Who's he marrying?" Mustappa demanded, and plucked another string.

The harp sang again:

> The Fairest flower in the land.
> He must be very smart and plucky
> To wed the Princess of Samarkand.
> He finally got lucky.

"No!" Mustappa said. "He got the lamp!"

Chapter Eighteen

"Things are never easy in your stories," Schahriar said.

Scheherazade smiled. "That's rather like life, don't you think?"

Schahriar sighed and rolled over. He reached across the bed to the nearest tray and took a biscuit. It had sesame seeds. He showed it to her, and then set the biscuit down. He still did not like sesame seeds.

"I guess it is like life," he said. "Although I should think that stories would be different."

"If things were easy in stories," she said, "no one would want to hear them."

He took a sugar biscuit. "I suppose you're right."

Scheherazade shrugged. "Well, I'm partially right," she said. "For example, on the morning after his wedding, Aladdin had no idea what fate had in store for him. . . ."

Aladdin woke as the dawn's light came across his wide marriage bed. The Princess slept beside him, warm and curled against him. But his movements woke her.

"It's too early," she said, pulling him closer to her.

"So it is, my love," he said, embracing her. Then he stroked her face and she caught his hand.

She ran her finger along the edge of his magic ring. "It's beautiful."

"It's yours." He took it off and put it on the Princess's finger before she could protest.

She held out her hand, admiring her new ring.

"You're so generous, my love," she said. "Have you always been rich?"

"Always," Aladdin lied. "My father was rich and his father before him. Our title is one of the most ancient in Zouman."

"It suits you," she said. "You're everything a prince should be but never is. You're handsome. You're gallant. You're generous."

He smiled. He had never been so happy in his life.

"But your mother—" the Princess said.

"My mother is what they call an eccentric," Aladdin said. "After all, she can afford to be."

"No, I love her for it," the Princess said. "She's different, like a breath of fresh air. I've never known anyone like her."

"And I've never known anyone like you," Aladdin said, as he kissed her and they drew the curtains around them.

While Aladdin and his new wife were enjoying their marriage bed, something was happening in Samarkand that would change their lives forever.

On the other side of town, Mustappa had arrived. He was driving an old carriage filled with new, sparkling oil lamps.

"New lamps for old," Mustappa called out from his wagon. "New lamps for old. We exchange new lamps for old."

Before he got too far, townspeople gathered around him. They all held old lamps.

"Why are you giving new lamps for old?" a housewife asked. "There's a catch."

"No catch," Mustappa said. "Just the bargain of the year. Where I come from, they prize old and ancient things."

"Can I trade in my wife for a new one?" a man asked. The crowd laughed.

"No, friend," Mustappa said. "Only oil lamps this trip. New lamps for old!"

"Didn't Aladdin sense something was wrong?" Schahriar asked.

He was lying across from her on the bed. They were so close they almost touched. Scheherazade felt a difference in him. There was not so much darkness.

She would have expected more, with Schahzenan's army coming toward them. But Schahriar seemed different this night—he had seemed very different ever since he called her a treasure.

"He was smart," Schahriar said. "He must've sensed some danger."

This point seemed to bother him a great deal. And then Scheherazade understood why. He had not foreseen his first wife's betrayal.

"Normally, Aladdin would have," Scheherazade said gently, "but he was in love."

"And that changes everything?"

"Yes," Scheherazade said. "Men and women act out of character."

"You, for example?" Schahriar asked.

Scheherazade had not expected that. She had thought he was talking about himself. He had actually been talking about her. How much about her did he know? How much did he remember?

"Oh, yes," Scheherazade said. "My father thought I'd never get married. He said when two people marry, each of them has to make sacrifices, but I was too strong-willed for that. But I've changed."

Schahriar propped himself up on one elbow and studied her face. "That must be love."

She felt herself flush. Schahriar touched her cheek with his fingers, as he had done on their wedding night, as he had done the night that he called the Chief Executioner. But instead of tightening his fingers on her skin, he leaned toward her, and kissed her.

It was a gentle kiss, tentative and questioning. Scheherazade answered it, and the kiss deepened. There was the tenderness she had known was within him, and the warmth.

And then, suddenly, Schahriar pulled away.

Scheherazade held her breath, wondering what he would do next. But he merely tilted his head back, closed his eyes, and said, "Tell me about Aladdin."

And so she did.

It took Mustappa most of the morning to work his way through Samarkand. Most of the morning and a lot of lamps.

Finally, he pulled up outside Aladdin's palace.

"New lamps for old!" Mustappa shouted. "I'm giving away new oil lamps for old. A once-in-a-lifetime offer. New lamps for old!"

A maid appeared at one of the windows of the palace.

"Did you say new lamps for old?" she called.

"It's a bargain," Mustappa shouted up to her.

The maid believed she would get praise for doing good work if she saved her master money. She crossed to the mantel and took the Genie's lamp. It still looked battered and old, worthless, just as it had before.

She carried it outside and exchanged it for a new, shiny oil lamp. Mustappa was careful not to act as if she had done anything special—until she left.

Then he clutched the lamp to his chest and laughed.

"Everyone loves a bargain," he said, and slowly began rubbing the lamp.

Chapter Nineteen

Scheherazade paused to get herself some water. Schahriar shifted on the bed, then rose on one elbow again, watching her.

She felt nervous with his gaze upon her. That kiss had distracted her, taken some of her concentration.

"Mustappa was smart," Schahriar said.

"Shrewd," Scheherazade said. "He knew how to appeal to people's baser instincts."

"You don't approve," Schahriar said.

Scheherazade shrugged and drank. The cool water soothed her throat. "I believe there is more to life than cunning," she said.

"Your stories seem to rely on cunning."

"In part, but there is more to them than that."

"What else is there?" Schahriar asked.

"Listen," she said, "and you'll find out."

* * *

Later that morning, Aladdin felt cold. He pulled up the blanket, but it didn't keep him warm. A breeze touched his face and he opened his eyes to discover—

—that he and the Princess were still in their bed, but their bed was outside. There were trees and bushes and grass around them instead of the palace.

The palace had vanished.

He slipped out of bed carefully so as not to awaken the Princess. At that moment, his mother came running over, pulling on her dressing gown.

"What happened?" they asked each other in unison.

Aladdin pulled his mother away from the bed so that they wouldn't wake up the Princess.

"Where's the lamp?" he whispered.

"Gone," his mother said. "Vanished. Poof!"

There was only one other person who knew about the lamp. "Mustappa!" Aladdin said. "Now my Princess will find out I'm not a prince."

"Worse," his mother said. "What happens when the Caliph discovers all the money we gave him has turned to dust? It's time to run, son."

"No one runs in our family," Aladdin said.

"Where did you hear that rubbish?" his mother said. "Taste my dust."

Suddenly a bell rang repeatedly. Aladdin whirled to see Mustappa leaning over the bed rail, tapping his ringed finger against the lamp. The clang was so loud that Aladdin wanted to cover his ears—and he was a distance away.

Before Aladdin could shush him, the Princess woke up, startled.

"What's going on?" She turned and saw Mustappa. She backed away from him and slid out of the bed on the other side.

"Where is everyone?" she asked, coming toward Aladdin. "Where's the palace?"

Before Aladdin could make something up, Mustappa spoke.

"Gone," Mustappa said, "like the snows of yesteryear. Everything's been a fake. There's no palace, no riches, and your husband is no prince. He's a thief, from a family of thieves."

"It's a lie!" The Princess took Aladdin's arm. "Tell him, Aladdin."

Aladdin opened his mouth, but nothing came out. Finally, he felt himself forced to speak the truth. "That's a bad way of putting it," he said.

"Don't be ashamed of it, son," his mother said. "I'm not. We're proud of our heritage, daughter. Our family are aristocrats, too, descended from the finest rogues in all Asia."

The Princess's eyes narrowed as Aladdin's mother spoke. Mustappa was amused. He sat on the bed and watched the show.

The Princess looked at Aladdin and gave him a chance to say something, anything, but he stood there, looking stunned.

So she punched him.

"That's for telling me you were a prince."

"It's Mustappa," Aladdin said, rubbing his jaw. "Don't believe everything he says."

"He has no reason to lie," she said. "You do."

She pulled off her ring and threw it at Aladdin.

"You're in trouble, lad," Mustappa said, chuckling. He was enjoying this more than he thought he would.

"Where did the palace come from?" the Princess asked. "And the money?"

"Magic." Mustappa rubbed the lamp like a gleeful child. Smoke poured out of its spout and then formed into the Genie.

"Ingrate," Aladdin's mother started across the field toward the bed. She pointed at the Genie. "How could you team up with this squelch? I couldn't warm to him if we were cremated together.''

The Genie cursed in an unfamiliar language, then threw chicken feed at Aladdin's mother. As the feed touched her, she began to grow feathers—and suddenly, she was a chicken.

She squawked indignantly and pecked at the ground.

The Princess covered her mouth. Suddenly things were quite different from anything she had ever experienced before.

All this time, Aladdin was on his hands and knees searching for the ring that the Princess had thrown at him. Finally, he found it, and rubbed it quickly.

The Ring Genie vibrated into being, looking very dizzy.

"What do you want?'' the Ring Genie asked. "I just got off my sick bed to be here.''

Aladdin turned him around to show him the Lamp Genie.

The Ring Genie screamed. "What in the name of evil are you doing here?''

"And you?'' the Lamp Genie said.

"You two know each other?'' Mustappa asked.

"Yes, yes, unfortunately,'' the Ring Genie said. "We're distant—very distant—cousins on my father's side.''

"I've hated you for centuries,'' the Lamp Genie said.

"Yes, that's right,'' the Ring Genie said. "You lying, bullying dog. You turn my stomach!''

"It would take the whole Persian Army to turn your stomach!'' the Lamp Genie said. "You pimple. You grease spot on the backside of a camel! I've waited a long time for this, blubber boy!''

There was a bright light, and suddenly the Ring Genie had on a pair of glasses.

"You wouldn't hit a guy wearing—" the Ring Genie looked at what he was wearing and shrugged—"whatever these are, would you?"

"Hold still while I think about it," the Lamp Genie said.

"Okay, bye-bye," the Ring Genie said, turning away.

Aladdin caught him. "No, no, no! My genie will challenge your genie," he said to Mustappa. "Winner takes all."

Mustappa smiled. "This sounds interesting."

"No, no, no." The Ring Genie faced Mustappa and spoke confidentially. "He's feverish. He's babbling."

"Done!" Mustappa shouted.

"Done?" the Ring Genie asked. He put his hands on Aladdin's shoulder. It was a pleading gesture. "You don't understand. I can't fight him. His magic is stronger than mine, which gives you some idea of how unfair Genie-world is, doesn't it?"

Then he started to moan and put his long-nailed fingers against his mouth. "Toothache! I have a toothache. I can't fight with a toothache!"

He started to walk away again, and Aladdin grabbed him.

Mustappa slipped the lamp inside his cloak. "Let's do this right," he said. "We must have the proper setting."

Mustappa waved his hand, and smoke covered everything. As the smoke cleared, Aladdin heard a great thudding noise. A coliseum, as old as time, formed around them. Aladdin, the Princess, his mother—who was still a chicken—and the Ring Genie were on the dirt arena of the coliseum, and Mustappa and the Lamp Genie were up in the seats.

The Lamp Genie flew across the center, as if he were watching the reactions below.

The Ring Genie turned in circles, stunned and a bit

frightened by events. The appearance of the coliseum seemed to make the fight even more real to him.

Aladdin saw an area near the wall from which he could conduct the fight. He tried to lead the Ring Genie there, but the Ring Genie dug in his heels.

"No, no, no," the Ring Genie said, "I'm not in good shape. I'm never in good shape. But I'm in worse shape now than I've ever been."

"You can do it, Master Genie," the Princess said.

Aladdin's mother clucked in agreement.

"You're our man," Aladdin said.

At that, the Ring Genie calmed. He seemed to know he wasn't getting out of this. He shook Aladdin off and adjusted his robe.

The Lamp Genie floated above them, getting larger and larger, so large that he blocked the sun. The Ring Genie looked up at him.

"Okay, I'm ready, Allah," the Ring Genie said, "Exalted Father, Creator of All, Granter of Wishes. You are my sufficiency."

Aladdin held his breath. The Ring Genie slowly made his way into the arena, never taking his gaze off the still-growing Lamp Genie.

"Pray for me in this moment," the Ring Genie said.

Mustappa made a small hand gesture—the way that a coach would guide a fighter. The Lamp Genie seemed to understand it, too, and moved his own hands accordingly. Aladdin watched and frowned, knowing that he should be guiding the Ring Genie, but not sure how.

As the Lamp Genie's hands moved, the Ring Genie's body turned into a sandlike substance and started trickling down. The sandlike substance formed a mouse's tail and then a mouse's body. The Ring Genie had become a mouse!

Aladdin's breath caught in his throat. He had a feeling this would be bad.

The Lamp Genie shrank suddenly and landed on the arena floor. As his hands touched the floor, they turned into paws. He became a white cat.

The Ring Genie mouse said, "Mommy!" quite audibly as the cat hurried toward him.

Mustappa chuckled.

Aladdin bit his lower lip thoughtfully. The Lamp Genie hadn't been looking at Mustappa when Mustappa signaled him. Maybe the Ring Genie didn't have to look at Aladdin. Aladdin made a small movement with his little finger.

The cat had almost reached the mouse. Then the mouse sneezed, and as it did, it transformed itself into a large, barking Rotweiler. The cat screamed and ran.

Mustappa looked upset. He clenched his fist, and the cat transformed into a huge dragon. The dog let out a whine that echoed through the entire coliseum.

Aladdin had no solution for that one.

The dragon breathed fire, and as it did, the dog changed back into the Ring Genie, who ran toward Aladdin.

Aladdin shouted up to Mustappa in the stands, "End of Round One!"

"Don't send me out there again!" the Ring Genie shouted as he hurried to their side. "I'm no match for blubber man."

"You're a pro," Aladdin said, cooling the Genie with a towel. "Get in there and fight!"

"Aladdin," the Princess said, getting as close to him as she could, "did you love me or was that another lie?"

"Not now, my love," Aladdin said.

The Ring Genie took a mouthful of water and gargled, then spat it out.

"Did you love me?" the Princess demanded.

The Ring Genie looked at her as if she were crazy to talk of that now. Aladdin wasn't going to answer, but the Ring Genie turned to him.

"Well?" the Ring Genie asked. "Did you?"

"Always," Aladdin said to the Princess.

The Princess smiled. She bent down and put her arm around the Ring Genie. "You heard him," she said. "Get in there and fight!"

The Ring Genie moaned and hurried toward the center of the arena. He was windmilling his fists as he ran in a vain attempt to punch at the Lamp Genie. Then the Ring Genie tripped.

Light flared, and he stood—as a camel—still wearing the Ring Genie's hat.

The Lamp Genie was still in his dragon form. The Ring Genie camel walked slowly toward the dragon. The dragon went down on all fours in preparation.

Mustappa grinned.

Aladdin nodded.

The Princess clasped her hands together.

The dragon took a deep breath and started to breathe fire. As it got close to the camel, the camel spat in its face, putting out the flames.

The dragon looked extremely disgusted.

Aladdin suppressed the urge to laugh.

Mustappa made a pointy gesture with his fingers, and the dragon transformed into an elephant. It trumpeted and rose up, clearly angry.

The camel started toward Aladdin, who nodded his next command.

Light flared again, as the Ring Genie transformed himself—back into a mouse.

The elephant took one look, screamed, and ran away.

Aladdin took the Princess's hand. She grinned at him.

Mustappa frowned and thought for a moment. Then he flattened his hands. The elephant stopped, as if it were frozen in its tracks. Large holes formed in its body until it looked like Swiss cheese.

Aladdin and the Princess saw the problem at the same time.

"No!" Aladdin said, gesturing. "No!"

But the mouse Genie sniffed the air, oblivious to the problem. Then it started forward.

"No!" Aladdin said again.

The elephant shrank to a single hunk of cheese. The mouse made little excited sounds. Aladdin kept gesturing, but the Ring Genie ignored him. Two of the Ring Genie's problems had merged: his mouse persona and his own love of food.

Oh, this wasn't fair!

As the mouse reached the cheese, a mousetrap rose out of the ground.

Mustappa clenched his fist, and the mousetrap sprang.

Aladdin and the Princess and the chicken all winced in empathy. The Ring Genie screamed. The force of the trap had transformed him to his own form again. He was lying on the trap, his face buried in the cheese, the metal part of the trap pinning his back to the wood.

"Lemmeouddahere!" the Ring Genie shouted, his mouth full of cheese.

"I win!" Mustappa shouted.

Suddenly the entire coliseum was filled with people, all of them cheering for Mustappa. He basked in the glory.

Aladdin bowed his head. The Ring Genie had warned him that he wasn't up to a fight with the Lamp Genie. The Ring Genie spat the cheese out of his mouth and started coughing, but Aladdin didn't go to him. He couldn't—not faced with this devastating failure.

The Princess knew now that he loved her, but would that be enough?

He couldn't let it end here. He didn't dare.

"I'm done for," the Ring Genie said. "Done for."

Mustappa was coming down the arena steps. He was using his arms to whip the crowd into a frenzy.

"Your champion's out," Mustappa said. "Out, out, out!"

The crowd echoed his words. Soon the entire coliseum was chanting, ''Out! Out!''

Mustappa had reached the arena, and as he did, Aladdin rushed to him and threw himself at Mustappa's feet. He grabbed Mustappa's coat and tugged.

''Mercy,'' Aladdin begged. ''Mercy for my wife and my mother, oh great Mustappa.''

Mustappa looked at the young man pulling on his clothes and grinned in triumph. ''No! It's winner take all.''

But Mustappa had already lost and didn't know it. You couldn't beat a man like Aladdin when it came to stealing. He was a master.

This time, he had stolen Mustappa's victory.

First, the crowd disappeared. Then the Lamp Genie's attention floated from Mustappa to Aladdin.

Finally, Mustappa understood what had happened. Aladdin had taken the lamp.

''You cheated!'' Mustappa shouted.

Aladdin laughed.

''Next time I will show no mercy. I will kill you. I will squash you like a bug!'' Mustappa was working himself into a frenzy. ''I will turn you into a—''

And suddenly, light flared as a spell was cast. Mustappa had turned into stone.

The Lamp Genie blew on his fingers after finishing the spell; then he raised his eyebrows at Aladdin to see if he would get into trouble. But Aladdin merely smiled.

The Ring Genie freed himself from the mousetrap. Aladdin's mother clucked and grew and slowly turned into herself again.

Aladdin had won. He had picked his last pocket.

He walked to the Princess. She was smiling at him.

''That was really clever,'' she said. ''Something I'd expect from a rogue.''

''He gets it from his mother,'' his mother said.

Aladdin put his hands on the Princess's shoulders, pulling her close. "Does it matter who I am?" he asked. "Villain or saint, I love you."

The Princess turned her face from him. "You told me you were a prince."

"Believe your heart, my love," Aladdin said.

She laughed, then kissed him. She had been toying with him. She would stay with him forever, just as she had vowed.

The Ring Genie approached, and as he did, Aladdin turned toward him. The Ring Genie looked sheepish. Aladdin pulled off the ring, and the Genie ducked, apparently expecting great anger.

But Aladdin said to the Princess, "I want to take the magic out of this ring and fill it with love for you, my sweet."

She frowned, not understanding. But the Ring Genie's eyes had brightened.

"So, Master Ring Genie," Aladdin said, "I'm giving you all the time in the world to rest and get healthy. I'm giving you permanent sick leave."

No one had ever been kind to the Ring Genie before. He didn't believe his pointed ears. "What do you mean?"

"I'm giving you your freedom," Aladdin said.

The Ring Genie blinked for a moment, then began to dance. A whirlwind twister formed beneath him and he sang loudly as he flew into the air:

> Farewell, good-bye!
> I bid you all a last good-bye!
> No tears, no sighs,
> it really is good-bye!

He kept singing as he floated away, maybe for days, maybe weeks, maybe more. Rarely in Genie-world had there been such happiness.

Aladdin put the ring on the Princess's finger and then kissed her. She kissed him back.

Finally, they let go of each other. Aladdin had one more thing to do. He beckoned the Lamp Genie, who flew over on a cloud of smoke.

"Master Genie," Aladdin said to the Lamp Genie. "We have a little business to finish. First, Mustappa."

The Lamp Genie laughed—and the stone Mustappa vanished.

"Now," Aladdin said, "restore my palace."

"And our *money,*" his mother added.

The palace reformed around them. They were standing in the courtyard, and, as a bonus, the cherry trees were blooming. The air was fragrant with their perfume.

Aladdin's mother laughed and touched the gilt walls. She had never sounded so happy.

But Aladdin still wasn't done. He crossed his arms. "You betrayed me," he said to the Genie.

The Genie shrugged. "It wasn't personal. I warned you I change sides like a weathercock to survive."

"You should give him his freedom," the Princess said.

"Careful, son," his mother said. "Think of what we'll be giving up."

"We've got everything we need," Aladdin said. "It will be too easy with a genie on call, Mother. Life will lose its spice. Genie, I give you your freedom."

The Lamp Genie chuckled. He did a mocking imitation of the Ring Genie's dance. "Free? I'm free?"

And then he stopped dancing and glowered at Aladdin.

"Freedom? What would I do with that? I would have to get a job, a fat wife, lazy kids. No, thanks. I've got power, total control. I'll decide when I want to be free."

He disappeared into the lamp. Aladdin and the Princess walked back into the palace. Aladdin's mother followed, pocketing the lamp along the way.

Chapter Twenty

"Would Aladdin really give the genies their freedom," Schahriar asked, "and give up all that power?"

He was lying so close to Scheherazade that she would barely have to move her arm to touch him—if she dared. She did not. Instead, she concentrated on his question. Somehow, she felt that it was extremely significant to him.

"Power isn't that important," Scheherazade said.

He raised his eyebrows. "What is?"

"Happiness," she said.

He stared at her for a moment, his eyes clear—as they had been all night—and then rolled away from her.

She felt as if she were losing his attention.

"Happiness is something that poor Amin Adbur didn't have," Scheherazade said quickly. "In fact, he had nothing. No peace, no comfort, no happiness."

She rose on her elbow so that she could watch his reaction. Without an expression change, Schahriar asked, "Who is Amin Abdur?"

"A young beggar in Cairo," Scheherazade said.

Schahriar sat up and grabbed the necklace as he did. "You're starting another story."

Only this time he didn't sound angry. But Scheherazade wasn't going to take any chances.

"No," Scheherazade said. "I was going to tell you about Amin because I thought you'd be particularly interested."

"Why?"

"Because he looked exactly like you," Scheherazade said.

Schahriar whirled. He was clearly fascinated. "Like me?"

"But the extraordinary thing about his story," Scheherazade said, "is that the other leading figure in it is Sultan Abraschild."

"So?"

"Abraschild looked exactly like your brother, Schahzenan."

She caught her breath after she said that. She was improvising, and she knew that if she wasn't careful, she would anger him.

"Like my brother?" Schahriar asked. "So I'm a beggar in this story, and my brother is Sultan of Cairo?"

She nodded. The sun was coming in from the Persian Gardens. Its rays were cutting across the bed.

"I suppose you'll want to save that for tonight," Schahriar said.

Scheherazade smiled. "How did you know?"

"I'm learning about you all the time, my love," Schahriar said.

Dawn brought the end of Scheherazade's storytelling, but across the desert, something else was happening.

Schahzenan's army moved out. It took a lot of effort to pack up the tents and the men, the camels and the horses, the supplies and the weapons, but it was done.

Schahzenan would win the kingdom that was rightfully his.

The desert wasn't warm yet. The sand still held the morning coolness. Schahzenan sat on his horse, on a sand dune, and watched as his army made its way.

The army looked like a black sea flooding the desert. More men traveled with him than Schahzenan realized he had. More men than his brother Schahriar could raise in a day. Schahriar was concerned with his new wife; he would have no time to prepare. He would lose before he even knew he was under attack.

Schahzenan had planned the last attack that way. It had only been luck that had saved Schahriar's life. Luck and a horrible throw.

Schahzenan turned in the saddle. Behind him was the wagon carrying his beloved. She marched with him wherever he went, as she should have in life.

Schahriar would pay for what he had done. His new Sultana, she who bewitched him with stories, would pay as well. It sounded as though Schahriar was becoming enamored of her. And if he was, then Schahzenan would make certain that Schahriar died *after* he watched his new Sultana die first—from a sword in the back.

The army continued to move. Slowly, so slowly. And purposefully. Schahzenan indicated to his aides that they should move on ahead of him. He would bring his beloved forward. But first, he wanted her to see what kind of troop they led.

He leaned toward the thick black netting that covered her small tent. He had been discussing with her the Chief Executioner's words ever since the Executioner left.

Schahzenan thought it fortuitous that Schahriar couldn't

live up to his vow, couldn't kill the woman as he had promised.

Schahriar had always been soft. Schahzenan would use that to his own advantage.

"Schahriar can't kill one helpless woman," Schahzenan said to his beloved. "Soon he will have to kill thousands to survive, and it will not happen."

He imagined her response. She would laugh at Schahriar's weakness, as she had laughed at Schahriar before. She had thought Schahriar nothing like his brother, not at all the kind of man who caught a woman's attention.

The new Sultana had to be interested in power, not Schahriar. No one could find a mad weakling attractive. No one.

"I'll cut his throat," Schahzenan said, "and Baghdad will be under our heel. How sweet it is, my love."

He peered through the netting, and he thought he saw his beloved smile.

She approved. And with her approval, he knew he could do anything.

Scheherazade had to get out of the palace. She felt as if she had been cooped up for days. Perhaps she had. She had lost track of time.

She needed to see the Storyteller. She needed help with the new story, and she almost sent for him. But, she decided, she would brave the bazaar. Sunlight would feel good, and so would the freedom of walking alone.

She knew the dangers, of course. That was what had prevented her from leaving the last time. But Schahriar seemed to be coming around and, she felt that things would be worse if he discovered she was seeing the Storyteller in the palace.

Scheherazade didn't want Schahriar to think she was getting her stories from someone else. She wanted to be indispensable to him; that seemed more important than getting caught outside the palace these days.

So she made her way to the bazaar, and as she hurried, heavy cloak over her clothing, veil over her face, she noted the large number of storytellers. She had forgotten, in the drama of her own life, that the storytellers' competition was being held this week. Once, before she had decided to marry Schahriar, she had wondered if a woman could enter the competition. She had asked the Storyteller all her questions to learn how to tell a story by this week.

She hadn't known then that she wouldn't be competing for money, but for her life.

Somehow, that threat seemed to be easing. That morning, when Schahriar had called her his love, something in her heart had warmed. She still wasn't going to relax around him. She didn't dare. But something had shifted— he had shifted—and he was less volatile than before.

Perhaps it was only the threat from Schahzenan. Perhaps that was all that diverted Schahriar's attention. Perhaps when Schahriar had dealt with that, he would remember what he had planned for Scheherazade.

She had to keep the stories interesting. She had to keep this *next* story interesting.

So she was at the bazaar. The Storyteller saw her and led her to his tent. He knew, as she did, the importance of keeping her identity hidden.

He let the flap fall and offered her some Turkish coffee. She took it with a shaking hand. She hadn't realized how worried she was until she sat down in a place where she felt safe.

"I've taken your advice," Scheherazade said. "I've told him an adventure, a comedy, and a fantasy, and now I want to tell something tragic. I hooked his interest by saying the chief characters resemble him and his brother. But where do I begin?''

The Storyteller poured himself some coffee. ''You begin at the beginning, and go to the end, and then stop. Just make sure he doesn't know what will happen next.''

He spoke without irony. Scheherazade shook her head.

''*I* don't know what happens next,'' she said, ''so I'm sure he won't. But should I go on? His brother, Schahzenan, is rising against him. Is this the time for storytelling?''

''It's the perfect time,'' the Storyteller said. ''Stories show us how to win. And in your case, defeat death.''

She let out a sigh. She hoped he was right. She hoped she had defeated death.

Perhaps she could help Schahriar learn how to win. Perhaps she could help in that one small way.

She sipped her coffee. It wasn't as rich as that served in the palace, but somehow the coffee here tasted better. She hadn't realized just how much stress she had been under, there.

She hadn't come just for the advice, but to have someone tell her a story as well. Besides, the Storyteller had her well hooked, and unlike Schahriar, she was a willing victim.

''How did your story about meeting Death himself end?'' she asked.

The Storyteller smiled. It was a sly smile, one that told her he knew she was hooked. ''You remember, my friend saw Death in Baghdad making faces at him. He was so frightened, he panicked and fled to Samara. I went back to the Street of Sighs to have it out with Death.''

Scheherazade sipped her coffee. She felt herself sink into the story.

''Death was a tall, weary man in a cloak and hood,''

the Storyteller said. "He asked me if I were looking for him. I told him I was. Then I asked him why he made faces at my friend, Kashir. I told him he frightened Kashir out of his wits.

" 'I wasn't actually making faces,' Death told me. 'It's the way I look. Actually, I was surprised at seeing him there.'

" 'Why?' I asked Death."

" 'Because,' Death told me, 'I have an appointment with him tonight in Samara.' "

Scheherazade let out her breath, and then she clapped. "Nice," she said, "short and well done."

"And with a point," the Storyteller said.

"One I should heed?" she asked.

"Only that Death is not easily fooled, Highness." The Storyteller put his warm hand on hers. "Be careful."

The handmaidens found yet another dressing gown for Scheherazade. This one was more beautiful than the last. Scheherazade was beginning to believe her father was the source of them, thinking that she might have a chance to seduce Schahriar with more than her stories.

She wasn't quite as confident as she had been that morning. The Storyteller's warning stuck with her. She would tell the best story she could.

And that was what was on her mind when she entered Schahriar's bedroom.

But he was speaking to a servant. They both looked surprised to see her, even though Schahriar had summoned her a few moments before.

"Come with me," Schahriar said to Scheherazade, and took her arm.

Scheherazade felt her heart start to beat hard. He wouldn't take her to the Chief Executioner at the beginning of the night, would he? She didn't know if she should start the story or if she should protest.

But Schahriar's hand on her arm was light, not the way it had been the morning when he dragged her out of the bedroom. He was walking beside her like an equal, not like a man bent on her destruction.

He led her through a passageway to the throne room. The servant followed them. Oil lamps had been lit, but Scheherazade had never been here so late at night. The throne room looked strange. It was filled with shadows.

Schahriar bade her sit on the smaller throne. Scheherazade did. It felt odd to do so in her nightgown and bare feet, her face uncovered and her hair hanging down her back.

Was he trying to see if the throne was a good fit?

He sat on the throne beside her and said to the servant, "All right. See why Giafar wanted to meet me here."

Scheherazade glanced at Schahriar at the mention of her father's name. But Schahriar did not look at her. Despite the fact that he was wearing his dressing gown, he looked strong on the throne, as if it made him taller somehow, more powerful.

A side door opened. Scheherazade's father entered. He was in his usual cloak and turban, which made her even more uncomfortable.

Behind him came several guards. They surrounded a single man whose hands were tied. It was the Chief Executioner.

His assistant trailed behind like a chastised pup.

Schahriar's posture changed slightly.

Scheherazade felt her heartbeat increase. What was this?

"What is the meaning of this, Giafar?" Schahriar asked.

"This man has betrayed you and told your brother everything," Scheherazade's father said. "Your brother's on the march now."

Scheherazade frowned. They knew that Schahzenan was gathering an army and would eventually attack, but she hadn't expected it quite this soon.

"Why?" Schahriar asked.

The Chief Executioner raised his bald head. He didn't seem subdued at all. "Because he thinks you're weak, Sayiddi. Show you're a true Sultan and kill your wife, as planned."

Schahriar glanced at Scheherazade. She made herself gasp as if she were surprised at the news.

"Kill me?" she asked. "But I thought you loved me."

Schahriar shifted in the throne. For a moment, she saw the man she had been with in his room, not the Sultan. "I do," he said.

She let out a small sigh. So he would leave her alone then.

But Schahriar was no longer looking at her. He had stood. He was facing the Chief Executioner. "But how I feel has nothing to do with this. You betrayed me, Chief."

"For your own good, Sayiddi," the Executioner said. "You have to be strong. If you can't kill her, kill me. My assistant stands ready."

The assistant made a little gesture of denial with his hands. "But, Chief . . ."

"Don't worry," the Chief Executioner said to the assistant. "I'll be there. You'll do fine. When I'm dead, everyone will know the Sultan is himself again."

"No," Schahriar said. "I spare your life."

"Why?" the Chief asked.

"Because you want to die," Schahriar said. "And I'm

not about to give you what you want, after what you've done.''

He made a banishing gesture with his hand, and the guards took both the Executioner and his assistant out of the room. After they left, Schahriar slowly sat on his throne again.

Scheherazade felt herself begin to breathe easily again. She hadn't realized that Schahriar had already made his decision to let her live.

She hadn't realized that he loved her.

Her father had his hands clasped together. His eyes shone with pleasure.

She had done it. She had made it through the nights.

''So,'' Schahriar said, shaking his head, ''Schahzenan attacks because I won't kill my wife.''

Her father would hate what she was going to say now, but she had to. She put a hand on Schahriar's.

''Perhaps you'd better do it, Sayiddi,'' she said. ''I'll give my life gladly if it means saving you and Baghdad.''

''What are you saying?'' her father asked.

Schahriar's gaze met hers. Scheherazade's did not waiver. She had meant what she said. If her death saved a thousand lives, then it was worthwhile.

''You have a remarkable daughter, Giafar,'' Schahriar said, not taking his gaze from hers.

''Remarkable and mad.'' Her father sounded angry.

''I know all about madness, Giafar,'' Schahriar said. ''Madness or not, she shames us all. But I have to show my brother that I am strong.''

''Then kill me,'' Scheherazade said.

Her father shook his head, but Schahriar didn't even notice. He was still looking at her.

''I'll never kill you because of my brother,'' Schahriar said. ''If I do it, I'd do it for my reasons, not his.''

So she hadn't won. She still faced death. That was what the Storyteller meant. Whether it was at the hands of her husband to save his soul or to save his people, she still wasn't sure if she would make it to morning.

"Your reasons, his reason," Giafar said. "She'd still be dead. And she's all I have. What are you going to do, Sayiddi?"

"I don't know," Schahriar said.

had been too drunk to notice people passing by, or crows scavenging the alley

Chapter Twenty-One

She had only one real chance, and that was to give
Schahriar something else to think about.

"Then listen to the story of the Sultan and the beggar,"
she said.

A smile played across Schahriar's lips, faint but visible.
Was he toying with her too, so that he could hear his
stories? Had he figured out her method, as he had said
the night before?

"All right, Scheherazade," he said. "But the story had
better be a good one."

Amin the beggar woke out of a drunken stupor. He had
spent the night, most of the following day, and the evening
in a dank, rubbish-strewn alley. He had been too drunk
to notice people passing by or crows scavenging the alley
for scraps of food.

When he woke, all he could think of was getting another
drink. He still had a few coins left, so he headed straight

for the nearest tavern, which was a sleazy place called The Cross-Eyed Man.

A moment after he entered, three men came down the filthy side street, carefully avoiding the camel dung piled on the dirt road. The three men were wearing what they thought poor people's clothes were like, although the clothes were still too rich for this particular neighborhood.

The men were the Sultan Abraschild prowling the streets in disguise, looking for adventure; the Commander of his Guard, Nouz; and his Grand Vizier, Moussel.

"Being Sultan is the most boring job in the world, Moussel," Abraschild was saying.

"Is that why your majesty has to disguise himself," Vizier Moussel said, "and rub shoulders with his subjects?"

"I find it amusing."

"As Commander of your Guard," Nouz said, "I have to say, it's a very dangerous amusement."

"That adds spice to the joke," the Sultan said. "When I mingle with ordinary folk, I'm laughing inside. If only they knew who I was, what tricks, what jests I can play on the poor fools. Here's entertainment to please the most jaded palette."

He led them down a side street toward the Cross-Eyed Man. He stopped in front of the tavern, peered inside, and thought it delightfully filthy and disgusting—as were most of its patrons.

"Let's go in here," he said to his companions, "and see what jollies I can conjure up."

The tavern had dancing girls, although not as beautiful as the ones at the palace, and wine, although it was watered down. But Sultan Abraschild wasn't there for the women or the drinks. He had other reasons for coming.

He sat down at the only table with room—Amin's table. Soon he and Amin were talking and laughing, and the Sultan was plying Amin with drink.

Moussel and Nouz watched from a discreet distance.

"Why does he do it?" Nouz asked Moussel.

"He likes practical jokes," Moussel said. "He'll sacrifice anyone for a laugh."

And his latest sacrifice hadn't even realized that his number was up. Amin was just enjoying the free drinks.

"I'll do the same for you when my ship comes in, friend," Amin said, waving a glass.

"What ship's that, friend?" Abraschild asked.

"My ship," Amin said. "My destiny. I have a destiny. That's why I drink. I drink while I'm waiting for my destiny."

"Which is?" Sultan Abraschild asked.

"I don't know," Amin said, "but it'll be great."

"If you could choose," Abraschild asked, "what destiny would you choose, friend?"

Amin thought for a moment and took the first idea that came into his head. Indeed, it was an idea that seemed to be in the air. "If I could chose my destiny," he said, "I'd choose to be Sultan."

"Look at yourself," Abraschild said. "Do you think you're fit to be Sultan?"

"What's fitness have to do with it?" Amin asked. "Sultan Abraschild was born with a silver spoon in his mouth. Everyone else had a tongue. He's about as useful as a glass eye at a keyhole."

"That's what you think of him, huh?" Abraschild asked.

"Abraschild has both feet firmly planted in the air," Amin said. "He's the invisible man. Ah, my friend, if only I were Sultan, you'd see."

"Perhaps it is your destiny, after all," Abraschild said, smiling.

To Moussel and Nouz's dismay, Sultan Abraschild staggered out of the tavern with Amin. The Sultan was only pretending to be drunk, but Amin wasn't. He was so drunk that he passed out leaning against the wall.

Moussel and Nouz caught up with them.

"Are you all right, Sayiddi?" Nouz asked.

"Never better," Abraschild said. "A jest, a jest. Take him to my palace."

"But, Sayiddi—this man?" Moussel said.

"Oh, Moussel, you dry stick, you desert cactus. Come on and be quick about it. I can't wait to start the game."

It was a sick joke. Amin was washed and perfumed so that even his mother wouldn't have recognized him. Then he was dressed in silk nightrobes and placed on the Sultan's magnificent bed.

Sultan Abraschild, Moussel, and Nouz watched as Amin was tucked in. Abraschild couldn't stop laughing.

"Everyone knows what to say and do when he wakes?" Abraschild asked.

"Yes, Sayiddi, but—" Moussel said, still trying to protest.

"No one spoils my fun," the Sultan said. "No one."

So Moussel and Nouz stopped trying. But they did not approve.

Hours later, when Amin awoke, Sultan Abraschild was in a nearby closet, watching and laughing. The whole palace went along with the Sultan's cruel jest. They had to. It was more than their lives were worth to object.

Amin had a terrible hangover. At first, he didn't even open his eyes. But the feel of satin beneath his fingers and the fresh perfumed air—something he hadn't smelled in a long time, if ever—caught his attention. He opened his eyes.

And found himself in the Sultan's bedchamber. It was gold and large and filled with riches.

It terrified him. He'd had daylight dreams before, with pink elephants and flying camels. And he thought this was one of them. He tried to make it disappear, but it did not.

Finally, Moussel entered the bedroom. His presence frightened Amin even more.

He backed away from Moussel and asked, "Where am I?"

"In the palace, Sayiddi," Moussel said.

"What palace?"

"Your palace."

"My palace?" Amin asked. He had no palace. Not even in his fondest dreams did he have a palace.

Or did he? It was hard to deny the evidence of his senses.

"Who am I?" he asked.

"Commander of the Faithful, Monarch of the World, the Prophet's Voice on Earth, the Sultan Haroun Abraschild."

"This is madness," Amin said. "I want to talk to someone in authority."

"You were up drinking last night." Moussel said. He walked around the bed and snapped his fingers. "It's affected your memory, Sayiddi."

Countless servants and harem girls started entering from various doors. Nouz was one of them.

"I do drink," Amin said, startled at this mass of humanity all coming to serve him. "And I do have a terrible head."

Sultan Abraschild giggled from his closet. He liked the way his joke was going.

"Your Majesty?" Nouz said.

"Who am I?" Amin asked.

"You're Commander of the Faithful, Monarch of the World—"

"No, I'm not," Amin said, as two female servants helped him put on his robe. "I'm Amin the Beggar."

"Is this another one of your jokes, Sayiddi?" Nouz asked.

"No!" Amin didn't like this. A man like him only had his identity, and now that was evaporating. "I'm Amin. Amin the Drunkard. They know me in every tavern in Cairo."

"I'm your Grand Vizier," Moussel said. "Don't you recognize me?"

"Yes," Amin said. "I've seen you riding through the streets."

"And I'm Abu Nouz, Commander of the Palace Guard for the last ten years. Have you seen me, Sayiddi?"

"Often," Amin said. "Why would you say I'm Sultan Abraschild?"

"Because you are," Moussel said.

"But I'm not," Amin said.

"Have you seen his Majesty, Sultan Abraschild?"

"No," Amin said.

"So how do you know you're not him?" Nouz asked.

"But I'm me," Amin said. "I know me, don't I?"

"It's the wine, Sayiddi," Nouz said. "It's clouding your mind."

Through the lingering alcoholic fumes in his wine-stained brain, Amin was already half inclined to agree with Vizier Moussel and the others. He had awakened in strange surroundings before, but this was different. It was all so real and so pleasurable.

Perhaps he didn't want it to end.

His first major trial came when he had to go to the throne room. He arrived to find the room crowded with courtiers, servants, physicians, astrologers, and numerous intimates of the court. Of course, Moussel and Nouz were there, and so was Sultan Abraschild, hidden in the crowd.

Moussel led Amin to the Sultan's throne and proceeded to conduct business as if it were a normal day.

Moussel went through the traditional greeting. "Pray silence for His Majesty, Sultan Haroun Abraschild, Commander of the Faithful, Monarch of the World, the Prophet's Voice on Earth—"

"I'm not any of those things," Amin said. "Not Commander, not Monarch, not the Prophet's Voice, and not Sultan Abraschild!"

Everyone in the court burst out laughing, no one harder than the real Sultan himself. The laughter only upset Amin more.

"It's one of Your Majesty's jokes," Moussel said.

"No," Amin said.

"It must be," Nouz said. "We're all laughing."

"I'm just a drunk from the back streets of Cairo."

The court laughed again. Yet no one except Sultan Abraschild was really amused.

"Why would the whole court say you were Sultan?" Moussel asked.

Amin had no answer for that.

Moussel gave Amin a hand mirror. "Look at yourself, Majesty. That's not the face of a drunkard. It's the face of a king."

Amin studied the reflected image. The man he saw in the mirror was neat and clean, his fingers manicured, his clothing beautiful. If he were not Sultan, how could he be here? None of this made any sense.

So he accepted, as best he could, his new identity and wondered why the old one was so stubbornly part of him. As he went through the day that Moussel prescribed— apparently the day he had always gone through—he tried to concentrate on his new job.

Or his old job.

In his study that morning, he realized that all he had thought of for years was where the next drink was coming from. But now, everything had changed. He was a different man.

He would do the best he could—for everyone.

After deciding that, Amin picked up the reports Moussel had left on the table and began to read.

Chapter Twenty-two

"A drunkard who could read?" Schahriar asked.

He was sprawled on the bed. Scheherazade was sitting in the center of the bed, telling the story. Her father had left long ago—early in the tale, in fact. He was still upset that Scheherazade had offered her own life in exchange for the kingdom.

Or perhaps he was upset that Schahriar made it sound as if he still hadn't changed his mind about executing Scheherazade.

Even though Schahriar played with the necklace as he lay on the bed, Scheherazade knew he had changed his mind—or nearly so. He had told her he loved her. He had kissed her. The Schahriar she had known wouldn't have been able to kill anyone he loved.

And the more time she spent with him, the more she knew that boy was still inside him.

"Drunkards and beggars were boys once," Scheherazade said. "They have childhoods. They learn things. Then they let poverty and drink take over their lives."

Schahriar grunted as if he did not entirely believe her. Then he waved the hand holding the necklace. The beads clicked together. "Go on."

So she did.

Later that day, Amin listened to the affairs of state in the Councillors' Chamber. He was silent and withdrawn as the councillors passed documents to each other. He was still thinking about all that had transpired.

Sultan Abraschild was hidden in a listening chamber, enjoying his jest.

The councillors were trying to conduct state business as if nothing were amiss.

"There is the matter of the Chinese Ambassador," Moussel was saying. "We have already decided to resume negotiations with the Great Khan—"

"You say I'm Sultan?" Amin interrupted. He had heard enough.

"Of course you are, Your Majesty," Moussel said.

"And I have absolute power?"

"By divine right," Nouz said.

"Then instead of talking of the Great Khan, we should be talking about my people. Their needs, their happiness."

His announcement made all of the councillors sit up in amazement. No Sultan in recent memory had ever said such a thing.

"Scribe," Amin said, beckoning to the nearest scribe. "Record this: 'I, Sultan Abraschild, institute the building of new schools in each of the major cities.' "

"But, Sayiddi," Moussel said, attempting to forestall this disaster, "you must consult and ponder this matter."

"If I consult and ponder, I'll do nothing," Amin said. "Scribe, another decree. We will reduce people's taxes by half."

"But, Sayiddi," Nouz said, "the Treasury—"

"Can afford it." Amin frowned at Nouz. "Commander, do you believe the army is underpaid?"

"Undoubtedly." Nouz could barely keep a smile from his face. He wagered that the real Sultan Abraschild hadn't bargained on this. "I've submitted reports indicating we can't expect troops to defend the nation if they're poorly paid."

"I accept all of your recommendations, Commander," Amin said. "And we'll start by doubling the pay of all the troops."

Again, the councillors gasped. Amin's actions were so right, so proper. Why hadn't the real Sultan thought of these things?

"How will we finance this, Your Majesty?" Moussel asked, figuring he would trip up Amin here. A beggar had no concept of how to run a kingdom.

"Cut out all the waste and extravagance, particularly here in the palace," Amin said. "Vizier, I've read your reports also. The state bureaucracy needs a radical overhaul. I propose to put your ideas into practice immediately."

"Sayiddi, I'm overwhelmed," Moussel said. "I've been trying for years to get you to read my reports."

The councillors were all pleased, but of course Sultan Abraschild was not.

"What a fool!" he muttered to himself.

But he couldn't miss Moussel's comment as all of the councillors left the chamber.

"We've got more done today than we have for years," Moussel said.

Sultan Abraschild was no longer laughing.

Meanwhile, Amin the Beggar was taking his role very seriously. Feed a grub royal jelly and he will turn into an emperor butterfly in an instant.

But Abraschild now wanted to complete the joke.

He waited until evening, when Amin was relaxing in

his rooms. He lay on a sofa, smoking a hookah pipe, drinking wine, and watching his concubines dance, while another beauty played the harp. The table beside him was laden with food—perhaps more than he had seen at one time in all his miserable life.

Amin smiled happily while a servant poured him another glass of wine. He was too busy watching the dancers to notice the servant slip white powder into the glass.

But the Sultan Abraschild saw it from his closet hiding place.

The drinking glass slipped from Amin's hand as he slumped back on the sofa, unconscious. The harpist stopped playing. The concubines stopped dancing.

Sultan Abraschild ran out of the closet, laughing so hard he was afraid he would make himself sick.

Moussel and Nouz followed him, reluctantly.

"What a jest, huh?" Abraschild said.

"I doubt he'll enjoy it when he wakes," Moussel said.

"I enjoyed it," Abraschild said. "That's what's important. Besides, he had his one day of power. That's more than most get in one lifetime."

"What will you do with him now, Sayiddi?" Nouz asked.

"Throw him back. That's the best part of the joke."

So the unconscious Amin, dressed in his own clothes—which had not been washed—was thrown unceremoniously into a stinking alley, worse than any he'd ever chosen for himself. He lay on garbage, and rats feasted around him. The night air was cold, but the drug put him out too deeply for him to notice.

When daylight came, the drug's effects slowly wore off. It was a rude awakening. It was terrible to go from extreme wealth to extreme poverty. That was enough to send any man mad.

Amin stood. His senses were speaking to him again,

only this time they told him he was back to his old self.
Amin the Beggar.

But he did not want to return.

"No!" Amin cried. "This is a dream. I'm the Sultan!"

He burst into the street, shouting hysterically that he
was the Sultan, hoping his words would make the alley
and all the people on the street staring at him disappear.

But they did not.

In fact, everyone ws frightened by his intensity. Someone shouted for the guards while the rest of the crowd
shrank from Amin.

He could hardly stand it. People shrinking from him
when the day before they were doing anything for him.
What was happening to him?

It was demons. It had to be.

Guards finally appeared and seized Amin, who fought
wildly. He knocked two aside. But they clubbed him over
the head with the hilt of their swords. As he fell, they
dragged him off, screaming, to the jeers of the crowd.

No one believed Amin's story, and he was thrown
into prison for disturbing the peace—and for his own
protection.

In the weeks that followed, he came to realize that only
a madman would think of himself as ruler of the world,
but it had all seemed so real. Although it grew less and
less real as the days passed. Soon Amin began to doubt
if it had ever happened.

But fate, and Sultan Abraschild, hadn't finished playing
with him yet.

One day, Sultan Abraschild came into Amin's cell,
disguised as a warder. He brought Amin a meal. Amin
was curled into a ball. His filthy clothes were even more
ragged than they had been before, and he was so dirty
that his dirt was covered with dirt.

"You should eat," Abraschild said as he crouched
across from Amin.

"I'm not hungry," Amin said.

The Sultan stood, unsure what to do. At the moment, the joke no longer seemed funny.

"S-stay and talk," Amin said. "No one will talk to me. They think I'm mad."

Ah, this was what Abraschild was hoping for. He crouched again. "Are you?"

"I was." Amin sat up. "I thought I was Sultan Abraschild. I dreamed of being Sultan for so long, it became real for me."

Abraschild's eyes narrowed. "Were you better than Sultan Abraschild?"

"Only in my dreams, friend," Amin said, and then laughed. "Only in my dreams."

His laughter was so infectious that Abraschild joined him.

"Laughter's the cure for all our ills," Abraschild said. "You'll soon be free."

"Thank you, friend," Amin said. "Thank you."

It took the Sultan a while to get away from Amin, but when he did, he rejoined Moussel and Nouz outside the prison. Moussel wasn't sure he wanted to hear how poor Amin was doing. He, in spite of himself, had liked the young man.

"He think's he's cured," Abraschild said, laughing.

"Now that you've found out what happened to him," Moussel said, "he can be left alone."

"He thought he did a good job as a one-day Sultan."

Moussel and Nouz exchanged looks. They agreed, but they didn't dare tell Abraschild.

"So," Abraschild said, "I'm going to give him another day of it."

"You're going to repeat the jest?" Moussel asked.

"A good jest is worth repeating."

"But, Sayiddi," Nouz said, "it could send him mad for the rest of his life."

"You two have no sense of humor," Abraschild said.

No. They didn't. At least not when it came at the expense of a man like Amin.

But they couldn't stop the Sultan. That night, he went back into Amin's cell with some wine.

He handed it to Amin.

"Compliments of the Sultan himself," said Abraschild. "It's his birthday. All the prisoners are given wine to celebrate the occasion."

Amin lifted his glass in a toast. "Long live Sultan Abraschild!"

And then he drank.

He passed out again, as he had before. Guards carried the unconscious Amin from the prison.

And so, Amin's torture continued.

Chapter Twenty-three

Schahriar did not move. He seemed so very far away that Scheherazade barely paused long enough to have some water. The night was dark, and dawn seemed a long time off.

She couldn't tell how the story was affecting him. Somehow, she felt that everything rested on the way that this tale went.

"It was a terrible nightmare," she said, "which was happening again. . . ."

When Amin awoke in the Sultan's bedchamber, perfumed, manicured, clean—he screamed. This time, he knew he was mad.

He was so agitated that he didn't hear a loud giggle coming from the closet. Sultan Abraschild believed that the joke was even better this time. He hadn't expected the scream, and he had liked it.

Amin careened around the room like a trapped animal.

"I'm mad again!" Amin shouted. "Save me!"

Moussel and Nouz hurried into the room. This time, they had kept the other servants away.

"What is it, Your Majesty?" Moussel asked.

"I'm Amin. This is a prison cell. I'm mad!"

"Calm yourself, Sayiddi," Nouz said. "You had another bad dream."

"But which is a dream and which is real?" Amin asked. "Is this the dream, or was that the dream?"

"We'll send for the Royal Physicians," Nouz said.

"It's the demons," Amin said. "They carried me here. They're in the air! Demons! Demons!"

He continued to pace as he spoke, and his movements took him near the closet. The advisors followed him, unhappy and uncertain about what to do. They hadn't expected this.

Neither had the Sultan, who was laughing so hard that he thought he was going to burst.

He wasn't quiet about it either, and Amin heard him.

"Listen!" Amin said, stopping suddenly. "It's the demons! The demons are laughing!"

He grabbed Nouz's sword and dashed to the closet, savagely thrusting the sword through the slats again and again.

"Death to all the demons!" Amin shouted. "Death! Death! Death!"

Then he withdrew the sword, and frowned. It was wet with blood. Demons didn't bleed, did they?

He turned around in his confusion and did not see the closet door swing open. Sultan Abraschild fell out, dead.

Amin dropped the sword and hurried to the bed, still confused by everything.

Nouz crouched beside the Sultan, but even before he checked to see if the Sultan was breathing, he already knew what he would find. "Dead!"

"There's one good thing," Moussel said. "No more jokes."

Nouz stood slowly. "And he died with a smile on his face." Nouz had never seen that before.

But he couldn't dwell on it. He and Moussel had a larger problem. "What do we do now?" Nouz asked. "Who is his heir?"

"He has none," Moussel said, having an idea. "There'll be a fight amongst the nobles. It will mean civil war unless we act."

"In what way?" Nouz asked. He glanced over his shoulder. Amin was still sitting on the bed, rocking back and forth, trying to sort out what was real and what was a dream.

Moussel looked in the same direction. "Sultan Abraschild ordered us to treat Master Amin as Sultan."

"He was meant to be Sultan for a day!" Nouz said.

"We know that, but others don't," Moussel said.

Nouz had spent weeks wishing that Amin had remained Sultan. He had liked the cool, efficient way that Amin had handled himself in that single day.

"If he keeps cutting taxes," Nouz said as he warmed to the idea, "he has nothing to fear from anyone."

"We'll say that Abraschild has gone on a holy pilgrimage to Mecca and asked his friend to take his place."

"It's true," Nouz said, glancing back at the Sultan's body, "in a way."

"True or false," Moussel said, "it's plausible. That's the important thing."

They walked over to the bed. Amin was still rocking back and forth. He was oblivious to all that had happened around him. He still didn't know that he had killed Abraschild—or that there was even a dead man in the room.

"Your physicians will see you later, Your Majesty," Moussel said.

"You've been ill," Nouz added.

"I have?" Amin asked. Somehow that news seemed to reassure him. He glanced over Nouz's shoulder and saw the body. He did not recognize it. "Who's that?"

"That was the Royal Jester, Your Majesty," Moussel said.

"What's the matter with him?" Amin asked.

"His last joke was a killer," Nouz said. He snorted, unable to keep the laughter back.

His snort inspired Moussel's, which then forced both of them to laugh. They started laughing so hard and so long that they confused Amin all the more.

"What's so funny?" Amin asked.

"He always said we had no sense of humor," Moussel said.

"And so Amin became one of the most beloved sultans in history," Scheherazade said, "and Abraschild was completely forgotten. Nobody noticed that he never returned from Mecca."

She was sitting close to Schahriar. He didn't seem to realize that the story had ended. Then his face changed, like that of a man coming out of a deep sleep—or a bad dream.

He got up and walked to the balcony, staring up at the night sky.

Scheherazade followed him, her heart pounding. She wasn't sure what about her story had provoked him, but she knew something had.

The balcony was cold. There was a slight wind. The stars were bright. It was one of the most beautiful nights that Scheherazade had ever seen.

"I saw myself as Amin," Schahriar said, "and as Sultan Abraschild. He was consumed by laughter. I was consumed by fear of betrayal. And I was prepared to do anything to feed my fear, as Abraschild fed his cruel humor."

"That wasn't you," Scheherazade said. "That was the darkness inside you."

"Is it still there?" Schahriar faced her. "Look into the windows of my soul. Look into my eyes and tell me."

Scheherazade looked into his eyes. He had beautiful eyes, dark and deep and filled with an intelligence that had seemed trapped before.

It did not seem trapped now.

"What do you see, Scheherazade?" he asked.

"Me," Scheherazade said, "looking at you, my love."

His entire body relaxed. It was as if the demons inside him were set free. He took her hands, and she recognized the touch. The gentle boy who had held her all those years ago, the boy she had dreamed of, grown into a gentle man.

"Sayiddi." The voice came from above them. Scheherazade recognized it at once.

Her father's voice.

Both she and Schahriar looked up. Giafar was at a window in the higher part of the palace. He seemed worried.

He said, "Your brother's army is camped outside the city."

Both Schahriar and Scheherazade turned as one. They looked not at the sky, but at the ground. Beyond the darkened city, they saw hundreds of bobbing lights from army campfires.

Schahzenan had arrived.

Schahzenan was looking at the lights of Baghdad, knowing that in the morning, he would have his victory.

He went over and over the plan in his mind. Nothing would get in his way.

It worried him that the Chief Executioner had not kept their appointment that night, but he could do little about it. The Executioner might finally have gotten his wish to execute Schahriar's new little wife. Or perhaps he would come later.

Schahzenan wanted to know whether Schahriar was expecting him. Somehow Schahzenan doubted that he was.

Schahzenan put his hand on the coffin beside him. His beloved was at his side, as she always was, as she should have been in life.

He was almost to his vengeance.

"Soon, my love," he said. "Soon."

Chapter Twenty-four

The arrival of Schahzenan prevented Schahriar and Scheherazade from having any more discussions. Schahriar had spent most of his time preparing for the attack, working with Giafar and with his army. Now he moved his entire staff to the camp that had been set up on waste ground inside the city walls.

He did not move Scheherazade or anyone else whom he valued. He had never planned to. He had always wanted her to be safe—a notion he had not examined until the morning after she had told the tale of Sultan Abraschild.

What a fool he had been. Schahriar had been looking backward, not forward. He had spent the last few years guarding himself and not his people. It had given his brother an opportunity to take over the kingdom, an opportunity that Schahriar would deny him.

Schahriar only wished he had spent more time with Scheherazade. He hadn't realized what a treasure she was until the last few nights.

What she had shown him the most was courage.
And courage was what he needed in facing Schahzenan.

Scheherazade spent most of the day in the palace, pacing. She hated feeling helpless, but she knew a woman
had no place with the army. *She* had no place there.

But she also knew that Schahriar was still fragile, especially where his brother was concerned. She had to find
a way to help him. Schahriar had only just come back to
himself. She had a hunch that if he faced Schahzenan
one on one, without some kind of support, he might
crumble again.

She couldn't allow that. She had to be at Schahriar's
side.

So, in the late afternoon, she put on her cloak and left
the palace, despite the protestations of the servants and
the guards Schahriar had left behind.

It took her longer to reach the camp than it took to
walk to the bazaar, but she kept a steady and even pace.
The soldiers were everywhere. She hadn't realized there
were so many in Baghdad.

Some gathered around campfires while other sharpened
their swords on grindstones, making sparks fly into the
night air. A steady stream of new recruits were showing
up and talking to officers. Horses stood near tents, camels
to one side. Merchants brought supplies, and all around,
the city prepared for war.

As Scheherazade made her way to her husband's tent,
she saw a group of soldiers forming a circle around one
campfire. The man standing near it looked familiar.

It was the Storyteller.

He was too old to be fighting against Schahzenan. She
veered toward the Storyteller to tell him that his services
were better used elsewhere.

The Storyteller smiled when he saw her, but she did not smile back.

"What are you doing here?" she asked him.

"On such a night," the Storyteller said, "men need stories to face the fear of dying."

She let out a small breath. He had come for the same reason she had. He was ministering to the troops; she would minister to their leader.

"That's why *I* was going to tell a story tonight," she said.

"That's good." The Storyteller understood what she was doing, then. "What kind of story are you going to tell?"

She had thought about it all day, and she knew the answer instantly. "Something full of magic and wonder."

"I shall be doing the same," the Storyteller said. "Go with God, Highness."

"And you as well." Then she hurried past him to Schahriar's tent.

She found Schahriar inside, his expression taut. He was being fitted by his armorer. The mail he wore over his chest was composed of solid metal, and it clinked as it moved. The armorer made adjustments, and Schahriar murmured things like, "Too low. Too high. It doesn't protect my heart."

Finally, the armorer removed the mail and left to make the proper adjustments.

Schahriar did not greet Scheherazade, even after the armorer left. Instead, he got himself a glass of wine and then poured her one. He did not tell her to leave as she had feared he would.

She sat down on the small bed. The tent seemed so close after the nights they had spent in his huge bedroom.

He seemed very tense.

"One of my stories will help," she said.

"No," Schahriar said. "One of your stories will not

help. This is not something you can talk your way out of, Scheherazade. The only danger you face now is from my brother. You won't be able to tell him tales to save yourself.''

Scheherazade felt herself blink in surprise. Had Schahriar known she was doing that all along? Suddenly she felt not quite as clever as she had earlier.

Or perhaps she *had* been clever. She was alive and beside Schahriar, after all.

''Schahzenan will cut your throat,'' Schahriar was saying. ''This isn't the time, Scheherazade.''

''It's the perfect time,'' she said, remembering her conversation with the Storyteller.

Schahriar walked toward the tent door. It was clear he was determined not to pay attention.

But Scheherazade had seen him like this before. She knew if she just started the story, he would get hooked. Schahzenan wouldn't attack at night.

No. The attack would come during the day. Schahriar wouldn't sleep, but it would be better if he spent those hours in some form of rest, even if that rest was listening to a fanciful tale.

She said, ''It's the incredible story of Princes Ahmed, Hussain, and Ali. They were brothers, too. They fought each other like you and Schahzenan.''

Schahriar let the flap drop. He paced to the other side of the tent.

''It happened long ago in far-off Yemen,'' Scheherazade said, ''before recorded time.''

Schahriar looked at her. She recognized the expression. He was hooked.

She smiled. ''The land was ruled by old Sultan Billah. And he had three sons, Ahmed, Hussain, and Ali. . . .''

* * *

Hussain was the best swordsman in Yemen. Ahmed was a master bowman, and Ali was a skilled fighter. He had enormous strength in his hands.

Most of the time, they fought each other. They rarely talked. They hit or punched or fell into a great fight over something trivial.

One afternoon, their father, Sultan Billah, a kindly old man, looked out of the window to see his three sons fighting in the garden. And for some reason, he finally had had enough.

He sighed and said to his wife, who was doing needlework, "They're at it again."

"It's just youthful exuberance, my love," the Sultana said. "They'll grow out of it."

"You've been saying that for the past ten years," the Sultan said. "Ahh, look!"

As he watched, his sons destroyed his prized hibiscus, then his favorite palm trees. The garden he had spent so long on was being ruined, just as the rest of the palace had been ruined at one point or another by his sons' fighting.

He summoned the boys to him. When they arrived, still slapping each other, the Sultan said, "Look what you've done to my prize plants!"

"It wasn't my fault, Father," Hussain said.

"It was their fault," Ali said of his brothers.

"No, it was theirs," Ahmed said.

"I don't care whose fault it was," the Sultan said.

"You boys are being very naughty, you know," the Sultana said.

"Yes, Mother," Hussain said.

"They're always picking on me," Ahmed said.

"What was the fight about this time?" the Sultan asked.

"The Princess Fatima loves me," Ali said.

"She loves me," Ahmed said.

"She loves me," Hussain said. "She said so."

"Rubbish," Ahmed said to his brother. "You could lose ten pounds of surplus fat if someone just cut off your head."

"Every time you look in the mirror, you take a bow," Ali said.

Ahmed elbowed Ali, who bumped into Hussain, and they fell into a new round of fighting—at least until the Sultan had his guards separate them.

"What happens when I die?" the Sultan asked the three. "You'll tear this country apart!"

"See what you boys have done?" Sultana said. "All this talk of dying. You're making your father ill."

"We didn't mean anything, Mother," Ahmed said. "Father's not dying."

"When I am," the Sultan said, "I'll name my heir."

"You should do it now, Father," Ali said.

"Don't forget," Hussain said, "I'm the eldest."

"And don't forget," the Sultan said, "that I have the final say, according to law."

"Who do you favor, Father?" Ahmed asked.

"I've got three blockheads for sons," the Sultan said. "How can I favor anyone?"

He had been thinking of this for a long time. The fight in the garden was the last straw. He had made his decision.

"Let it be proclaimed throughout Yemen," the Sultan said, "that I'm sending my sons on a quest. Whoever brings back the greatest wonder in the world will be my heir."

"How long have we got?" Ali asked.

"One year," The Sultan said. "You all leave together and return together."

And so, the brothers went forth into the unknown to find the greatest wonder in the world. They rode across the desert together, and stopped at a place called The Traveler's Rest. There, they managed to have lunch without hitting each other.

"We should meet here on the same day next year," Ahmed said, "and go home together."

"And may the best man win," Ali said.

They raised their wineglasses and drank to Ali's toast. Then they grinned at each other. Superior smiles on all three faces.

"What are you smiling at?" Hussain asked Ahmed.

"I'm obviously the best man," Ahmed said.

"The only thing you're best at is shoveling camel dung," Ali said.

Ahmed threw wine in Ali's face. Ali punched him. Hussain roared with laugher, and Ahmed and Ali punched him. All three fought furiously.

It was their way of saying good-bye.

The next day, they galloped to a rocky canyon together and pulled up when it divided into three paths. Ahmed took the path to the right. Ali took the path to the left, while Hussain galloped straight ahead.

They had no maps to guide them, no stories to follow. Instead, they followed their hearts, and each one believed that he, and he alone, would win.

Chapter Twenty-five

Schahriar sat beside Scheherazade on the small bed. He put his arm around her and pulled her close as he listened.

Ali found himself in a fabled land: the bronze city of Zirog. It is all gone now—the bronze rusted and the fountains dried up—but then it was a wonder to behold.

In this marvelous city, Ali found a shop that sold antiques. He went inside and explained to the owner, Schaca, his quest.

"So," Ali said, "my brothers and I are searching the world for wondrous objects for my father."

"I have something wondrous," Schaca said.

He went toward a table at the side of the shop and brought out a bronze box. He opened it to reveal a bronze telescope.

Ali was not impressed. "I've seen a telescope before, Master Schaca."

"Not like this," Schaca said. "Put it to your eye. You only have to ask and you'll see anything you want to see."

Ali tentatively put the telescope to his eye. As he did so, he said, "I'd like to see the Princess Fatima of Yemen."

The image in the lens focused down until he saw a beautiful woman dancing in the palace garden. He recognized her instantly.

"That's her!" he said, stunned. "That's Fatima."

He stared for a long time at this piece of home. Finally, reluctantly, he took the telescope from his eye and said, "All right, Master Schaca. It's a wonder. Can I buy it?"

"It's not mine to sell," Schaca said. "I'm delivering it to Hari ben Karim."

"Would he sell it?"

"Ask him," Schaca said.

So Ali accompanied Schaca to Karim's bronze palace. Hari ben Karim turned out to be the richest man in Zirog— and he had more interest in things than in money.

"The telescope's not for sale," Karim said. "As you can see, I don't need the money. But I might give it to you as a gift."

"What would I give to you in return?" Ali asked.

"Entertainment," Karim said. "Schaca tells me you're a master fighter. Would you fight my champions for the telescope?"

"Gladly," Ali said.

Karim clapped his hands five times, and five warriors emerged from the flaming bronze pool at the far side of the room. Ali was not impressed by them. He had fought his brothers; he knew he could fight—and defeat—anyone else.

Karim's warriors advanced, but Ali attacked, swiftly dispatching each warrior with extraordinary speed and dexterity.

"The telescope's mine," Ali said, breathing hard. "I've killed your champions."

"What makes you think they're dead?" Karim asked.

He clapped his hands and the five dead warriors sprang to their feet.

"This time," Karim said, "knives."

"Knives?" Ali said. "That's cheating!"

But he had no choice. The champions were all carrying knives—long, sharp daggers that would make for a terrible fight. Ali was skilled in the art of hand-to-hand combat, not in knife fighting, which was a different skill. He pulled his own knife, then made a decision.

He flung his knife straight at Karim.

The knife hit Karim in the throat. Karim looked surprised. "That's cheating," he said.

Ravens flew out of his chest, and then he slumped forward, dead. His champions disappeared as if they never had been.

Ali hurried forward and grabbed the telescope. Schaca was too shocked to stop him. Ali put the telescope under his arm and fled Zirog.

As Ali made his way back to The Traveler's Rest, Ahmed was heading north.

He found a great monastery that housed, he had heard, one of the world's great wonders.

Buddhist monks led Ahmed inside the monastery to a hall that was lit by a thousand candles on the polished floor. Ahmed made his way past the candles to the Holy Seer, who sat cross-legged at the far end.

"I am Prince Ahmed of Yemen," Ahmed said. "I've learned you have a rare fruit. A holy green apple that is said to cure all illness. I'd like to buy it."

"It's not for sale," the Holy Seer said.

"Is there something I can give you in exchange for it?"

"Perhaps," he said. "You have a special skill?"

"With the bow," Ahmed said.

"Then you will undergo a test to see if you are fit to own the Apple of Life."

The monks set up a large wooden target at the far end of the hall. Almost without looking, Ahmed took his bow and fired. His arrow hit the target dead center.

Then he shot another arrow, which split the first arrow in two.

The monks did not seem greatly surprised. The Holy Seer nodded toward a young monk, who set a burning candle on the ground. Another monk blindfolded Ahmed.

Ahmed took careful aim and fired.

The arrow snuffed the candle out.

"I'm impressed, Ahmed," the Holy Seer said. "I have one more test and the Apple of Life is yours."

Yet another monk joined them with the green apple in a wooden chest. Ahmed looked at his prize and knew having it was close at hand.

Then an eight-year-old boy appeared at the far end of the hall, where the original target had been. The boy put a red apple on top of his head. Ahmed stared at the target. He had never tried anything like this before.

The monk blindfolded Ahmed again, and Ahmed raised his bow.

But he could not fire.

He brought the bow down and raised his blindfold. The boy stared at him, unafraid.

"It is a risk," Ahmed said.

"The prize is worth it," the Holy Seer said.

"Not for the boy," Ahmed said.

"Then you lose and go away empty-handed."

Ahmed glanced at the Green Apple of Life and slowly replaced his blindfold. He raised his bow and carefully drew back the bowstring to shoot.

He tried to release the arrow, but he could not. Nothing was worth the boy's life.

This time, Ahmed deliberately pulled off his blindfold. "I lose," he said.

"No, you win." The Holy Seer nodded to the monk holding the Green Apple of Life.

"What?" Ahmed asked. "How?"

"You win by losing," the Holy Seer said. "You weren't prepared to win at any cost. The Apple of Life is yours."

The Holy Seer gave Ahmed the Apple and some words of advice before he left.

Meanwhile, Hussain was riding toward the vain, fabulous city of Petra. Petra has since disappeared into the sand. The Earth forgot her. But in those days, she was the jewel of the East.

Hussain discovered the most amazing thing about Petra. It was two cities, not one. A second city lay under the first. Underground Petra survived many years after the other one, but that too is gone, swallowed by the sand.

In Petra, Hussain found a street packed tight with people and stalls selling all kinds of goods. He walked through them, seeing nothing amazing.

But at the end of the street, he saw a stall that was empty except for a single carpet. The stall owner seemed completely uninterested in selling it. That intrigued Hussain.

"Is this the only carpet you have to sell?" Hussain asked.

"For fifty pieces of gold," the stall owner said.

"You must be mad," Hussain said.

"Have you enough gold to pay for it?"

"If I want it," Hussain said.

"You'll want it," the stall owner said. "Follow me."

The stall owner rolled up the carpet and went into the shop behind his stall. Hussain followed.

The shop was filled with hundreds of carpets, each more beautiful than the last.

"Why're you out there trying to sell one old carpet when you've got hundreds like this?" Hussain asked.

"Because it's a flying carpet," the stall owner said. "It can take you anywhere."

"I may be a stranger in Petra," Hussain said, "but I'm not a child. There are no such things as flying carpets."

"There are thousands," the owner said, "and this is one of them."

The stall owner spread the carpet on the ground and chanted over it, "Rise, carpet, rise!"

The carpet rose off the floor and moved with a strange ripple. As it moved away from the stall owner, the owner pulled out a carpet beater and gave the carpet a whack.

"Down, down. Come to rest."

Trembling, the carpet settled back on the ground.

"All you have to do is tell it where you wish to go," the owner said.

Hussain was astonished. He had never seen anything like it. "Fifty gold pieces, you say? It's worth every penny. I'll pay cash."

He undid his shirt to reveal the money belt around his waist. As he started to open the belt, a man entered the store—and not a savory man either, but one who was clearly up to mischief. A man who wore knives as easily as other men wore turbans.

"What's this?" Hussain asked.

"We're going to rob and kill you," the owner said. "It's nothing personal, but I can't sell a magic carpet for a paltry fifty in gold. It wouldn't be good business."

"Just you two?" Hussain asked, laughing. "You're not enough. You lose."

The unsavory man drew one of his knives and slowly aimed it at Hussain. The man threw the knife, then drew another and another. His pace was relentless.

The blades shot through the air so quickly that the average eye could not see them.

But Hussain did not have an average eye. He deflected each knife with his sword.

Then he snatched up the carpet and ran from the shop, sword in hand. The stall owner hurried to the doorway and shouted to the crowd outside, "Stop the thief!"

Hussain, hearing this, looked behind him, and immediately stumbled into some jars. He dropped both carpet and sword. A man in the crowd grabbed Hussain's sword, suspecting he was the thief.

The carpet unfurled and flapped in front of the startled Hussain. He stared at it, as did the crowd.

Behind him, the stall owner and his murderous friend hurried toward Hussain. Hussain only had a moment to make a decision.

He leapt onto the carpet and said, "Take me to The Traveler's Rest!"

The carpet shot off. Hussain had to work to keep his balance. The stall owner and his companion caught up to him. The carpet hurried into an alley, and as Hussain looked up, he realized they were at a dead end.

The carpet turned back on itself, flipping Hussain off his feet. Miraculously, he landed on the carpet's other side, and they changed direction, heading back into the crowd. The carpet did not go any higher, and the crowd was forced to fall to the dirt to avoid getting hit.

The stall owner, sword in hand, darted to the edge of the alleyway and, using boxes for leverage, took a flying leap at the carpet. He boarded. The force of his landing on the carpet catapulted Hussain upward. He reached back for his sword—but it wasn't there.

So he drew his dagger instead. The stall owner lunged with his sword, and the battle was underway.

They fought through the streets, up the stairs, and out of the underground city. They fought in the gorge outside Petra. They fought in the rocky cliffs, and all the while the carpet took them toward The Traveler's Rest.

Finally, the stall owner lunged at Hussain. Hussain jumped, and the stall owner missed, falling forward and cutting the carpet. He rose and knocked Hussain's dagger free.

The stall owner moved in for the kill, but at that moment, the carpet spun around, throwing the stall owner forward. He fell off, but he managed to grab on near the tear in the carpet.

The carpet tried to shake him off, but he clung tightly. The tear started to unravel and the owner found himself clinging by a thread. The thread got longer and longer, and the owner was dragged and bounced on the desert floor.

Hussain thought the man would never give up. He would hang on until there was no carpet left at all.

Then the carpet rounded a corner. Ahead was a huge statue of a naked man. Hussain maneuvered the carpet so that it took a hard right around the statue. The turn was so quick that as Hussain and the carpet took their right, the thread and the stall owner continued to move forward.

The thread wrapped around the statue, and the stall owner was spun wildly around and around until he was deposited unceremoniously between the bare buttocks of the statue.

Hussain laughed as the carpet flew across the desert toward The Traveler's Rest.

Soon he was reunited with his brothers. They had dinner and discussed their prizes.

"We've all done well," Ahmed said. "A magic apple, a flying carpet, and a wondrous telescope. Have you tested the telescope yet, Ali?"

"Of course I've tested it," Ali said, slightly offended. "Just tell it what you want to see."

He handed the telescope to Ahmed. Ahmed raised it, feeling foolish, but he put it to his eye anyway.

"I'd like to see our father, Sultan Billah," Ahmed told the scope.

The image in the lens showed Sultan Billah, but he was lying on his bed, his face gray, his body emaciated. He was surrounded by grieving courtiers and his wife.

"It's Father!" Ahmed said.

Ali took the telescope back and peered into it. He saw the same thing that Ahmed did. After a moment, he handed the scope to Hussain.

Hussain had the same vision. Slowly he let the telescope down.

"He's dying," Hussain said. "We have to be there."

"It'll take us a week to get home," Ali said.

"I have a quicker way," Hussain said.

He unrolled his carpet and all three sat on it.

"Rise, carpet," Hussain ordered, "and take us to Sultan Billah's palace. Fast!"

Chapter Twenty-six

"They arrived in time to save their father with Ahmed's Apple of Life," Scheherazade said.

She was still cuddled against Schahriar. The tent had grown dark, and the sounds from outside it had stilled as the army fell asleep. She had tried to keep this story short, but it had taken several hours to tell.

Schahriar seemed awake and fascinated by the story.

"United now and for the rest of their lives," Scheherazade finished, "they ruled in peace and harmony."

Schahriar waited a moment, as if making sure that Scheherazade was really done with the story. Then he asked, "What advice did the Holy Seer give Ahmed when he handed him the magic apple?"

"He said the world was an inferno full of darkness and evil," Scheherazade said. "And there were only two ways of dealing with it. The first was easy and wrong: to accept it and become part of the darkness and evil."

Schahriar sighed and looked down. Scheherazade took his hand.

"The second," she said, "was harder and right: You fight it and recognize those who aren't evil and help them endure."

Schahriar looked up at her. His gaze was both humble and grateful.

"You've taken the second way," he said softly. "You've helped me, and saved me from the darkness. Why, my love? Why did you sacrifice yourself to save me?"

"I love you," she said.

"Is that the answer?" he asked.

She smiled. "It'll have to do—"

But Schahriar didn't let her finish. He leaned forward and placed his hands in her hair, pulling her close. Then he kissed her so intensely that her senses swam.

She expected him to stop as he had before. But he did not. He drew them closer than they had ever been—only his method require no words, no stories.

Just the two of them. Together. Forever.

The hour before dawn came too early, and when it arrived, Scheherazade woke alone. Schahriar was already outside. She dressed and joined him.

His men were wrapping the hooves of the camels in strips of carpet. Scheherazade had seen nothing like it before.

When Schahriar saw her, he smiled and beckoned her close.

"Remember Hussain and the flying carpet?" he asked. "I'm putting the story to good use."

Scheherazade slipped her hand in his. The idea was brilliant. The camels would move silently across the desert. If Schahriar's army started moving before Schahzenan's was even awake, Schahriar's would get close without attracting any attention at all.

Schahriar squeezed her hand. "I've learned something from the other stories too."

He looked beyond her. She followed his gaze. She had never been in a military camp before, but it seemed to her that the preparations going on around her were unique. Men were filling jars with oil. Others were attaching quivers to their backs.

Still others were heading into the desert wearing dark clothes and carrying swords. They were not riding at all.

She looked questioningly at Schahriar. He smiled at her.

"Ali Baba was lucky," he said. "I was lucky finding you, but you're right. Being lucky isn't enough. You have to be smart, too."

Her heart leapt. He had a plan, and he was confident in it. Her work, then, was done. She had helped him in the only way she knew how.

He didn't let go of her hand. As he walked through the camp, encouraging his men, he kept her at his side.

The wind was kicking up. Scheherazade didn't know if that was a good thing or not. Sometimes the wind got so severe that it created a sandstorm. She doubted that was part of Schahriar's plan.

She was about to ask him when her father and two captains rounded one of the tents. The men were clearly looking for Schahriar.

When they saw him, they salaamed.

"We've had reports the enemy is being led by Schahzenan and the former Sultana," the first captain said.

"The Sultana is dead," Schahriar said coldly. "I killed her."

"Even dead, she still wants to destroy you," the second captain said. "The army thinks she's good luck. They make a powerful combination."

"Tell them we have one even more powerful," Scheherazade said. "I'll be riding into battle with my husband."

"No!" Giafar said. "It's too dangerous."

Schahriar pulled Scheherazade close and said so softly that only she could hear, "You don't have to prove your love."

"It would rise the spirits of the men," the first captain said. He hadn't realized that Schahriar had spoken. "The enemy has a dead Sultana. We have a live one."

It took another hour of preparation before the troops headed out. Schahriar took Scheherazade to the armorer and got her outfitted in her own suit of armor. It didn't quite fit, but it would do. It would protect her more than her own clothing would.

He also found her a horse, a powerful one, and, despite her protests, he gave her both a sword and a dagger.

"I will not have to fight, my love," she said.

"In case," he said to her. "Just in case."

The wind was kicking up even worse, but that didn't seem to deter Schahriar. In fact, it seemed to please him, but he did not tell Scheherazade why.

Finally, the troops went out of the city gates. Schahriar, with Scheherazade at his side, led them, his captains behind him. The troops moved more silently than Scheherazade had imagined they could.

Scheherazade felt as if she were in an army of ghosts.

Outside the city, the wind was even stronger. They were in a sandstorm. She brought her veil over her face, not to hide her visage, but to protect herself from the blowing sand.

The dawn was obscured by the blind sheets of sand. Sand devils, whirling and twisting, moved across the desert like advance columns.

Somehow Schahriar seemed to know where they were.

After they had ridden deep into the desert, he raised a hand and stopped his troops.

Scheherazade's eyes stung in the storm. The sand coated her. She could barely see Schahriar as he turned to one of his captains.

"Guard my wife!" Schahriar shouted, his voice almost taken by the wind. "She is more precious to me than my life."

And before she could react, he leaned over and kissed her. Then he continued forward with a small party of his men, leaving Scheherazade behind.

It took Schahriar and his advance guards longer than he had planned to make it through the sandstorm. Eventually, Schahzenan's camp rose like a mirage out of the darkness.

As Schahriar had suspected, Schahzenan's troops were protecting themselves from the storm. Apparently Schahzenan believed the element of surprise was on his side, and he had put off attacking that day.

Schahriar had learned that it wasn't wise to put anything off. Schahzenan would learn the same lesson—but if Schahriar had his way, Schahzenan wouldn't live long enough to apply it.

The camp was deep behind a bluff. Schahriar knew there had to be guards. Before he started the attack, he looked over his shoulder and saw the second advance team approaching. Mostly, it was composed of camels and riders.

At that moment, Schahriar gave the signal. His men moved forward and silently attacked the guards. Schahriar dismounted and hurried forward on foot.

His target wasn't the army, but its leader.

He climbed over the bluff and saw a guard ahead of him. He slit the man's throat so fast that the guard didn't have a chance to draw a breath, let alone scream. Then

Schahriar attacked a second guard, and suddenly he was inside the camp.

On all sides, his camels were running forward. They all had large jars tied behind them. The jars were spilling oil throughout the camp.

Schahriar waited until he couldn't see the camels any longer; then he reached into the pouch he had at his side. He removed an oil lamp, like the one Scheherazade had described to him when she told him the story of Aladdin, and he lit it. He tossed the lamp as far as he could.

It landed in a puddle of oil in the center of camp. The oil ignited, the flames racing along the oil trails in all directions. The fires were large and terrifying, mixing inky black smoke with the sand from the storm.

Finally, Schahzenan's worthless army seemed to realize something was wrong. They hurried out of their tents to discover fire raging all around them.

Schahzenan's men panicked, allowing Schahriar's men to escape.

The advance team had done its work, all except Schahriar.

Schahzenan's men started screaming. Some were on fire. Others grabbed spears from the spear racks in the center of the camp and tried to fight the attackers. Except Schahriar's men were gone. Schahzenan's men were fighting each other.

Schahriar watched all of this with his telescope, waiting for the one face he needed to see. And finally it emerged from the tent. Schahzenan, looking as if he had just awakened, stepped out into the chaos.

He stopped one of his guards and shouted at him. Schahriar could read his lips: *Gather your men!*

The guard nodded, and soon what remained of Schahzenan's army headed—on foot—toward Schahriar's.

Schahzenan was alone.

Schahriar put his telescope away and made his way

through the burning camp. When he arrived at Schahzenan's tent, he found the flap down.

Schahriar slashed the tent with his sword.

"Open sesame," Schahriar murmured.

He stepped inside to find Schahzenan staring at a corpse at the back of the tent. Schahzenan had his sword in hand.

He seemed completely surprised by Schahriar's appearance.

"It's time to take responsibility for your actions, brother," Schahriar said, "and die!"

"You killed my only love," Schahzenan said.

"You betrayed me," Schahriar shouted back and lunged for him.

Schahzenan brought his sword up. Schahriar thrust at him, but Schahzenan parried. They were evenly matched—had been since they were boys—and they moved across the tent, thrusting, parrying, slashing, taking advantage of every opening, but not succeeding in any way.

Then Schahzenan lunged for Schahriar, and Schahriar moved out of his way. Schahzenan tumbled into a table filled with fruit. Schahriar stepped toward him, but Schahzenan rolled and got on his feet, sword in hand. He stabbed at Schahriar, and Schahriar blocked him, feeling the power of the blow in his arms.

Sweat was pouring down his back, and the air stank of smoke. Schahzenan lunged for Schahriar again, and Schahriar dodged—but this time Schahzenan's sword caught the tent's central pole instead.

The tent collapsed on them both, pinning them beneath its weight.

Sitting astride her horse in the middle of the dying sandstorm was not how Scheherazade had planned to spend the battle. She had wanted to be at Schahriar's side.

A column of troops fanned out on either side of her, and the captain whom Schahriar had admonished to take care of her was beside her.

No one had moved since Schahriar left.

After a while, the sandstorm eased even more, and they saw smoke rising from Schahzenan's camp. In the distance, they heard screams and shouts.

It took all of Scheherazade's strength to remain still. She wanted to urge her horse forward, but she did not. She knew that Schahriar had to defend himself.

And then, over the dune near Schahzenan's camp, a blackness arose. Scheherazade squinted her sore, sand-filled eyes. It took a moment for the image to register.

Troops—Schahzenan's troops—running across the desert like crazy men.

The captain beside Scheherazade shouted, "Draw your swords."

All around her, the troops raised their swords. The ground troops moved ahead of her and lined up, fifteen deep. Another group moved even farther forward. They had bows over their shoulders and quivers on their backs.

Scheherazade felt her breath catch in her throat.

Schahzenan's troops screamed and waved their swords as they ran across the desert.

"Hold the line!" the captain shouted.

None of her troops moved. Not a one.

The sandstorm cleared, and the sun came out, as if there had never been a wind. She couldn't see Schahriar's footprints on the smoothed-over sand.

Schahzenan's troops were getting closer. Ahead of her another captain nodded. The archers in the very first rows dropped to their knees, put an arrow in their bows, and aimed the bows high over each other's heads.

"Hold!" the captain beside her yelled.

The army was getting very close. Scheherazade felt her hands tighten on the reins.

"Ready!" the captain yelled.

The sound of Schahzenan's army was overwhelming—the screams, the shouts, the cries were almost growls. Like wild animals on the attack.

"Now!" the captain yelled.

The archers let their arrows fly, and every fourth man in the front of Schahzenan's army dropped as the arrows found their targets.

So impressive, like Ahmed in her story.

Then, behind the army, Scheherazade saw movement. The ground appeared to be shaking. From it emerged another half of Schahriar's army.

She felt a laugh catch in her throat. Half of Schahriar's army had been hiding like Black Coda's men, under the sand. Schahriar! That was what he had meant when he said he used the stories. He had used them all to fight Schahzenan.

Schahzenan's army was caught in a pincer movement with hostile forces front and back. At first, they tried to fight, but they could not. They had no idea how to attack in two directions at once.

Finally, they gave in.

They surrendered.

Schahriar cut his way out of the tent. The air was black with smoke, and fires still raged around him. He nearly staggered into the rack of spears.

Men were running in all directions—his men, mostly, and he saw that as a good sign. His men wouldn't be there if Schahzenan's troops had been able to prevent it.

But Schahriar couldn't see Schahzenan anywhere.

Then he heard a cry behind him, a familiar cry, one he had grown up with.

Schahzenan had freed himself from the tent and was running toward Schahriar, sword in hand. Schahzenan seemed to have superhuman strength. He was fighting like a madman, growling the entire time.

He used both hands to wield his sword, giving its blows a power they had lacked before. Schahriar parried, but he was getting tired. He had dominated the first part of the fight, but it seemed that Schahzenan was dominating this part.

Then Schahzenan struck a hard blow, and Schahriar's sword slipped through his fingers. He fell to one knee, and Schahzenan kicked him in the chin, sending him backward.

He was dazed, trying to catch his breath.

Schahzenan tossed his sword away and grabbed his dagger, then jumped on top of Schahriar, pointing the blade at his throat.

Schahriar managed to grab Schahzenan's shoulder, holding him back, but Schahzenan had the advantage. He would, eventually, break Schahriar's hold.

With his other hand, Schahriar cast about for something, anything, to help him. His fingers found a rope. He spared it a single glance, and felt Schahzenan's blade get even closer.

The rope led to the rack of spears behind Schahzenan.

Schahriar's elbow buckled. The blade grazed his throat. With all his strength, he tugged on the rope.

He could feel blood on his skin. Schahzenan's eyes were rolling, mad. The brother Schahriar knew had always been cruel, but never mad, not like this.

And Schahriar would die at his hands.

Poor Scheherazade.

Then Schahriar heard a sound like giant footsteps, just as he had imagined the soldier statues from the tomb in Aladdin's story had sounded as they fell against each other. Schahriar glanced over Schahzenan's shoulders and saw the spear racks hitting each other, one after the other, falling toward Schahzenan.

Schahriar grabbed a handful of dust and threw it in Schahzenan's eyes. That was enough to break his brother's grip, only for a moment.

Then Schahriar kicked Schahzenan in the belly so hard that Schahzenan went flying backward—

Into the falling spears.

Schahriar sat up.

Schahzenan was impaled on the spears, his mouth open in surprise. He looked at Schahriar for a moment, and seemed to see him clearly.

There was no regret in Schahzenan's eyes.

Schahriar stood.

By the time he reached his brother, Schahzenan was dead.

The camp was a blackened ruin. Scheherazade rode through it, her heart pounding. All of Schahriar's men seemed to have come out of this fine, but none of them had seen her husband.

She had no idea if he were alive or dead.

Then she saw him, his gold uniform sparkling in the sun. He was standing next to a body, spread out like that of a thief who had died for his crimes.

Schahzenan.

Schahriar had won.

Scheherazade rode toward him. As she did, she passed a collapsed tent. The wind caught its edge, and the canvas flew up, like a magic carpet about to fly, revealing something ugly beneath.

The corpse of the Sultana, Schahriar's first wife. The woman who had betrayed him.

She no longer looked human. A ghoul, a ghost, something that should sink and disappear into the sands.

Scheherazade did not spare her a second glance. Instead she rode to her husband and dismounted.

* * *

Schahriar left Schahzenan to the vultures. His brother would not receive a proper burial. It would be better to let the desert take him, to let time and history forget that Schahzenan ever lived.

That would be Schahriar's revenge.

He had wasted too much time on his brother's evil already. What had Scheherazade said? That there were two ways of dealing with the world's darkness. The easy way was to become part of it, as Schahriar's brother had done. Or there was the hard way, which was to fight it, as Scheherazade had done.

As Schahriar had done this day. And he would continue to do so for every day forward.

Then he raised his head. A vision appeared to him out of the smoke. A beautiful woman in the desert, just like in his dream.

But not like his dream. For this woman was real. She was good, and she loved him.

Scheherazade.

He hurried toward her and looked into her familiar face. He could grow old with her, and she would keep him happy, and wise, and sane.

Very sane.

He kissed her gently, then cradled her against him.

His wife.

His treasure, more precious than anything.

Even his own life.

Epilogue

"The battle was over," Scheherazade said.

Somehow she ended up lying on the bed. Her sons, who should have been asleep hours ago, were sitting on their knees, staring at her.

How many stories had she told in this bed? Her bed. Schahriar's bed. And unlike those first stories, the ones she told now often began in twilight and went until darkness, as she tried to convince her sons to sleep.

Her sons always managed to get her to talk too long.

"And Father won?" her oldest asked.

"Yes," Scheherazade said. "Father won and Baghdad was saved."

"That was very exciting," her oldest said. "You're very good at stories, Mummy."

"Tell us another," her youngest said, as he always did.

That excited both of them. They bounced on the bed, demanding another one. Another one. Another one.

Sometimes she imagined Schahriar would have been like this, if he had been raised in a loving way.

He too liked to hear more stories, always more stories.

Her sons still hadn't quieted. They were still bouncing on the bed, demanding another tale.

"Tomorrow night," she said to her boys. "I'll tell you another story tomorrow night."

She smiled and pulled them close, and said the words she always used to end their time together.

"Wait until tomorrow night."

An enchanting television event on ABC.

ARABIAN NIGHTS
by Kathryn Wesley

The knowledge that his dead wife and his brother were having an affair has unbalanced the Sultan Schahriar of Baghdad. Convinced that all future wives will try to kill him and having to marry again or lose his kingdom, Schahriar decides to kill his new wife first. He appoints the Grand Vizier Giafar to select a woman from his harem to be his bride. Giafar's independent daughter, Scheherazade, vounteers to marry Schahriar, having loved him from afar since childhood. She thinks she can stay alive by telling suspenseful stories to the sultan and he will let her live so that he can find out how they end. To this end, she tells the stories of Ali Baba and the Forty Thieves; Bacbac, the hunchback jester who is seemingly killed by a whole series of people; and Alladin—each time managing to come to a suspenseful stopping point just as the sun comes up.

Coming soon on video from
Hallmark Home Entertainment.